PULSE

DANIELLE KOSTE

Danielle • Koste

PULSE

ISBN 978-91-984252-1-5

Edited by Autumn Lala

Cover design by Divine Michelle © YONDERWORLDLY DESIGN

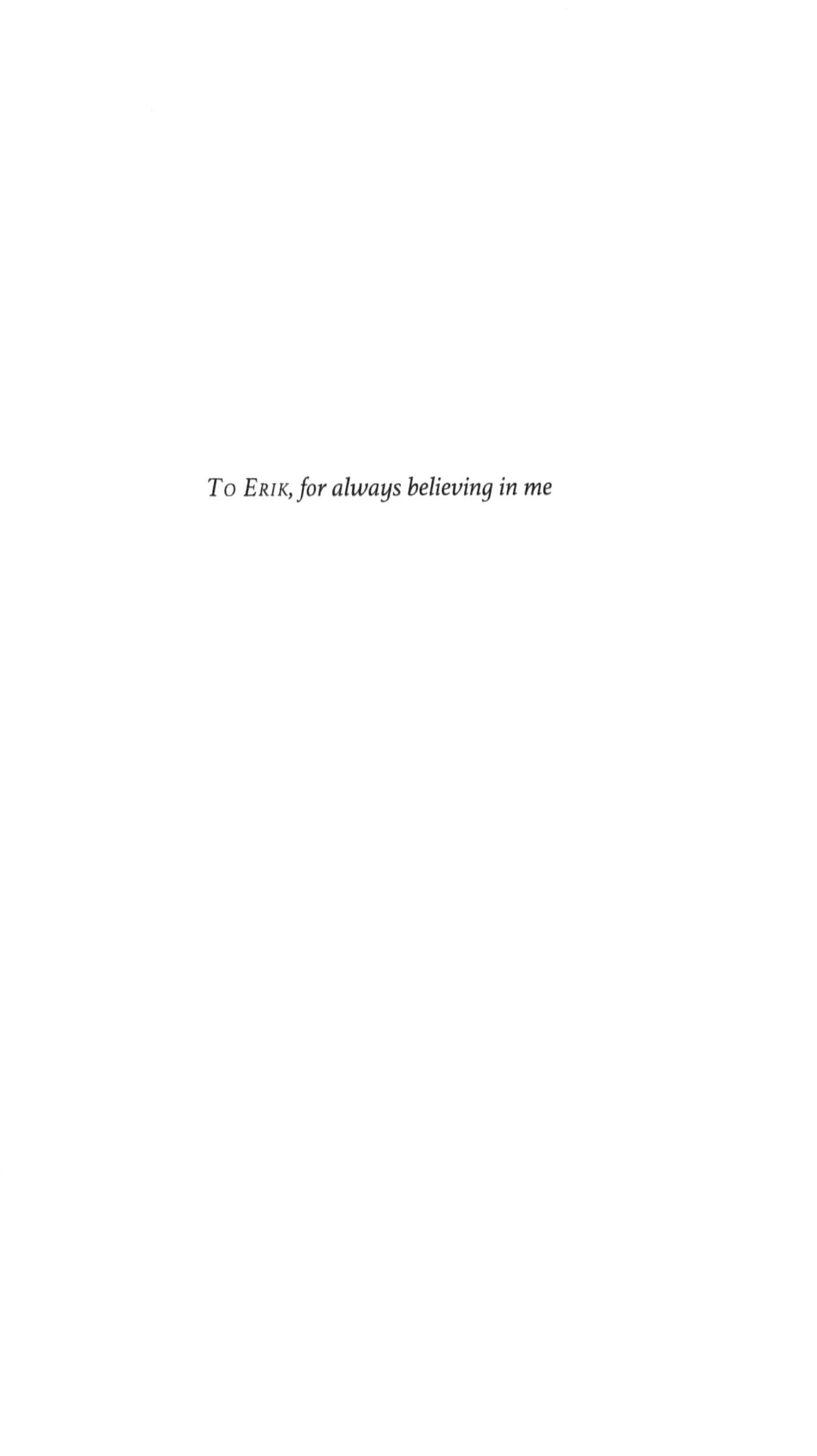

To Erik, for always believing in me

ACKNOWLEDGEMENTS_

Huge thanks and love go out to the following people, who without, this book would not exist.

My wonderful parents, for always making sure I knew that absolutely no dream was off limits.

My amazing friends, for their unwavering kindness, compassion, and excitement that always kept me motivated.

My great big inkie family, for sticking together and lifting each other up, my guardian angels during times of need.

And Autumn, for always sharing a frequency with me.

"His chart, Doctor."

The attending nurse handed off a clipboard to a tall man in white, then circled to the other side of the patient's bed to adjust an IV and check vitals. Nodding in thanks, the doctor's gaze turned down to the paper in front of him, a furrow passing his brow as he read.

"Looks like anemia," he mused aloud, seeking the nurse's input. He had only been out of medical school for a few years, obvious in his under-weathered skin and the way he still second-guessed himself.

"All the symptoms point to it. He's developed severe koilony-chias, and when the ambulance arrived, these cracks on the side of his mouth were bleeding. His body temperature is abnormally low. Don't think I've seen someone so pale outside a morgue." The nurse folded her arms across her chest, letting the straight line of her mouth twist upwards as the doctor smirked at her quip.

The second of humor dissolved. It was always disheartening when someone younger than himself showed up in such a serious condition. He had yet to see a patient survive after arriving so lifeless.

He ran a hand through his hair as he thought, then put the chart back in its holder at the end of the patient's bed with a sigh. The eighteen-hour mark of his shift approached and it wore on him; he could feel the black circles under his eyes, pulling down his tired face and attempting to coerce his puffy eyelids shut. "Seems the most likely case. We should wait for the blood work, but get him ready for a transfusion. I'll give you the go ahead once I get the lab report back."

The nurse confirmed with a curt nod, and he dismissed himself, heading to the waiting room at the end of the hall, craving a coffee.

The night had other plans for him, though.

"Dr. Andrews!"

He glanced over his shoulder, another white-coated colleague jogging towards him from down the corridor. The technician already started speaking well before he reached the doctor's side. "I got those tests for the kid in ICU finished up. I think you should take a look at them." Uncertainty in his voice and apprehension on his features, he handed over the papers.

Frowning, the doctor took them and skimmed over the results. "This can't be right," he said, giving a firm shake of his head. "The patient is obviously iron deficient. With the high levels of iron you have recorded here he would be—"

"In cardiac arrest," the technician finished. He took back the papers and ruffled through them to show his thorough investigation. "Believe me, I'm as baffled as you are. I checked five times. The numbers are correct."

"But these are high enough to kill a person," the doctor protested, bewildered.

"These are high enough that the person would already be dead," the other corrected gravely.

They shared a brief look, one that all doctors knew: hesitancy. When someone had to make a decision even while having no confidence in the options.

"Karmen!" The nurse stuck her head out of the patient's room, and while turning to head back towards her, the doctor commanded, "Start the blood transfusion!"

Reading the urgency in his voice, the nurse ducked back into the room without question.

"Wait, Andrews. Are you sure about this?" The lab technician offered a timid objection, hurrying to keep up. "If he's anemic with high levels of iron, it could be that he's used to much higher. Giving him regular blood... It would have a fraction of this. It could kill him."

"Symptoms are not science, Kenneth. Just because it seems like he is anemic doesn't mean he is. The numbers suggest iron toxicity. Those numbers need to be brought down, or else he's going to die anyway." The doctor's face went hard, insecure with the decision, but one had to be made. He would not have a death on his conscience simply because he was unable to get past his fear of making the wrong choice.

A scream from the patient's room interrupted the mens' disagreement, and they sprinted the last few yards to the doorway. When they turned sharply into the room, the nurse stood cornered against the far wall, wide-eyed and paralyzed.

"Karmen, what—"

"He just— he just woke up." Her voice shook behind her palm. "I was preparing the blood for a transfusion, but the moment I punctured the packet he woke up and snatched the blood from me and started— and started..."

Across from her, the patient sat upright in his bed, shoulders hunched, knees bent to his chest, his already thin frame bunched up even smaller, little more than a skeleton. Tight in his desperate grasp, the blood packet bulged out between his long fingers as he held it firmly against his mouth. It took them a moment to understand what was happening, but the two men realized in unison, covering their mouths in disgust along with the nurse.

The boy sucked the blood from the plastic bag, his guttural growls overpowering the quickening beep of the heart monitor. He seemed oblivious to the other people in the room as he gorged; his eyes shut, his breathing slow and long through his nose as he swallowed thick, wet gulps, like he was starving for it. The doctor thought of his early days working nights at the rehabilitation center, the patient reminding him of a drug addict going through withdrawals. A tremor of anxiety shook his bones, recalling the violent and unpredictable behavior he experienced there.

All three professionals found themselves too horrified to act, able only to watch as the boy sucked the blood pack dry. When he finished, his hands fell down to his sides, limp against the mattress, the empty packet slipping from his grip. He took a few deep breaths, keeping his eyes closed, as if still far too weak to completely awaken from his former coma. Lips stained red and glossy, a drip ran down his pale skin from the corner of his mouth to the sharp edge of his chin.

A lull soaked the room in unease, forcing a small, almost inaudible noise of discomfort from the nurse's throat, and in response, the boy's eyes shot open. The professionals flinched, the nurse whimpering as she retreated further into the corner, away from his stare.

The boy scanned each one of them with a piercing, unnaturally blue gaze, before his lips twitched upwards into the ghost of a smile.

"Forgive me," he rasped, his voice barely there. They had to hold their breath just to hear him.

"I'm still starving."

He left only a brief pause after his words, perhaps to make sure they heard, or perhaps to enjoy the confusion on their faces. Then lunged from the bed.

CHAPTER ONE

Rowan woke to a loud slam, shooting her upright in her chair and jumpstarting her heart. Blinking the sleep from her eyes, she searched for the source of the noise through the shadows of the empty research lab. When had it gotten so dark? She wasn't sure what time she fell asleep, but by the look of her coffee mug, she was about halfway through her fifth cup. She hurriedly brushed through her flat hair with her fingers to erase the evidence of napping, but unfortunately, her interrupter already saw more than enough for an accusation.

"I'm sorry, sleeping beauty, did I wake you?" Cameron teased from across the room, where he stood innocently next to the door he had just thrown closed. When he flipped on the lights, Rowan squinted.

"I was just resting my eyes," she insisted.

"You were drooling," he countered.

Rowan scowled, her cheeks going red with guilt and embarrassment. "No, I wasn't." She wiped at her mouth.

Cameron crossed the room as Rowan picked up where she left

off, tapping the screen of her tablet to wake it up as well. "What are you even doing here this late, Row?"

"Phelps needs these reports proof read for tomorrow," she explained, scrolling up with her finger, pretending to read even though the words were nothing but a blur to her sleepy eyes. She only had a couple more to finish. A little while longer, that's all she needed. She'd be ready for work the next day with a couple hours of sleep, even. It's not like it was that late yet, anyway.

Rowan checked the time on the tablet to confirm, cringing when she was proven wrong.

"If Dr. Phelps knew you were working at two in the morning, he'd tell you to go home. So I'm going to do it on his behalf."

"I just need—"

"Go home, Rowan."

She gave him a pointed glare for interrupting, starting again. "I just need to finish with this, and then, I'll go home."

"Sure." His skeptical tone and eye roll said how often he'd heard that excuse. "You know, I'm a security guard here. I can *make* you leave, if I have to." With his casual threat, Cameron adjusted his utility belt around his hips and gave a smug grin.

It was Rowan's turn to roll her eyes at his faux professionalism. "And I'm a doctor here. I have the hierarchy over you."

That wasn't entirely true. Rowan didn't have her Ph.D. yet, making her little more than an intern. Her mentor, the renowned biologist Dr. Robert Phelps, who was an integral part in creating the first successful treatment for the common cold virus, was the only doctor at the Eureka Center for Biological Studies who actually had superiority over the security personnel. Rowan was sure nobody would argue against her right to be there after hours though, if only because she practically lived at the facility with the amount of overtime she put in.

"But I have the gun," Cameron said, his eyes laughing when

Rowan offered nothing but an unimpressed expression in response. "Besides, what kind of friend would I be if I let you work yourself to death? How're you going to finish your dissertation and become a *real* doctor if you're six feet under the ground?"

"I'm a body donor, so when I die, I'll be used as a medical cadaver, not rotting away in a hole." Rowan looked up from her tablet when she realized her tone had went pretentious, giving Cameron a guilty grin. She offered some self deprecation to bring herself back down off her high horse. "And you know I'd find a way to work even from the grave."

Cameron opened his mouth to keep up their banter, but through the early morning silence of the facility, the two of them were both distracted by an approaching commotion outside: The rumbling engine of a large vehicle. Odd, because besides Cameron, who was supposed to work nights, and Rowan, who wasn't but did anyway, the building and surrounding area was generally deserted after hours.

They exchanged a curious glance, then Rowan rose from her chair to follow Cameron as he rushed over to the window. The research lab she had been hiding out in was on the second floor, which looked out over the parking lot, giving them a clear view of the interruption.

An armored truck approached the front entrance, followed closely by a jet-black SUV with tinted windows. Both had their headlights off despite it being nearly pitch black this far out from the city, and both parked near the doors rather than any of the numerous, designated parking spots. The engines were left running as several, armed men in SWAT gear emerged from the vehicles, assault rifles hugged in their arms.

Upon seeing the weapons, Rowan and Cameron immediately ducked down under the window, getting out of the line of sight.

"What the—"

Cameron could only gasp, frozen in shock next to Rowan, a dreadful uncertainty filling the air between them as they continued to survey from over the window sill. Out of the SUV came four more men, resembling secret service agents in their matching black suits. As the armed men moved for the doors of the facility, the suited ones approached the back of the armored car, opening the vehicle's rear doors.

"Aren't you going to do something?" Rowan asked in an urgent whisper.

Cameron gave her a defensive glare. "What do you want me to do?"

She hesitated. "I don't know. You're security. You said you have a gun!"

"Yeah, and they have six!" Cameron said, struggling not to raise his voice in his growing hysterics. "Do you think they're here to steal some equipment or something?"

Rowan tried to remain calm despite her racing heart. It wouldn't help them to panic, that was certain. She peeked over the window sill again, shaking her head. "No, they don't seem like criminals..."

As she continued to watch, they wheeled something out from the back of the vehicle. Cameron gathered enough courage to look out the window again, just in time to see what arrived in the car.

"Holy shit. Row. Is that— is that a body?"

It was a medical gurney. The SWAT team surrounded it as the suited men pushed the cart inside. Even covered with a sheet, it was hard to mistake the shape.

"What's going on?" Cameron swore under his breath a few more times.

Rowan didn't have an explanation, so she didn't answer. Her head swam with questions as she tried to decipher her way through the anxiety sitting in her throat. If it was indeed a body, was it alive or dead? And what was it doing there? Someone important maybe, a celebrity or politician? It would explain the suited men but didn't solve the question of why they were at a research facility and not a hospital.

A cadaver was a more reasonable explanation, since they often studied dead bodies in the facility, but not many deceased were transported by a posse of armed guards. That fact alone made Rowan's stomach twist with an ill dread. She tried to remind herself it was not like a scientist to fear what she could not explain, but it was unnerving nonetheless when her logic failed her. After all, it didn't happen often.

As Rowan fought to piece together an answer, a third vehicle approached. Cameron swore again when he heard it, but once it came in from the distance, Rowan sighed in relief.

"It's Phelps' car," she explained, standing and hurrying for the exit.

Cameron stumbled to his feet and raced after her, his hand on the gun at his hip. "Are you sure?"

"I would recognize that dirty old lemon anywhere," she affirmed, jogging out into the hall to the stairs.

Rowan was reassured with Phelps arrival, positive she simply missed the meaning of everything happening. Phelps would be able to fill them in once she spoke to him, and all this commotion would be resolved.

Speaking to him would be the problem though, with guns aimed at them the moment they left the stairwell and arrived at the main entrance.

"Stop there! Who are you?" One of the armed men demanded, the others halting to aim their guns also, stopping Rowan and Cameron in their tracks.

The fear Rowan managed to shake off at the appearance of Phelps' car came roaring back as the small army of assault rifles pointed at them. Somewhere within her reasoning she'd forgotten for a moment that while Phelps knew them, these men didn't, and whatever they were doing, it was clear they wanted no one else involved.

Rowan never expected to be at the barrel-end of a gun, and it was more immobilizing than she could have imagined. She wanted to explain, to de-escalate, but her words caught in her throat as she tried to speak, stumbling on the panic knotted in her throat. All she could do was raise her hands along with Cameron, hoping the gunmen weren't trigger happy.

Cameron took a step forward to answer in her place. "We work here. I'm security, and she's a doctor. Who the hell are you?" He held a strong stance but his voice was still unsteady.

The man that addressed them previously lowered his gun, but the others kept their aim. "Civilians," he announced. "Leave the premises immediately or I'll be forced to remove you."

Rowan burned with a moment of offense, sparking her voice back to life. "We're not civil—"

Cameron shushed sharply through his teeth, having the better judgement to just shut up and listen. Rowan had never been good at biting her tongue, but managed to silence herself, and when the man motioned with his weapon, they followed begrudgingly towards the exit.

While passing closer to the other men, Rowan peeked around Cameron's shoulder, seeking a hint to satiate her curiosity. Whatever came out of the back of that gigantic vehicle, they weren't meant to see it, only making Rowan's interest grow. For a brief second she managed to catch a glimpse of the gurney through the wall of thickly armored shoulders, confirming exactly what was under the sheet.

The man that addressed them stepped into her line of sight, and Rowan felt the barrel of the gun nudge her ribs, her back instantly straightening. She was already staring ahead when he ordered her, "Eyes forward."

The glimpse was too short. Unfortunately, all it left Rowan with was more questions. The only other hint to go off of was a sharp scent in the air, distinct from the gunmetal of the weapons, wafted away once the entrance doors were opened to usher them outside the facility.

Phelps approached as they exited, and Rowan felt a wave of relief again despite having a gun to her back. Phelps would sort out this misunderstanding. He'd explain everything, and maybe they'd all have a laugh about it in a few moments. She even smiled warmly as she called out to him, a habit after growing so fond of the man while working under him for so long. " Dr. Phelps, sir!"

He did not return his usual warmth. Whatever was going on, it had Phelps tense even before seeing the two of them led out by gunmen; she saw it in his hurried steps and straight shoulders. When he neared, the apprehension already on the doctor's deep wrinkled face shifted to shock and concern.

"Rowan, what on earth are you doing here so late?" He quickly waved away the gunman's excessive force. "There's no need for that, good lord."

The tension on her spine released ever so slightly as the weapon lowered from their backs, but Phelps fidgety behavior had her on edge.

"I'm so glad to see you. I was just trying to finish those reports and—"

"You two should leave immediately." Phelps cut her off with an urgent, definitive tone.

She stumbled on her words a second time. This response was not what she'd grown to expect from Phelps. Warm, open, honest Dr. Phelps, who more often than not said too much rather than too little, and who she could always worm more words out of with a bit of not-so-subtle prodding. It was strange to see him push up his thick glasses with an unsteady hand and put the other on Cameron's shoulder to push them a few steps further away from the building.

Rowan insisted, once she got over her bewilderment. "But, sir, what— what's going on?"

"Nothing for you to concern yourself over. Go home now, both of you. Get some sleep. Regular work hours tomorrow." Phelps' words were not as casual as the expression he was attempting. In fact, they dissolved as he continued, into something that resembled more of a beg, only baffling her more. Even Cameron was left slack jawed next to her, too surprised by the doctor's brush off to speak.

"Sir, please, you can't just send us off like nothing has happened." Rowan pleaded, but Phelps was already being ushered inside by the same man who forced them out.

He looked back at her, torn for a moment between his instinct to share and his obvious obligation to keep quiet. Before being led the rest of the way inside, he dismissed himself with a forced, "We'll see you tomorrow, Miss Platts."

The doors closed behind them, and the lock latched, leaving Rowan and Cameron alone in the dark parking lot.

After a moment of standing there together in their joint dejection, Cameron gave a heavy sigh and turned for his truck.

Rowan frowned hard. "Hey. Where are you going?"

He slouched his shoulders in defeat. "Come on, Row. We're not getting any answers tonight, we might as well go home and get some sleep. I'll drive you."

Like she could sleep, after what just happened. Rowan scoffed, the sound of it going frustrated with her caving will. As much as she wanted to stand there and pound on the facility door until she got her explanation, she knew that the spoiled brat way of handling this wouldn't get her anywhere. He was right. If her mind wasn't going to settle, they were at least better off speculating at home, where she could at least lay down and give her aching back a break.

Reluctantly, she turned and followed Cameron to his truck, hopping in the passenger side. She kept her eye on the facility as he pulled them out of the parking lot, weak hope that she'd get one last clue before leaving, but the building remained as dark and deserted as she'd expect it to be that late at night.

As they pulled out onto the dimly-lit, forest road back to the city, Cameron kept quiet and let Rowan stew in her thoughts. The silence sat until they reached the part of the road lit with street-lamps, signaling their return to civilization. Even with the warmth of the orange lights flashing by, Eureka was still mostly dead past eight-thirty, little more than a graveyard as they drove through it.

"So. Figured it out yet?" He probed finally, smirking when his question left a crease in Rowan's forehead.

"It doesn't make sense. A cadaver is the most logical explanation, but why would they need to get rid of us? It's not like we haven't seen them moving bodies in and out of the facility for research before."

"Yeah, it's a pretty regular thing." Cameron hummed. "A famous body?"

Rowan sighed, shaking her head. "Famous or not, once the person is dead, usually a body is just a body."

"I guess you're right. Security guards are mostly there to keep a person *alive*." His grin widened when his reasoning made Rowan roll her eyes.

"That's the other thing, too. What the hell were the guns for? A dead body doesn't need protecting and a live one… doesn't really have much reason to be at ECBS." She hoped that bouncing her thoughts off Cameron would lead her to a new conclusion but unfortunately it was the same old circles.

Analysis wasn't exactly his specialty.

He let the silence between them stretch again for a second before adding, "What if the gunmen weren't there to protect the body but instead, to protect others from *it*."

It took Rowan a second to wrap her tired brain around his words, and when they still didn't make sense, she gave him a confused look.

"I'm just saying what if the gunmen were there because *whatever* was on that gurney, dead or alive, it was dangerous."

With Cameron's specific choice of words, Rowan finally clued into what he was implying, letting her head drop down to the dashboard. "Not this again..."

"Listen, it would explain a lot." He was only half joking now, and Rowan was too tired to argue.

"Ok. Humor me."

He beamed with her cooperation, however reluctant it was.

"What if the body was an alien—" Interrupted with a heavy groan from Rowan, Cameron raised his voice to talk over her. "You can't keep denying the facts, Row. Secret late night transportation. Scary government guys in suits. Research lab conveniently out in the middle of nowhere. Tell me that's not a recipe for an alien."

Rowan teased, "An alien conspiracy, maybe." Which happened to be Cameron's favorite out of the long list of conspiracy theories he subscribed to. For how much of a jock he looked on the outside, Cameron had always been even more of a nerd than her with some things.

Unexplained phenomenon being one of them.

He ignored the fact that she was obviously not taking him seriously. "They are probably bringing the body down to the underground labs to do super secret government research on it. Dissect it like they did with the body they found in Area 51."

Rowan couldn't help but laugh this time. "Cameron, the secret labs are just a story they tell the newbies to scare them. You're not saying you believe that?"

"Have you ever been there, Rowan?" He asked, exaggerating his seriousness.

"Of course not, because it doesn't exi—"

"I have no proof it exists but you also have no proof that it doesn't." He grinned an I-rest-my-case grin.

Rowan wanted to point out that the burden of proof laid on the one making the claim, but she was far too exhausted to properly debate. "Ok. So if there's a secret lab under the ECBS accessible by only elevator, as the stories say, then how would anyone get out of the lab if there was an accident?"

"Maybe if there's an accident, they wouldn't want anyone getting out. Maybe it's a security feature, to make sure that whatever they take down there never gets out." Cameron put on his spooky voice, getting another laugh out of Rowan.

"Is it an alien, or a monster now?"

He shrugged, trying his hardest to suppress his own laughter. "Either one. It could be anything. Who knows?"

"We certainly don't," Rowan responded, their giggles deflating into a disgruntled sigh. Because as wild and ridiculous as his theory was, at least it was some sort of answer. When she tried to stick to logic and facts, it didn't get her anywhere other than frustrated.

Rowan gnawed on her lip, unsettled despite Cameron's attempt at lightening the mood. Because all his joking did this time was make her curiosity for the truth that much more unbearable. What if it was something else? Something she hadn't thought of. Something so unlikely, so unbelievable that her logic wouldn't allow it to be a possibility. What if it was something more sinister, like her gut told her?

"Whatever it was... Corpse or famous celebrity, or a damn alien, I have to know." Rowan paused to give Cameron a serious look. "I'm going to confront Phelps tomorrow about it and make him tell me what's going on."

Cameron practically beamed with her resolve. "I mean, we've already seen too much anyway, right? You can play the teacher's pet card. I bet he'll make you head of the super secret government project."

A grin cracked through Rowan's attempt at seriousness. "And if it's an alien, I'm going to study the shit out of it."

"I'm so jealous, why do you get to dissect the alien?" Cameron whined, leading Rowan into a fit of laughter.

"Scientist privileges," she responded with a sly grin.

CHAPTER TWO

WITH BARELY ANY sleep that night, Rowan still arrived at the ECBS bright and early the following morning with two, large cups of coffee in hand: one for herself to keep the eye bags subdued and another, she hoped, to loosen Dr. Phelps' lips.

She had spent the rest of her night constructing the case she would make once he arrived for work. Rowan was top of her class, excelling in his program, the best assistant he's had, and not to toot her own horn, but definitely his personal favorite. She deserved, at the very least, to know what was going on after last night's confusion.

He owed her that much.

Even with her speech all planned out, Rowan sat outside his office with her back tense, legs bouncing with anticipation and gnawing rough on her lip with her nerves. Because something about what happened felt important. Important in a way she didn't understand yet, but felt in her gut like a sixth sense. Like there was a reason she stayed late that night, seen what she saw. A reason beyond simple coincidence or probability.

Whatever it was, whatever the cause for his secretiveness, for the guns and the armored vehicles, she could handle it. Rowan was ready for something bigger. Bigger than a research analyst job at a small facility in the middle of nowhere. Phelps wouldn't be able to argue. He knew her drive, her passion, her ambition, and she could tell this was her chance.

Of course, "chance" suggested a certain amount of luck Rowan did not believe in. Rather, this was an opportunity waiting to be taken, and Rowan wasn't going to just sit around and let it pass her by or hope it would be handed to her. She'd gotten this far in her career only by hunting down every single opportunity that came, so this would be no exception. She wasn't even sure what she was going into his office to ask for, but she knew she wasn't leaving without a yes.

There was no way to argue against "chance" when it came to what she happened to hear while waiting for Phelps, though. Unintentionally eavesdropping on a conversation between doctors as they passed by, Rowan picked up a name she knew, a name she shouldn't have heard, a name that turned the nervous fluttering of her heart into hard, heavy pounds against her eardrums.

"Did you hear? Adam said he saw Dr. Miller in the building this morning."

"Yeah right. Adam likes to exaggerate."

"Miller and Phelps went to school together, and they worked together on the influenza anti-viral. Maybe it was a friendly visit."

"Even so, doesn't Miller work for HHS now? Why would anyone on a government wage set foot in Eureka? The only way I'd show my face in this town after leaving would be if I lost a bet."

Rowan didn't have enough time to process the information. The rest of their conversation moved further down the hall, and approaching from the other end was Phelps, at a pace noticeably quicker than his usual mosey, similar to how he had rushed inside the building the night before.

His steps faltered when he saw Rowan waiting for him, knowing why she was there and reluctant to face her. He managed to push through the apprehension, though, and went right for his office door, fumbling with the key as he greeted her politely.

"Morning, Miss Platts."

Stuck in a moment of disbelief, Rowan almost allowed Phelps to escape into his office completely unharassed, but managed to shake out of it just in time to keep him from closing the door behind himself.

"Is it true, sir?"

A flash of panic swept over his face at her question. "Is what true?" he asked, like there were a number of things she could be asking about, and her knowing any one of them was highly undesirable.

"Was Dr. Miller here?"

Rowan's question came out too loudly, and Phelps shushed her, tugging her into his office and shutting the door behind them before someone overheard her.

"Does this have something to do with last night? This isn't a coincidence, it can't be. Miller was here because of the body, right? It was a body, wasn't it?"

Phelps shushed her again to try and get her to lower her voice. He seemed worried at first by exactly how much information had just come out of Rowan that she probably shouldn't know, but he gave in quickly. Dropping his pretenses while collapsing into his high-back desk chair, he gave a defeated sigh while adjusting his bowtie straight again.

"You're too perceptive for your own good, you know that, Rowan?"

"Please, sir. You can't lie to me. You know how I feel about Dr. Miller. Please."

Rowan hurried to discard the coffees onto his desk and collect a chair to sit across from him. Although, it was barely sitting, with how rigid in anticipation she was.

Phelps gave her his "tough" look, an attempt at a scold he could never quite manage because he didn't have kids of his own. Offering another defeated sigh, he muttered that he'd be hearing about this later before answering.

"Yes. Miller is here, and as much as I'd like to say it was just to visit an old friend, I've never been paid such a pleasantry. And... And that's already far more than you need to know so that's all you're getting out of me."

His words were meant to sound like putting his foot down, but it came out more like a plea not to push it further. As if Rowan needed anything more to start piecing together a picture of what was going on. She was on her feet again, pacing across Phelps' office as she put together the puzzle he'd presented.

"If Miller is here that means... That means this is something big. The government wouldn't just send one of their top scientists off to the middle of nowhere for nothing." Rowan couldn't help her over-exhausted mind going to places it probably shouldn't have, reminiscent of the alien talk the night before with Cameron. The possibilities made her head spin with foolish fantasies, and put a giddy, girlish grin on her face. "Something big, here in Eureka. Holy sh—"

"I'm stopping you right there before you get ahead of yourself. This has nothing to do with you and will have nothing to do with you. You've already seen too much, but I'm *trusting* you to not tell anyone about it. I can trust you, right? Rowan?"

Rowan brushed away his words, unable to help herself from prodding further. "Are you going to be working with Miller again, Dr. Phelps?" She couldn't help the stars that were no doubt in her eyes at the prospect of the old colleagues reunited.

Her excitement only softened Phelps up further. He hesitated, but caved too easily, a less than humble smile crawling onto his face. "I have been asked to be of assistance, yes."

Rowan couldn't breathe through her excitement. "This is history in the making."

Phelps chuckled, trying to brush her off. "Come now, it's not—"

She scoffed at his attempt at regaining some modesty. "You two cured influenza the last time you worked together! This is *huge*."

Rowan was trying to calm down her shaking, because he wouldn't take her seriously if she was in hysterics, and an idea was starting to form. An idea of her, his assistant for over a year, shadowing him on this secret project. Or maybe... Working with them? She didn't even know what the project was, what the study would be based around, what the gurney and the body and the armed men had to do with any of it.

And she didn't care.

Whatever it was, it would be groundbreaking if Miller had anything to do with it.

While fantasizing, Rowan's expression shifted to the big, doe eyes she'd use to get in Phelps' favor, and once he realized what she was doing, he immediately protested. "No. Absolutely not. Get the thought out of your head, Rowan, because it's not happening."

"Please, Dr. Phelps. Please. This is everything I've ever wanted. A project like this could make my career. And to work with my idols. Sir, you and Miller were the reason I went to university, why I pursued biology, you're the reason I am where I am. If I can so much as be involved in something with the both of you..." Rowan paused because she didn't even have words to express the rest of her thought.

It was unfathomable.

Phelps stared hard again, like he was trying to muster up the last bit of his will to withstand her. Rowan promised herself a yes, though.

"Please Phelps, you can't just let me not be involved. I can't miss out on this, especially after knowing all this. Knowing about Miller. I'd spend the rest of my life wondering exactly what I missed out on."

Rowan sat on her last attempt, waiting for Phelps to crack with her racing heart pounding away in her throat. She steady her wringing hands on her thighs, and watched the deep lines of the hard frown on his forehead loosen.

"You're lucky that I've always liked giving Miller a hard time."

PHELPS SENT Rowan home early with a thick folder of papers and specific instructions: read the lengthy contract front to back, think seriously on what it included, and return the next morning with it signed if she still wanted to be involved. When Rowan pressed about how Miller would react, he assured her everything would be handled when she arrived the following morning, leaving Rowan little more to do than sit down and get some reading done.

She had some errands to run, and since she expected to be tied up from the next morning forward, Rowan decided to make some pit stops before heading home with the contract. She'd have to pick up some groceries since she tended to fall into bad eating habits when work took over, and there wasn't proper food in the house. She'd also have to pick up some migraine medication; she got them when she would forgo sleep, which she anticipated would be happening often.

Rowan was so caught up in her excitement and fantasizing, she didn't notice the black SUV following her until she parked at the market and saw that it stopped at the other side of the parking lot, as well.

A chill seized the back of her neck, remembering the night before: the security personnel in dark suits and the feeling of a weapon to her spine. Rowan reminded herself that lots of people had SUVs, and everyone needed to shop. She was just being paranoid. That was all. With a deep breath, she forced the thought away.

She almost completely forgot the unpleasant idea, but it burrowed deeper into her bones with every nervous glance over her shoulder, leaving a chill that made her stiff and uncomfortable as she shopped. There was never anyone when she looked, but when she'd turn back, the hairs stood up on her neck like there was. The discomfort rushed her through the aisles, definitely forgetting something while counting the times she involuntarily checked behind her.

When she left the market, the parked SUV seemed empty, and Rowan felt momentarily relieved. She was being foolish, hyper sensitive in her exhaustion, and still dwelling on Cameron's foolish fantasy from the night before. Maybe she'd allow herself to take a nap when she got home before diving into the contract, just to clear her head.

That was a short lived plan though, she realized, while exiting the pharmacy after picking up her migraine medication and seeing the same black SUV parked down the street, in plain sight of the exit she used to return to her car.

Rowan tried not to let her panic get ahead of her, but a churning dread in her stomach reminded her of the night before. This time though, it was the middle of the day, the sun was up, and she was surrounded by people. She would be fine. She *was* fine.

Even as she tried her best to act normal, to take deep breaths and calm herself down as she got back in her car and pulled out onto the road, the first thing she did once out of the parking lot was dial Cameron's number.

"Row, what's the occasion? You never call me during working hours. How'd it go with Phelps?"

"Cameron, are you home?"

There was a pause over the line. *"I had to pick something up for the truck. Why?"*

"Ok, no problem. I'll just—" Her voice cracked. "I'll use my key, then."

He saw right through her weak facade. *"What's wrong, Row?"*

"It's not a big deal, it's actually kind of stupid. You'll think I'm going crazy." She tried to brush off his concern, holding her phone between her ear and her shoulder as she adjusted her rearview mirror, the SUV four cars behind her as she drove.

"Why would I think you're going crazy?"

Rowan laughed nervously. "Because I think I'm going crazy."

"Try me." Cameron snorted.

She forced her eyes back onto the road ahead of her, exhaling shakily. After another breath, she swallowed hard and said, "I think I'm being followed."

CHAPTER THREE

"Rowan, you here?" Cameron barely got into the apartment before she sprinted from the living room, rushing to the door to close it behind him, locking the latch. When she leaned against the door and gave a heavy sigh, he offered a concerned chuckle. "You ok?"

"Did you see them?" She asked, then rushed back into his apartment, over to the window in the living room that faced out towards the road.

"Who?" He followed, finding her peeking past the curtains she had drawn shut, her shoulders going straight and immediately beckoning him closer.

"Look, look!" She pointed discreetly as he neared, directing his eyes to a black SUV parked down the street. "It's them, from last night. The suited men. They followed me here."

Rowan let out an unsteady sigh and returned to his couch, where she laid out papers across the entirety of his coffee table, sweeping her eyes rapidly across the text.

Cameron stayed at the window to keep a lookout. It certainly seemed like the car from the night before, but it could easily just be a coincidence. It was the more likely conclusion in fact. It was unlike Rowan to be so irrational. That was usually his thing.

"Hey, Row, have you slept?" he pried gently.

She growled. "I'm not crazy. They followed me, ok?" Her head fell into her hands, sighing again.

Cringing, Cameron sat and pulled her closer to him by her shoulders. "I'm sorry, I'm not doubting you, just… Maybe you need to clear your head a little." She deflated with his arm around her, shaking her head as she rested in his collar. While she tried to settle her racing heart, Cameron glanced over the papers. "What is all this?"

"I talked to Phelps today. About what happened. He gave me this contract to read over." She answered with a weak, tired voice, realizing after a moment the information she shared was disjointed and probably didn't make much sense.

She tried to clarify, pulling away from his comfort to collect the papers in order and hold them out for him. "It's a project, Cam. Whatever we saw last night, I guess they are researching it or… *something*. Phelps didn't say, and the contract hasn't been much help. All I know is that Miller's heading it."

"Wait. Miller?" Cameron took the papers from her but paused with disbelief at the name. "You mean, *Miller*, Miller. The author of all those science papers you couldn't put down while in school?"

Rowan gave him an eyeroll at his attempt at knowing what he was talking about. "They're called scientific journals, Cam. And yes, *that* Miller." She was about to add to the thought, but Cameron was on his feet with excitement for her, interrupting.

"Rowan, that's huge!" He beamed, looking at the contract in his hand and laughing. "You're going to be working with one of your idols, Row. That's amazing." He turned to her for a reaction, but his grin faltered when all she could manage in response was a strained smile. "Why aren't you more excited? I thought you'd be losing your mind over this."

"I am! I mean... I was." She tried harder to be grateful, but when she failed, Rowan let the pretenses fall off her face, allowing the concern constricting her lungs to show. "This is a really amazing opportunity, absolutely. Something just feels... *off*."

"Off like, how?" he asked, sitting again to listen.

Rowan inhaled deep to try and shake the discomfort away, running a hand through her hair and letting her eyes stay shut for a moment too long. "Well, the men following me is a little unnerving, for one."

Cameron hummed. "Are you sure it was the same people from last night?" It was clear he didn't want to doubt her, but he was also trying his best to encourage her to be a bit more logical. She didn't blame him.

Even she knew it sounded insane.

"No one ever left the car, but it followed me all over the city. I came here because I got so nervous to go home alone. After reading some of the contract, I'm even more convinced that it's them." Rowan feathered the papers in Cameron's hand to point out how much reading she had been doing, before directing him to the first page. "The whole thing is really vague. It never names what we're working with. Just 'the subject,' and it doesn't say anything about what *kind* of study we're doing."

"Isn't it kinda common with contracts though? Like, general language, so they can recycle the contract for all their projects?" Cameron tried his best to calm Rowan's nerves by being the rational one for once.

She nodded. "Yes, but... It also stresses more than once that I'm possibly at risk of *death* during this study."

He laughed, although a hint of discomfort leaked into it. "I'm sure they're just covering their asses. I mean, when we have to put warnings on coffee cups that the contents are hot..."

She ignored his interjection, determined to prove her concerns now. "It talks about the necessity of being 'discreet' regarding the project. Basically, I can't talk to anyone outside of my colleagues about it, which is fine, I understand, but usually there is some sort of clause about the consequences for breaking the agreement, and it will outline the process of your removal from the team and whatnot. In this contract it's all very vague wording... I get the feeling that it's threatening me, with much worse outcome than just being removed from the project."

Once again, Cameron's concern showed on his face, but he attempted to smile it away, shaking his head. "I'm sure you're just reading too much into it, Row."

Huffing at his stubbornness, Rowan grabbed the contract back from him and flipped through the pages to find her proof. Pointing out a section she highlighted previously, she gave the paper back and read aloud from next to him.

"One should be with the understanding that leaks of information will not be tolerated, and those suspected or guilty of sharing information, or suspected of being likely to, will be dealt with accordingly. By signing this contract, one is agreeing that one understands and gives consent to any form of consequence seen fit if the mentioned agreement is broken."

Cameron met her expectant gaze after she finished reading, the discomfort twisted up in her gut ghosting across his eyes. He tried to banish the expression by giving a dismissive snort and a casual, "Ok, so... Maybe they are trying to scare you a little," but the damage was already done.

Rowan's stomach tied itself into another knot. "They're succeeding," she groaned, letting her face fall into her hands once more. "What am I getting myself into, Cam?"

Her defeated tone triggered something in him, driven to prove her doubts wrong. "The contract is a little unsettling, I'll give you that. But what does it have to do with the suits following you?"

She paused a moment, realizing it wasn't really a question she had asked herself quite yet. "Well if the contract is anything to go by, then I guess... To make sure I don't say anything problematic before signing? I wasn't supposed to be part of this, after all. Maybe they think I can't be trusted and are keeping an eye on me."

"But you said you don't even know anything yet, really." Cameron pointed out, doing his best to counter her arguments, likely for her own sake. It was strange, having him switch roles with her and act as the rational one, rhyming off logical questions to try and relieve her concerns. It wasn't working, but she appreciated it regardless.

"I know enough. We saw a body, afterall. Remember?"

Cameron nodded, a chill shaking up his spine at the unsettling memory.

Rowan groaned again, rubbing at her tired eyes and kneading the headache from her temple. "I just can't stop thinking about it. Like... If they are so worried about the details of the project getting out, what on earth are we studying?"

The worst part was, even with all these reasons to be terrified, Rowan also couldn't help herself from feeling hungry: desperately aching for an answer to all the questions that were cycloning around in her head since the night before. It was crazy, but the longer she thought about it, the more reasonable Cameron's alien theory kept getting, and it was a troubling sign when she settled for conspiracies to satiate her curiosity. She hoped it was only the exhaustion getting the better of her, but she couldn't shake the possibility from her mind.

She sighed, defeated. "Whatever it is, maybe I should be scared."

Cameron wrapped his arm around her shoulders again to offer some comfort. "It's not like you to let your imagination run wild, Rowan. Normally you leave the crazy theories up to me," he teased, offering a gentle smile when she laughed in self deprecation.

"Besides... Since when do you let a few scare tactics get in your way? So what if all signs clearly point to it being an alien?" He paused to hammer in his joke with a sarcastic look. "How fucking cool would it be to study an alien? With one of your idols? And you have that chance, Row. You're going to let some stupid contract and some assholes in tailored suits and an expensive car spook you out of a once in a lifetime opportunity?"

Cameron's pep talk worked wonders, stifling her nerves for a moment and allowing a grateful smile to tug at Rowan's lips as she leaned into his hug. Determined to rid her of her last bit of apprehension, Cameron flipped through to the last page of the contract and held it out for her to take.

"Sign this. We both know you'll spend your life regretting it if you don't."

It's like he was putting to words, loud and clear, the logical part of her thoughts that her fear was refusing to listen to. He knew her too well. She was already going insane with curiosity, with the ache of the unknown; it was only her timid fingers keeping her from guaranteeing the answers she knew she needed.

If she didn't get them, she'd always wonder.

Rowan glanced at him, his dark brown eyes so naive and honest, and her heart swelled with all the times he had been there to support her and push her in the right direction, even when she wasn't always there for him. The thought stung bittersweetly though, when she remembered this was an opportunity she'd have to go at alone.

His earnest encouragement helped though, letting her push

that negativity down along with the rest of her previous worries, at least long enough to take a pen from the coffee table and scribble her name across the final page of the contract with the last bit of nerve she had left for the night.

When she exhaled definitively, turning to Cameron for a reaction, he beamed and raised his arms into the air in celebration, shouting, "Get ready to be studied, ugly, alien scum!" The expression forced Rowan into a fit of tired giggles that made her stomach ache and cheeks burn.

CHAPTER FOUR

ROWAN STAYED the night with Cameron, sure she'd be up once again, but her body thankfully took pity on her, and she was out like a light once her head hit the pillow. She woke rested and alert, albeit slightly achey from sleeping on his couch, buzzing with a sickening mixture of nervousness and excitement the moment her consciousness caught up to her opened eyes. She opted to skip breakfast, fearing her stomach wouldn't hold any food in its twisting state, so instead, she fueled with some instant coffee from Cameron's cabinet and set off for ECBS.

Phelps met her at the entrance, a flat palm on her shoulder blade and a wide smile she could never quite muster so early in the morning. The type of warm welcome Rowan was used to receiving from him.

"I'm quite excited, Rowan. I'll admit, it was a particular pleasure watching Miller dance around the news of my 'assistant,' trying to be polite about the sudden addition while likely having a mild panic attack."

Rowan tried to chuckle despite being mildly horrified by the prospect of Miller not liking her before even meeting because of Phelps desire to yank on some chains.

Her honest reaction must have been written across her face though, because Phelps waved away her concern quickly with another comforting pat on her shoulder and a laugh. "Don't you worry. Miller will warm up to you once you two meet. Just a little bit of a control complex is all."

"I hope so. I'm not trying to step on any toes. Just getting to observe is already more than enough. Thank you for doing this for me, Phelps. It's an amazing opportunity." She wanted to make sure it was well known how grateful she was.

Phelps wasn't having her gratitude, though. He waved it away as he had her earlier worry, directing her to follow him as they headed for the elevators. "My pleasure. To be honest, I'm glad you forced me into the situation. It will be nice to have someone there I'm used to working with. Comforting even, since I was finding myself a little apprehensive about the whole thing. It's... Well, it's complicated. Better left explained after you know all the details."

Rowan tried her best to not let her thoughts run away with the hint of Phelps' concern. Hers were still only just below the surface and waiting for the opportunity to rear their heads again, so she stifled them as best as she could. It tightened her throat to know something had Phelps uncomfortable as well, but she assured herself. If he could be so cheerful, then so could she.

Luckily, a distraction presented itself just in time, as they entered the elevators. Phelps used his security card as usual, necessary to access the other levels of the facility, but unlike usual, instead of choosing one of the upper floors as he did every single day since Rowan's first one working there, he entered a six-digit code onto the elevators touch display. The speaker chimed in confirmation, and the elevator started moving.

Down.

Rowan's breath caught in her throat. It was real. The underground. It existed, and she was going there. She would get to see it with her own eyes. A myth, a legend, that just a second ago she was certain was just a dumb story, turned out to be real. In that case, what else had she previously written off that could prove itself to be real in a matter of moments?

With a grin, she thought about how she'd tell Cameron this later, then remembered from this point forward, everything was completely confidential, and felt her heart sink with disappointment.

"Dr. Phelps."

They were greeted by an armed security guard when leaving the elevator, and Rowan recognized him as the same man who stopped her and Cameron the night all this began. He was tall and built, the bullet proof vest around his chest accentuating his stature, and the assault rifle in his grip caused Rowan to take a subtle step away from him in unease.

"Good morning," Phelps replied, nodding and smiling politely at the man. The guard missed the friendly cue though, his eyes darting over to Rowan with suspicion on his face. Rowan fidgeted under his scrutinizing gaze, feeling out of place.

Phelps intervened. "Miss Platts here will be accompanying me as my assistant. It won't be a problem." He spoke confidently, words holding his authority. The man looked apprehensive, but nodded curtly and directed them down the hall.

Rowan tried to shake off the encounter, following briskly after Phelps, but the lump stayed stuck in her throat. She'd been working at the ECBS for a while now and had grown comfortable with Phelps and her colleagues, despite most of them being twice her age. A mutual respect radiated among the regulars at ECBS;

she hadn't even thought about how she would have to earn her place all over again among Miller's chosen, who were no doubt an even more elite group of intellectuals and would likely pass judgement on her swiftly.

She tried to keep this in mind, to hold onto her previous confidence and let her abilities speak for themselves, but she could feel her will beginning to crumble under the already immense pressure she put on herself to succeed.

The uncharted territory of this new lab was not helping Rowan feel any less uncomfortable. Everything was much more high-tech than she was used to above-ground. The dry, recycled oxygen, and smell of sterilizing agents that she had become too familiar with over the years were absent. Instead the halls were fresh and cool, the barely-blue tone of the walls only intersected by the metallic shine of each new doorway they passed. Electronic beeps and chimes of security codes and scanners echoed through the halls, and the gentle swishing sound of the sliding glass partitions connecting the corridor to each room, automatically opening and closing as people moved in and out.

They turned down another corridor and stopped at a frosted glass door which Phelps used his security card to open. He entered, and Rowan followed, but she ended up lagging behind him as she absorbed the surroundings, awed.

The room was modest in size, but the air was clean and cool despite the multiple, high-end computers lining the back wall. Powered on and whirring quietly, they added a familiar ambiance behind the chatter. If this room was anything to go by, this underground laboratory had to be where most of the ECBS profits were going.

In the middle of the space sat a number of long tables, curved into a semicircle facing the left, towards the only blank wall, which, along with the number of bodies, didn't do any favors for the room's size. A couple computers were occupied, but most of the white-coated doctors stood, idly chatting with each other to occupy their time. She recognized a few faces, but most were strangers, likely members of Dr. Miller's research team.

Someone called Phelps by his first name, and Rowan's attention redirected. She hurried to catch up, only to falter again as she realized who Phelps was shaking hands with.

"Margot, it's been a long time."

Margot Miller had aged a few years since the most common photo of her circulating the internet were taken, but it was undoubtedly her standing in front of Phelps, their hands clasped over each others in a warm, friendly shake between old friends. Rowan was left in disbelief, breathless and staring with starstruck eyes.

Even though signs of seniority crept in, with the crow's feet at her eyes and peppering of silver strands in her dark hair, she wore her age much better than Phelps. While he had grown fluffy around the waistline and let his beard go less tended to, Miller was a vision in a crisp, white coat: tall, dark, and thin, with deep set eyes hiding behind a pair of rimless glasses.

Miller smiled wide and friendly just as Phelps did, but her body stayed straight postured and precise, noticeably less fluid than Phelps flamboyance as she answered. "It has. Talking is one thing, but finally seeing each other after all these years... How have you been?"

"Well, while you've been stirring the pot with controversial topics, I've been settling my career and working towards retirement. Perhaps if you did the same, you'd have your own laboratory and wouldn't have to get me involved in your affairs." Phelps spoke in his usual chipper tone, but the sarcasm was hard to miss. It would normally have concerned Rowan that her mentor was being so open about his apprehensiveness, but she was too caught up in her awe to be worried.

"You know I've always been insatiable, Robert. Settling down is out of the question." Miller laughed at the double meaning of her own words, patting Phelps' arm with a slender-fingered hand. "And besides, why would I have my own labs when I know you'll let me use yours whenever I need it?" she added with a sly grin, discreetly poking fun at Phelps for his well-known weakness of never being able to turn down someone.

When the conversation lulled between them, Miller's eyes moved from Phelps to Rowan, and she froze all over again under the older woman's gaze.

"And you must be the wonderful Miss Rowan Platts." She side-eyed Phelps with a curl of her lip. "Robert's told me a lot about you, albeit only just yesterday."

Rowan swallowed hard, somehow forcing herself out of her stunned silence as she reached out for a handshake. When Miller took her hand, the nerves bubbled out of Rowan's mouth in embarrassed blubbering.

"I'm such a big fan, Dr. Miller. I own all your scientific journals. If there were more photographs of you, I probably would have posted them all over my walls as a kid. Being a woman in the field and being so successful just... It was a huge influence for me. I'm really excited and grateful for this opportunity to work under you and Phelps."

Rowan could feel her face going red with her over-talk and tried to pull back her outburst into something a little more professional. Miller seemed entertained though, chuckling a little after Rowan managed to reel in her rambling.

"And with how highly Robert speaks of you, I thought I'd be the one sucking up. After all, any assistant of Robert's must be pretty special." Miller smiled warmly, glancing around the room for a moment before adding, "I'd really like to talk with you more later, Miss Platts, but for now, we have to get started. If you'll excuse me."

Rowan's heart fluttered at the exchange, the embarrassment on her face going red-hot from the praise and the prospect of speaking even further. She never thought she'd be standing in front of Margot Miller, let alone getting to shake her hand and exchange compliments. She had to fold her fingers together to keep them from shaking, wanting to hold onto her professional aura, but barely keeping a grasp on it.

Miller crossed the room to the blank wall behind them, and as some of the other doctors noticed, they turned from their conversations so the quiet murmur of the room gradually died off. Many took the opportunity to sit at the desks provided, but a few stayed standing, so Rowan opted to keep her spot next to Phelps.

Although she refused to show it, she was terrified to stray from him. She was walking into a lion's den, and while she had been warmly welcomed by the leader, the other doctors were as good as predators, yet to notice her. She feared once they did, they would tear her apart with her own insecurities, so she pushed it away into the deep corners of her skull in hopes they wouldn't smell it on her.

"Good morning, friends."

The moment Miller spoke, claps from her team members interrupted her. She soaked up the praise with a humble smile, however, letting the applause go for perhaps a little too long before putting up a hand to stop them. As she started talking again, Rowan noticed Miller's change in demeanor. She was relatively soft spoken and warm when exchanging pleasantries with her and Phelps, but as she addressed the room, a certain hardness found her tone.

The steady and confident voice of a leader.

"It's wonderful to see you all here today. I understand the sacrifices many of you are making to join me on this study, but I want to promise, and prove to you today, that your time and effort is not in vain."

It was a bold statement, a buzz of curiosity circling the crowd, but Miller had spoken in front of others before, and she was good at it, that much was obvious. Rowan felt her stomach twist, but instead of her previous nerves, it was a tight anticipation, excited for what Miller would present them with.

"Most of you know each other, but you'll notice we have some new faces, courtesy of Dr. Phelps, the owner of this fine facility. Normally, I would start with introductions, since I like my team to work together as one big, happy family, but I think we'll have the opportunity to get to know each other personally at another time. I can see most of you are eager for me to dive into the juicy details, so I won't keep you waiting." When she finished, Miller gave a gentle head tilt to the technician waiting at a computer in the corner.

Rowan's heart picked up an extra beat. The technician returned a curt nod and swung around in his chair, typing in a line of code and pressing enter. Her eyes jumped around the room when the lights dimmed. Miller stepped aside, presenting the wall behind her as it began to move.

Starting at the center, the wall glided apart in sections, folding under each other in panels. Rowan attempted to conceal her shock, to little avail.

No one else in the room seemed impressed. Miller's team must have been used to such advanced technology, and to Rowan's side, Phelps' face turned to cold disconnect, suggesting something grave. The concern didn't quite manage to pierce Rowan's amazement, though.

The eight panels tucked snugly away into the adjacent corners, and left in their place was a wall of glass, floor to ceiling, and almost invisible in clarity. Beyond the glass, another room, stark white and lit by fluorescents, housing a bed, sink, toilet...

And a body.

CHAPTER FIVE_

IT WAS A BOY, a youth, surely no older than twenty. In the farthest
corner, he was curled up, his knees to his chest and his eyes closed,
a hard expression marring his sharp features. He was pale,
perhaps the palest person Rowan had ever seen in Northern California, and his dark hair hung to his jaw-line, stringy with grease
and grime. A thin robe covered his navy hospital scrubs, but even
with the layers, she could tell he was thin, too thin. Underfed. She
would have assumed him dead if she hadn't seen him flexing the
fingers of his hand into a brief fist, knuckles spiking out from his
taut skin.

Breathless, Rowan stared, wide and unabashed into the room
as confused and anxious chatter started among the doctors
around her. She felt sick, and the tension in the air made it worse.
She wasn't the only one to feel the sudden regret. She turned to
Phelps, and he refused to look at her, his brow fighting a frown. He
already knew, but that didn't seem to make the reveal any less
disturbing for him either.

There was another human being locked up in a room across from
them. They were not studying an alien or some other, strange creature

they'd never seen before. It wasn't just a body. They were studying a living person. A boy younger than herself. And somehow, that was more unbelievable than Cameron's prospect of an extraterrestrial.

Rowan's insides twisted in disgust as the bits fell together. This was the secret that needed protection. The contract insisted discretion because they didn't *want* awareness. She wondered if this was even legal, or if she had just agreed to take part in poking and prodding information out of an innocent victim.

Presumably, anything was "legal" as long as no one knew about it.

Miller came forward to settle the growing conflict, gathering everyone's attention before they grew any more restless. "Please, do not be put off by the appearance of our subject. I understand your apprehensions, but know first, what you see on the other side of this glass is not human like you and I."

She had a way with words, and Rowan's curiosity crept back. Her eyes jumped between Miller and the youth. When she gazed at the boy, she saw a human, she saw a victim, but Miller was suggesting otherwise.

"At about two a.m., the morning of Friday, August twenty-third, our unconscious subject was admitted to the emergency department of a small town's hospital about a hundred miles from here. The doctor's write up suggested he suffered from a severe case of anaemia, but blood test results conflicted, reading very high iron levels. When our subject was about to receive treatment, he woke up and became hostile. Within moments he attacked and killed the attending nurse and doctor."

Miller paused briefly for a reaction, but the room held a chilled silence, and Rowan felt cold chills crawl up her spine.

"The laboratory technician who handled the subject's blood work attempted to sedate him with a high dosage of morphine.

The subject retaliated and killed the lab tech, as well as another nurse who came to investigate, and a wandering patient, before the morphine set in."

The room stayed completely silent. Rowan's eyes wandered back to the boy in the room, her mind racing with questions. It seemed impossible for this obviously unhealthy teen to murder five people with his bare hands, let alone with a dose of morphine in his bloodstream. He looked near death, and likely couldn't even hold his own weight up, but Miller expected them to believe he was capable of a rampage?

A young man who sat at one of the desks closest to the exit broke the silence. "A human wouldn't be able to do the things you're claiming. Doctor, are you saying that this subject is not human?" A certain tone of sympathy lightened his voice, as if he was also unable to see past the boy's helpless appearance.

"He's right, Doctor. I apologize, but I can't quite understand how *that,* managed to do what you're claiming." Another member of the group piped up as well, trying her best to keep her doubtfulness polite, but unable to completely hide her disgust. The room murmured a quiet agreement, all turning to Miller for an explanation.

"I know about as little as all of you do, but I can confidently say, this subject is definitely not like you or me. At the very least, we have a dangerous killer, who perhaps has a serious mental or physical illness causing him to act out in violent, powerful fits of aggression." The room filled with growing whispers again, but Miller continued despite the chatter, talking over them. "But, of course, I understand a number of you require some sort of proof for the grand claims I'm making. We're prepared to provide this for you."

These words silenced everyone yet again, the air around

Rowan growing thick as their interest piqued. She wasn't the only one holding her breath now.

"When the subject came into our custody, we were desperate to find a secure holding place for him, considering the situation he was taken from. Dr. Phelps' facility was offered to us last minute. Though it is a wonderful place for research, it is unfortunately not equipped for what we need. As you can imagine, few laboratories would be. This means we will limit our interactions with the subject, without putting lives in danger, of course. We have no permanent ways of restraining or sedating the subject, and at the moment, the only interaction possible is verbal, which has proven less than effective. We had security cameras, but he has since destroyed them. We have only audio recordings now.

"There is one tool at our disposal though, which will, at the very least, do a wonderful job at showing you all exactly what we're dealing with."

Stopping to assess the room, the warmth previously on Miller's face when they shook hands was now completely stone. Along with Rowan, a number of the others' initial disgust morphed slowly into consideration. She wondered how Miller would prove this boy was more than the underfed, wraith he currently was. Rowan's stomach churned though, sickened by her own curiosity.

"You should all see a cuff on his ankle. This device, on our command, delivers an immobilizing electric shock. We've applied this cuff primarily as a safety measure, to have an external power in case we ever need to disable him in some way. But it's proven to be an effective antagonizing mechanism, also."

Miller didn't continue this time, choosing instead to let the proof speak for itself, and gave another glance to the technician at the computer. Reaching for a tiny remote when acknowledged, he pressed a button the size of his thumb after Miller gave another tilt of her head.

Rowan's eyes flashed back into the room where the boy stiffened in his spot. His thin arm flew up, and his hand flattened firmly on the wall to brace himself against the pain, but it didn't help. He shook uncontrollably, and as the shock became unbearable, a howl of sheer agony broke through his attempts at resisting, his head stretched back until she saw the veins in his neck pulsing against his transparent skin.

Her heart swelled to a painful pound in her head, keeping count of the long seconds. Two, three, four...

"Stop! For God's sake!"

The words escaped without her consent, like vomit, to accompany the horror and disgust knotting her throat. Miller's previously kind eyes flashed something dark at Rowan's interruption, but she signalled to the other man, and Rowan stared as the boy's muscles slacked, the electricity stopping. He writhed in the afterpain until he crumbled, his face pressed against the floor, recuperating with deep, labored breaths. The ridges of his spine jutted through his layers of clothes, and his skin under the cuff flared raw and red, suggesting this wasn't the first bout of pain he'd endured.

Rowan's chest tightened, and her hand gripped the back of a chair to keep herself standing, feeling suddenly faint. She had just taken part in the torture of a sick and innocent youth. They could have killed him. He could die. Right there in front of them, he could die, and it would be her fault for not stopping it sooner. She found herself staring at the boy, willing him to rise from his spot on the floor, to show her he was alright. Her breath shuddered further with every passing moment, her heart still pounding away, hard in her throat.

Finally, a movement, and the entire group of doctors flinched simultaneously. At an unnatural speed, the boy shot out his arm and grabbed the bed's metal foot rail, using it to support his weight as he rose to his feet. Rowan blinked a few times, making sure her eyes were working correctly after what she'd just seen.

She was not the only one to noticed the speed of his movement, either. Shock etched on the faces around her, some twisting to their close colleagues to confirm they were not crazy, a stunned buzz enveloping the room.

The boy stood, more feeble than ever, a bony hand clenching the thick, aluminum bed frame. His sharp shoulders rose and fell with each deep, controlled breath. Rowan, who had been holding her own from nerves, sighed quietly to herself, thankful that he was alright. And, as if he heard, he glanced up from the floor through his stringy fringe, right at her, and her previously relieved breath was snatched from her lungs.

The reveal of his piercing, unnaturally blue eyes surprised everyone. He wasn't looking at any of them, though. He looked right at her, gaze furious.

His thin fingers flexed around the foot of the bed, and Rowan saw his weight shift. Something about how he held himself was different than before; he didn't seem thin and feeble anymore. Even with his malnourished appearance, his feet were now grounded, and a muscle tightened in his forearm as he adjusted his grip.

Rowan predicted his next move just before everyone else, twisting her body away as he lifted the whole bed frame off the floor. With a fluid motion he launched it, matress and all, towards the glass.

Screams filled the air, and everyone hurried to hide behind chairs and under desks, preparing for the storm of shattered glass. Rowan had already hid her face behind the collar of her lab coat, but she couldn't resist glancing back. She saw the bed hit, but instead of crashing through, it simply bounced off and landed roughly on the floor again, resulting in nothing more than a loud clatter as it settled.

To the side, Miller chuckled lightly at their reactions. "No need to worry, friends. That glass is nearly indestructible, and only one way. As you can imagine, he knows we're here, but he cannot see our face or hear our voices, so there is no need to fear him from this side." Miller seemed pleased with herself, knowing her method of torture received the outcome she required, thoroughly spooking them all into comprehension.

The others seemed to settle again, some of them even laughing at their own reactions. Rowan wished she could relax as easily as those around her, but it was impossible when the boy in the other room still stared at her with those sharp, blue eyes.

She assured herself he couldn't see her. Miller said the glass was one-way; it was just an illusion. He stared right at her like he heard her though, like the glass wasn't even there, like they were facing each other across an empty room. He stared until standing became too difficult, then fell back to the wall, sinking to the floor and curling up, resembling a wounded animal once more.

"He's strong." Finally, someone from the crowd broke through the quiet buzz going around, dragging Rowan away from the boy and into her new, overwhelming wonder.

The others were alive with it also, and it fueled the fire in her. She wished she was uninterested. She wished she could say she felt only disgusted by the idea of locking up a young boy for observation, but she could not deny her curiosity after what she just saw. Whatever this boy was, she wanted to know.

She would be the first to know.

"How can he have so much strength, though? He looks like he's ready to die." A doctor on the other side of the room posed the question, a notepad and pen in his hand, scribbling a note as he asked.

"Glad you both brought it up. The subject you're seeing right now is quite underfed. We can only assume that given a proper diet his strength would increase dramatically." Miller's explanation turned excited now that the rest of her team was ripe with the same amazement.

Near Rowan, another member of the group lifted a hand to interrupt. "Why has he been underfed?"

"Another good question, one that brings us to our first task, which we'll start on tomorrow. Our subject has proven quite *unco-operative*. We've been trying to provide him with different foods, but he refuses to eat what we've given and will not give us any hints on what he will eat. It's possible he doesn't know English, but since he's made no attempts whatsoever to communicate with us, we can't be sure of anything. We're definitely not interested in starving him, so our first order of business will be figuring out how to get him eating."

Miller paused to step a few paces to the side, gathering up a large stack of papers, and splitting them to be distributed around the room.

"Coming to you is a copy of the observation reports from the last few days. Normally it would have a copy of the surveillance video, but we've already discussed that. Tonight, you can all get up to speed on the details we already know about him, which are few, unfortunately. Read over them, and we'll have a group brainstorm in the morning to see if we can't come up with a solution."

Rowan took a booklet of papers and passed the pile on, flipping through the pages but finding herself unable to focus on any words. Instead, she stored it away in her bag for later study.

Miller didn't have to openingly dismiss anyone; her team understood the directions, gathering their belongings and shuffling towards the exit. Many debated and theorized, a new found interest in their tones. A few lingered, glancing into the containment room briefly before following colleagues out. Rowan shared the excited emotion, but mingled with it was a noticeable discomfort she couldn't shake.

She didn't want to stick around in that room for any longer than necessary, her thoughts a mess, but when she went to duck out, someone called for her.

"Miss Platts." Miller crossed the room to meet Rowan as she stepped aside from the exit. When Miller smiled, it was all friendly and unintimidating once again. "If you have somewhere to be I don't want to keep you, but I thought maybe we could speak more before you leave. I'm quite curious about you, to say the least, after all the wonderful things Robert had to say."

It took Rowan a few wide-eyed blinks to finally respond. "I would love to talk."

CHAPTER SIX

"Phelps told me you haven't been down to these parts of the facility yet, and you'd need a new security card."

Rowan nodded as she followed Miller into a small room acting as a temporary office. Miller circled the desk in the middle of the space and started rummaging through a drawer. She resurfaced with a crisp, new card and another contract, then sat, and Rowan followed her lead, taking the edge of a chair across from her.

Miller grabbed a pen and started filling out a few blank places on the paper. "Just a standard security agreement we'll need you to sign. Basically all it says is you understand that misplacing this card means paying for an entirely new security system here," she explained while recording the long number on the back of the card. When she finished, she turned the papers in Rowan's direction and held out the pen.

"Right. So, don't lose the card unless I'm looking to be millions of dollars in debt," Rowan repeated as she reached for the pen and signed her name, garnering a grin from Miller.

"That sums it up."

Reminded by the signing of her name, Rowan twisted to

rummage in her bag for the folder holding the contract she slaved over the night before, handing over the two signed documents together.

Miller straightened as she took the papers, pleasant surprise taking over her face. "Does this mean you're staying, Miss Platts?" Rowan tilted her head slightly, giving a nervous smile, and when Miller noticed her confusion, the woman offered a tiny laugh and a wave of her hand. "Sorry it's just, after your outburst... I worried that you thought ill of me. Like Phelps does right now."

Rowan shook her head, giving another curious expression. "It didn't seem like you two were on bad terms a moment ago."

Miller corrected quickly. "Oh no, not bad terms. Never. Rather, simply haven't seen eye to eye on this project so far." She paused to give a careful smile as she considered something. Deciding, Miller let her guard down and allowed her shoulders to drop, a sigh and an eye roll as she offered a fairly accurate imitation of worried-Phelps. "It's not right, Margot. Having him locked up like that. It's inhumane."

Rowan couldn't help the tiny laugh that bubbled from her lips, which she stifled behind her palm.

Encouraged by the reaction, Miller relaxed further, her eyes dancing behind her glasses. "You're not much like Robert, though, are you, Miss Platts?"

She wasn't sure what it was supposed to mean, but Miller's tone sounded like a compliment. It brought a flush to Rowan's face. "I'm sorry?"

Miller smiled further, like she meant to tease and was pleased it stuck. "No need to get defensive. It's a good thing. I'll admit, while I adore Phelps, I was a little worried when he told me he wanted to bring on an assistant. We can butt-heads sometimes, and I honestly didn't want another mini-Phelps backing him up and undermining my authority on important decisions." Realizing she had been distracted by her own ranting, she fixed her focus back to her original point. "You're not like that though, are you? Phelps thinks you are, and you like it that way, but I can see it in your eyes."

Rowan stared for a moment, speechless at Miller's forwardness. She didn't have to ask to know what Miller was talking about, but she didn't appreciate how easily her intentions had just been read, and chose to act oblivious. "See what, doctor?"

Miller leaned forward onto her elbows, a knowing gleam in her gaze. "Your drive. I see it all over your face. With Phelps, his morals come first. It gets in the way of his success. It's a shame really, because if he could just put his emotions aside, he'd be where I am. You have a softness to you, there's no doubt there, but you're still willing to set your emotions aside to succeed. After all, you wouldn't be here if you weren't interested in succeeding, would you?"

Left tripped up on her tongue again, Rowan could do nothing but sit silently, unable to deny her very accurate evaluation. While her fear made her apprehensive at first, Rowan had always wanted success, and she couldn't ignore the fact that this project would give it to her.

Miller took her silence as apprehension. "I could be wrong, of course. Maybe I'm getting ahead of myself. I guess I just get excited at the idea there might be someone else here seeing this as the opportunity I see, not just senseless cruelty."

Rowan shot her eyes up, not liking her nerves being so noticed and interpreted as wavering commitment. Rowan respected Phelps, but she didn't want to be him, letting the apprehension in her gut define whether she reached her goals or not. She wanted to be the person that Miller said she saw: driven to succeed against all odds.

She certainly wouldn't become a successful virologist by being scared of finding answers.

Rowan knew what Miller wanted her to say. Swearing to her overwhelming curiosity would impress her, and in that moment, she wanted nothing more than to impress her. So, choosing to snub out the lingering doubts in the back of her skull, Rowan embraced success instead.

"Whatever the boy is, it's obvious he would be a danger to civilians, and maybe even himself if he was anywhere but here. I also imagine he might be treated substantially more inhumanly by the public. To be honest, it's a miracle he's not dead, considering his rampage, and his death would have been a shame, because we can obviously learn a lot from him. My outburst today was triggered by what seemed unnecessary torture, before we were shown his unusual nature."

Rowan punctuated her words with a steady gaze, willing Miller to read her determination. The itching need to prove herself in the other woman's gaze, and the desire to be the first to figure out this boy's mysteries, smothered the embers of any previous apprehension.

Miller nodded after her words, glancing down for a moment, as if to hide a bit of shame. "Yes. I admit I can see why you might have thought it was cruel at first. I hope you can understand my actions."

"However cruel it seemed, you needed something big to get our attention. I can't ignore the possibilities now. I *did* work hard to get here, doctor. I have no intention of having that work go to waste. So, I guess you were right with your initial analysis of me."

From across her desk, Miller's face stretched into a satisfied grin. After watching Rowan for a moment, she leaned over and held out her hand.

"I look forward to working with you, Miss Platts."

ROWAN DISMISSED HERSELF, exiting Miller's office with her new key card and a restored sense of determination. Phelps' approval was one thing, but Miller's parting words left Rowan with a fluttering in her chest that she couldn't shake. She never even fathomed the possibility of meeting Margot Miller, let alone working under her, or even, dare she say it, alongside the woman. The prospect left Rowan feeling like she was in a dream, floating on air, up on cloud nine.

She quite nearly skipped down the hall to return to the observation room, intending to retrieve the pile of observation notes she had forgotten while flustered by Miller's attention. At the door, Rowan tested out her new key card, and it confirmed its working order with a cheerful beep.

The room was much quieter this time, with the lights dimmed and only the gentle hums of the computers occupying the space. When she realized the wall to her left remained open, allowing her to gaze into the containment room, her stomach twisted, the previous unsettlement leaking back into her chest and making her lungs suddenly tight.

Rowan attempted to not be distracted, letting out a breath and hurrying across the room to gather her papers. She couldn't deny her curiosity though, and as she slipped the notes into her bag and slung the strap over her shoulder, she felt her eyes gravitate towards the glass.

The boy hadn't moved. Still sitting tight in the corner like a scared animal, he slumped forward, using his body as a shield. His expression no longer read hard and angry. Instead, he seemed tired. Perhaps he could sense that he no longer had a group of people observing his every move, allowing himself a moment of vulnerability.

She felt a pull in her chest, and her feet moved without permission, giving her a closer vantage point as she neared. When Rowan reached the glass, she leaned against it to watch him closer despite herself. The purple circles under his eyes made his face look sallow and sickly, and she wondered if he was deteriorating so quickly, or if it was just her sympathy playing with her eyes.

He took in a strained breath, and Rowan felt her throat knot. She reminded herself of what she saw him do earlier: his quick reflexes, his abnormal strength, the unwavering rage in his gaze. It was difficult to see past his current victimized exterior, though. She sighed, fogging the glass in front of her.

"What *are* you?" she said the words to herself, barely a whisper on her lips as she casted her eyes down with a moment of empathy.

When she checked again, his eyes were open.

The fresh memory of his icy blue eyes finding her through the one-way glass caused Rowan to stiffen, a tremor of fear rushing up her spine. She reminded herself that he couldn't have seen her. It was impossible.

But he proved to be capable of a few impossible things that day.

He wasn't looking at her this time. He wasn't looking at anything, in fact. His eyes stared straight forward into nothing, gaze unfocused, one eyebrow turned down just slightly. His tired expression was now inquisitive, a question on his parted lips. He tilted his head, and Rowan's breath went shallow when she realized.

He was listening.

Against her better judgement, she tried at confirming the hypothesis, speaking again in another barely-there whisper.

"Can you hear me?"

She felt foolish. Surely her own imagination exaggerated. She refused to believe it.

An astonished breath fled her lungs when he straightened his neck, and his gaze jumped to the exact spot she stood. He placed the location of her voice so expertly she had to question his outward exterior. No human was so good with their ears. He was something else entirely. An animal. A predator.

As if he meant to confirm that thought, he unfolded his gangly limbs like a spider and rose to his feet. Keeping a hand mounted on the wall next to him for balance in his weakened state, he followed it around the room, shuffling towards her.

Rowan held her breath, unsure whether she appreciated him knowing where she stood, or worried that he was heading in her direction. His eyes moved to the floor, searching again with his ears, waiting for another noise to hold onto. As his supporting hand moved from the wall to the glass, he stopped, and a hint of a grin passed his lips. He closed his eyes, savoring something.

"I can hear your heart beating."

Rowan saw his lips form the words and heard them through the automated telecom, playing through the speakers on her side of the glass. She prayed he only heard her because the telecom was on, but a dreadful terror inside reminded her that the little device would have never picked up her racing pulse.

As her heart quickened in tempo, the barely there smirk spread further onto his mouth. The pale, dry skin of his lips cracked with the motion, his worn-down body even more clear to Rowan with how close he had come. Yet, he stayed upright, moving even closer, managing the smoothness of a snake with each step. More words flicked across his lips, like a serpent tongue.

"Are you scared?"

His question made her conscious of the terror that froze in place. Until then, she had been overwhelmed with her disturbing fascination, like the immobilizing amazement of watching a wild animal as it takes down it's prey. There was a dangerous beauty in the way he stood, the way he fought, despite being obviously broken and exhausted. Though he held himself straight and strong, Rowan felt like he might collapse at any moment. Through the telecom she could hear the dry rasp of his voice as he inhaled before speaking again.

"You are. I can smell the fear on you."

His words settled on her like a pair of hands, tight around her throat. She uprooted her feet, taking a step back as he closed in on the spot directly in front of her, reminding herself that he couldn't touch her, that she was safe. Somehow she still felt uncertain, the way his eyes found where she stood and how he claimed to smell her even through the thick glass between them made her second guess.

He stopped and faced her, lifting a hand and leaning onto his forearm. Adding to the disturbing intent of his last words, he set his forehead against the glass and closed his eyes, taking a deep breath.

His nostrils flared. "Delicious."

Rowan threw a hand to her mouth as she felt sick rise in her throat. She took another step back, and the back of her thigh hit a desk, causing her to stumble.

The boy had been smiling, but now as he stood there, the expression turned sour. A hard line formed between his brows. He clenched his jaw, tucking clawed fingers into a tight fist, his breath shifting from controlled to labored and heavy, fogging the glass just as she had done.

Rowan gripped hard on the edge of the table she leaned against, her pulse pounding in her skull like a drum. It pushed her, willing her to run, but she couldn't. Her body trembled terribly, and she knew her legs would give under her if she fled.

"I'm starving," he said, the whispered admission sounding broken and hopeless. Then, in stark contrast, anger bloomed as he banged so hard against the glass with his fist that the whole panel convulsed with the force, and Rowan stifled a scream with her palm.

"Give me your blood!" he bellowed, demand blazing in his frigid gaze, the desperation of a dying animal trapped in his huge, black pupils.

He banged again, harder, another growling roar with it, and her fear finally ignited her. She didn't want to know if he was capable of getting through. She didn't want to know anymore at all. Rowan had seen enough. Her confidence and curiosity were gone.

She bolted for the door.

CHAPTER SEVEN

Rowan never experienced this type of terror before. It had her fleeing to her vehicle in a irrational panic, intending to drive as far from the ECBS as she could on her half-empty tank of gas. All that kept her there were her trembling fingers, refusing to set her key in the ignition.

This wasn't like her. Normally, she'd want to share this information. That *thing*, who refused to communicate until then, had spoken to her. No, not spoken. Yelled. Threatened with the intention of terrifying. This was important. Someone needed to know, and she would be rewarded for telling. This was a *good* thing. It would move their research along, would give her the positive attention she wanted.

An opportunity. That's what this was. She repeated the thought in her head, pushing down the fear, stomping on it. She pulled out her phone, intending to call someone, but despite her valiant attempt at fighting it, her nerves kept her fingers stiff.

Who was she going to tell, even? Everything that happened was now confidental, so she couldn't speak with Cameron, even though he was the first person to come to mind when she thought about who would best help settle her panic. And Phelps would worry, maybe even pull her from the project if she put up a fuss.

Miller... She should tell Miller, but it would mean going back inside the facility, and with just the thought, her back went rigid with refusal. No matter how hard she tried, the driven spark that Miller said she saw in her failed to reignite. Something deep in her gut stifled it, a primal instinct, urging flight rather than fight.

So she put her phone away, and let her pounding heart settle in her chest before returning home in an unresponsive daze.

Her numb state of mind lasted well through the night, her restlessness manifesting as dark circles under her eyes the following morning. Instead of sleeping, she spent the night mentally preparing herself, building up the determination to meet Miller first thing in the morning and recount what happened. That's what the motivated, career-driven Rowan would do, and it was clear she needed to find that inside herself again.

It seemed like a simple enough plan, but when Miller arrived, Rowan immediately noticed the woman's hurried pace and the frown line between her brows. The fear from the night before seeped under Rowan's skin in a dreadful chill.

"Doctor, is there something wrong?" Rowan asked as the woman rushed by her. She picked up her steps to follow, almost jogging to keep up with Miller's wide strides.

"Possibly," she replied, a grave tone on her voice. Rowan felt dread sink in her stomach like a rock. Something happened. She hadn't said anything, and something happened because of it.

Rowan followed behind Miller in an awkward silence, wanting to speak but too nervous for words, and far too scared to ask further questions. Anxiety nipped at her heels, making her move quicker, despite being unsure if she wanted to know the reason for the concern on Miller's face.

The observation room buzzed with chatter, the dismay pungent in the air. Miller pushed past, marching towards the corner where Phelps and another, older doctor stood, and they dove immediately into a serious discussion. Rowan couldn't find the will to eavesdrop.

Instead, her discomfort dragged her eyes to the left wall, even though she didn't want to look. Everyone was crowded around the glass, pointing, talking with their neighbours in worried, hushed voices. She couldn't fight her thirst to know.

Her feet approached the glass without permission, working her way around bodies until she saw him. Sprawled over the stark white floor of the containment room, pale as a ghost, the boy laid, completely unconscious.

"What's happened?" Rowan asked on a breath, not intending to have the question answered, but another doctor near her offered a response.

"They found him this way early this morning. He's completely unresponsive. They think he might be dead."

Rowan's first reaction was relief, but that emotion went sour immediately. If he was dead, the amazing opportunity she was so excited about slipped from her fingers overnight, and she had only herself to blame. This failure was her own doing, because of her stupid fear, her irrational mutism, because she allowed herself to be spooked silent.

Rowan turned her attention to Miller and Phelps. They were arguing in a hushed tone, Phelps making it clear that he was adamantly against whatever Miller suggested.

Miller took little heed to Phelps' protests. "It has to be done, Robert. I have no choice. Perhaps if we were in a facility better equipped..."

Rowan hadn't liked the bit of the argument she managed to pick up. She could read in Miller's tone her annoyance, upset over the commodity that laid unconscious on the floor in the room across from them. Phelps didn't understand. Whatever made that boy able to lift up a bed with one hand and kill multiple people while heavily sedated, it was important. It was groundbreaking. They couldn't let this opportunity go so easily.

Miller stepped away from the conversation to address the room, leaving Phelps mid-retort. "Welcome back, everyone. I'm sure you're all wondering, so no beating around the bush. Perhaps it would be easier to take if I could sugar coat it some way, but we have no time for sweetening today."

Dr. Miller was deathly serious, a drastic difference from her warm demeanor the day before. It unsettled Rowan, perhaps just as it intended to.

"As mentioned yesterday, we have no way of interacting with the subject other than through vocal communication and the shock cuff on his ankle. In any other situation, we might give him a shock to try and jolt a reaction from him, but it's too risky at the moment. If he's not dead, shocking him could possibly kill him, and we can't risk his death."

The room buzzed with apprehension, but Rowan decided mentally that whatever they needed, she would do. It was her responsibility to right this wrong. She even moved past a few of her fellow doctors to approach Miller, preparing to offer her assistance.

"We need a group to enter in with the subject, to inspect his vitals and perform emergency CPR if he is experiencing heart failure."

The room reacted with objections, and Rowan found herself retreating back into the crowd of her peers, that crippling fear chilling her bones frozen again.

Miller had more to add, continuing over the chatter as if

getting the bad news out quickly would make it less offensive to everyone.

"We hoped never to need it, but we have a line of defense for doctors to use to enter the room. It's a cuff for the wrist similar to what he is currently wearing, which will give a shock if a connection is made between the subject and the doctor. Unfortunately, these cuffs cannot be used effectively in this situation since we will need to touch the subject directly to assess his vitals. Anyone volunteering would have to be aware that they are putting themselves in severe danger of injury. "

As she described the "safety" cuffs, everyone was unanimously relieved for a moment, but once Miller confirmed their uselessness the other doctors fell back into scepticism. They agreed with Phelps, who had clearly been against sending anybody in to help the subject. To each person, Rowan included, their own life was far more valuable than whatever was on the other side of the glass.

Miller tried to calm the tense air, lifting her hands to gather everyone's attention again. "I know what I'm asking of you is drastic, but we cannot just leave him. I'm volunteering myself, to show you all that I'm willing to put my life on the line for the success of this project, and to keep one of you from having to make the decision, so all I need is two more volunteers to assist me."

Miller's willingness stirred some debate in the room, a few of the doctors turning to each other with unsure glances, but still, no one step forward.

"I assure you, we have taken all the precautions possible to reduce risk. All we need is to confirm a heartbeat so we can choose the next plan of action. We will be in and out, no time at all."

Unfortunately her attempts were doing little to sway the room. Everyone was too scared, seeing first hand what the boy was capable of only the day before. No one wanted to be a lab rat.

Rowan found herself once again torn between the driven, career focused woman she usually was, and the girl who had been scared stiff the day before by the boy lying unconscious in the next room. If this was yesterday, when Rowan was blinded by excitement and driven by her urge to prove herself, she might have stepped forward. She knew that normally she would jump on this opportunity to show her dedication, to impress Miller once again with her commitment. Something had her rooted to the floor, though. She imagined it was her natural instinct of self preservation.

She was not the only one. The apprehension around her was thick, most of the other doctors directing their gaze to the floor to avoid Miller's expectant gaze. The doctor wasn't about to let them ignore the situation, though.

"This project, and our subject, will die if no one steps forward. Not only will we have the blood of a living being on our hands, but we will also have failed all of humanity. We could have something groundbreaking here. We could change the world with the secrets this subject has to offer, and if no one offers themselves, you're all letting that opportunity die. You all will have to live with that."

Miller's words started desperate but deteriorated into a stifled outrage instead. She believed in what she was saying, so much so that she was offering herself up to die to keep this project going. Perhaps she had every right to judge the others in the room for not making the same commitment, no matter how crazy they all thought her own was.

However, Miller's accusations weakened their resolve, and another round of quiet rustles spread across the group of doctors. Whispers and glances exchanged among them until two men stepped forward.

The others in the room watched in amazement, dumbfounded by the bravery of their colleagues. Or perhaps contemplating their intelligence. Rowan felt a twist of guilt in her stomach, knowing these two volunteers would never have stepped forward if they knew what Rowan experienced the afternoon before.

"Good men, William, Vincent. Let's get in there and finish this quick, so we can get you two back to safety."

Miller led them to the far left side of the glass wall, where there was a double-doored security entrance into the containment room. The entrance consisted of a small area with two doors parallel to each other, one connecting to the observation room, and the other, to the subject. The purpose behind the entrance was to disable any attempted escapes. Anyone looking to enter or leave the containment room would enter through the first door, have it securely locked behind them, and then continue through the second. The double doors meant that even if the subject managed to get through one doorway, he would have nowhere further to go.

Miller took a moment to assure Vincent and William, who were showing their regret. "If anything goes wrong, our technician will be on standby to give the subject another shock, just like yesterday. So really, there's absolutely nothing to be concerned over." She gave a convincingly warm smile, but Rowan felt her nerves bloom into a full bout of anxiety.

She knew she should say something, stop them before it was too late, before her omission put people in danger, but her throat constricted, and everything was moving so quickly. The words never came.

The three entered, the automated doors shutting behind them. With the sound of the lock securing, Rowan's heartbeat became heavier. She took a step forward to the glass, waiting to see the three doctors emerge from the other side of the entrance. On the floor, the boy continued to lay motionless, and Rowan prayed for a moment that he was as expired as he appeared.

Miller exited into the containment room first, quickly, and with determination. The two volunteers lagged back with apprehension.

"Vincent, check for a pulse. William, check for signs of breathing or obstructions in the throat. I'll get him positioned for CPR." Miller called orders to get their feet moving; Vincent and William shaking themselves out of their nerves to follow instructions. Miller flipped the subject flat on his back, and Vincent moved for the boy's wrist first to test for a pulse there. William hesitated, but forced himself into action and joined them on the floor.

"Can you find a pulse, Vincent?" Miller asked, strong and confident, taking lead of the situation. If she had any concerns, she hid them well.

Vincent swallowed, his eyes wide with fear. "I— I don't know. I can't tell. I feel something, maybe. My heart's beating so fucking fast, I can't tell if it's my pulse or not." He panicked , the stress cracking his voice.

"What about you, William? Can you tell if he's breathing?"

When Miller addressed him, William froze up, but managed to shake himself from his nerves and continued pressing his fingers along the boy's throat, checking to make sure his airway was clear. Still unsure, he leaned towards the body, to perhaps hear or feel a barely there breath. Rowan held hers.

Everything went quiet as he hovered an ear over the body, the rest of the room holding the air in their lungs just like Rowan. The seconds slowed, her heart seemed to stop, and before the next beat pounded in her chest, she watched the boy's eyes open.

In disbelief, Rowan blinked, and around her the room exploded with screams. In that split second, the subject leapt off the floor, pinning William to the glass by the neck. His frail arm supported the doctor's entire weight, and William choked as he struggled roughly against the one-handed grip trapping him.

Rowan stared, frozen, for what seemed like forever, even though it all happened in one fleeting moment. The subject stared, a curiously vacant expression in his gaze, before reaching out with his free hand and ushering William's head aside. With the doctor's throat exposed, the subject lunged forward like an animal. Despite choking, William yelled, although the sound was reduced immediately to a sickening gurgle as blood exploded from his torn jugular.

The color knocked Rowan from her terrified trance like a hard punch to the gut, leaving her unable to breathe, as if she'd been winded. The cries of helplessness around the room flooded into her head. William's blood ran down his chest and dripped to the floor at his feet, the subject still buried in the wound he created with his mouth.

"Do something!" Rowan shouted to the computer technician upon finding her voice, shaking him out of his own shock. He turned to the computer in a panic and administered a dose of electricity.

In the observation room, the subject seized up against the voltage, writhing and collapsing to the floor. The now unconscious William followed, but he was quickly gathered up and dragged out of the room by Vincent and Miller.

Rowan hurried forward to help, but a number of the other bystanders beat her there. She stood back and watched instead as Miller ordered for the wounded William to be brought to the infirmary. Someone had taken off their white coat and wrapped it around the open wound on his neck, but the blood was already soaking through and dripping onto the floor. Everything smelled thick and metallic. She could taste the scent in her mouth, sharp on her tongue.

It was the same smell she noticed the night the subject arrived. The one she couldn't place in such a brief moment.

The smell of blood.

Past the red smeared glass separating them, Rowan could see the subject still on his knees, facing away from her. He was no longer disabled with electricity, but his shoulders continued to shake. Rowan took a step towards him, a disturbed curiosity getting the better of her, and witnessed the thin boy as he let his head fall back, a grin plastered wide and grizzly on his blood-stained face.

He was laughing.

As he sat there in the carnage of someone he had just almost killed, with red staining his mouth, neck, and arms all the way up to his elbows, dripping from the strands of his dark hair, he laughed. He laughed like he just pulled off a well-planned prank, not like he just pulled a man's jugular opened with his teeth.

White hot rage flamed in her chest, and before thinking, Rowan banged her fist hard against the glass. She didn't know what she was doing, just that she wanted to interrupt his elation. He didn't deserve to sit there and stew in his own sick pleasure. In the panic around her, no one else noticed her angry fit, except for him.

Before she withdrew her hand, he shot his eyes to where she stood, their blue color even more vibrant against his stained skin. His gaze cut through her like a knife, and her breath caught in her throat. She had wiped the grin off his face, but it lingered in his dilated pupils, a smiling monster hiding just out of sight.

She blinked, and he was standing in front of her on the other side of the glass, dark and sinister and covered in red. A smirk twitched at the corner of his mouth after Rowan's heart stopped in panic, but she assured herself that there was absolutely no way he heard. She watched, her breathing shallow, as he reached up to the patch of bloodied glass that stood between them, extending a pointer finger and dragging it through, drawing a frowning face.

He pouted, then his lips quickly stretching into another satisfied smile when Rowan swallowed down her horror. With his finger covered in the blood from the glass, he secured her terror by sticking the digit in his mouth and licking it clean.

CHAPTER EIGHT

WILLIAM WAS RUSHED to the infirmary in critical condition. Miller and Phelps left the group to assist in his care. The rest of the doctors, Rowan included, moved to the floor's lounge to wait for news on their co-workers hopeful recovery.

For how many people were in the room, it should have been a louder commotion, but a somber silence reigned. Every so often, Rowan heard hushed murmurs of reassurance being passed. In the corner of the room, Vincent was shocked into silence. Blood still soaked his clothes, and a few of the other doctors tried to offer comfort, but he was lost in his head.

Rowan was also somewhere else. She couldn't stop seeing the blood bursting from William's neck, replaying it over and over again in her head. The ice blue color of the subject's gaze was burnt on the back of her eyelids, his laugh on repeat like a skipping record, echoing off the corners of her skull. She could smell the blood, a coppery tang lingering in her throat, and it made her stomach turn in sickness and regret. It was her guilt that sat the heaviest in her gut, though.

If she had just said something, if she told Miller that the

subject had spoken, bellowed at her like a wild animal, perhaps something could have been different. Perhaps William wouldn't be near death, and Vincent wouldn't be traumatized, and Rowan wouldn't feel like she was suffocating.

It was difficult not to eavesdrop on people's conversations in the quiet room, even though the topic of discussion just made Rowan feel more ill. The doctors debated the safety of the project, bringing into question Miller's leadership, and even considering the repercussions of quitting. The idea festered in her head the day before as well, and now circled around the rest of her thoughts like a vulture. It was the only way out of this.

But the contract also made it clear that, at the very least, a break of the contract meant her career was as good as over.

She felt cheated, played for a fool. Fate offered her a dream, and she was too busy trying to catch it to notice the strings attached. Now she was tangled up in them. She was stuck in a hell she could have never predicted, where the people around her were suddenly dying and suffering, and the demon set to torture her was a bloodied, laughing boy locked up behind glass. With no option to back out, she felt caged herself, much like the subject of their observation.

Feeling like the walls were slowly closing in on her, Rowan stood and left the room, intending to get some air and clear her head with a walk around the halls. Her thoughts were so clouded with her guilt and fear that she could barely put together a logical thought. Her natural instinct to flee consumed her. At that moment, it seemed worth it to throw everything away just to avoid tumbling deeper into this hell.

It was while pacing the halls, struggling with her resolve, that Rowan almost ran into Miller as the woman turned around a corner from deeper in the labs. Shaken back to reality by the near collision, Rowan immediately began apologizing. "Dr. Miller, please excuse me. I'm a little out of my head."

"Aren't we all? With what happened..." She put a hand on Rowan's shoulder, her concerned expression switching focus as she surveyed Rowan. "You look pale. Maybe you should sit down a moment."

Miller's office was just down the hall, and she led Rowan over to the door with her statement. Rowan accepted a seat, feeling faint and sick as she tried to calm down. Miller retrieved a small bottle of water from a drawer and handed it across the desk. Rowan took a sip, but it only made her feel worse.

"I understand if you're shaken up about what happened. Not many people can witness something so gruesome and not be affected. You should know, though, William is alright. I was on my way to tell the others the good news."

Miller's attempt at some comfort was appreciated, but it didn't relieve her of the bile sitting in her throat.

"That's good to hear." She managed the words by taking a deep breath to try and settle her racing heart, but when she opened her mouth next, her thoughts escaped on a trembling exhale. "I think I have to quit this project, doctor."

Miller sat stunned for a moment, and then the worried line in her forehead chiseled deeper as she leaned forward onto her desk, folding her fingers together. "I'm... very sorry to hear that, Miss Platts." Miller paused for a moment to gather her thoughts, continuing after she swallowed down a thick emotion. "You had so much potential."

Rowan tried to bite back the tears stinging at her eyes, Miller's words confirming more than enough about what would happen. "I'm... sorry..."

She muttered the words, more for herself than for Miller. She was failing herself. She would regret this, she knew she would, but she'd never been so scared in her life, and her body screamed at her to do whatever it took to escape.

Miller leaned back in her chair and sighed heavily, staring at the wall for a moment, like she was trying to comprehend. She had seen something in Rowan that wasn't there. Something unmovable. Something that maybe she *wanted* to see in Rowan, and now her disappointment was palpable. It hurt almost as much as the regret sitting in Rowan's stomach.

"I'm very sorry this happened. I should have expected that an accident like this so early would dwindle my numbers but... It's a blow nonetheless. I was looking forward to having you on my team, Miss Platts."

Rowan shook her head, feeling guilty for causing Miller more distress. She offered an explanation before she even thought her words through. "It's not just what happened to William."

Miller frowned in reaction, begging silently for further explanation.

"I was going to tell you, but everything happened so quickly this morning, I just... I froze up." Rowan let her head hang in shame, unable to look the older woman in the eye, shutting her own tightly. "Yesterday, after leaving your office, I returned to the observation room to retrieve some things. While I was there, the subject... He spoke to me."

Rowan heard Miller inhale a sharp breath, shifting to sit up straighter in her chair. "If that's true, this is a big deal. He hasn't spoken to anyone since arriving." A different emotion snuck into Miller's tone, and when Rowan lifted her gaze again she identified it in the woman's dark eyes. She tried to stifle it, but excitement shined in them as she asked, "Well, what did he say?"

Since the attack on William, Rowan's mind had been occupied by other thoughts, and with Miller's question the memories she repressed from the day before flooded back and caused a cold chill to sweep up her spine. She was sure by the look on Miller's face that her color went a shade paler.

How was she supposed to express what the boy said? That he could hear, through a glass wall and from the other side of a room, her lungs and heartbeat? That he could smell her blood, like some sort of predatory animal? It sounded delusional.

Somehow, she managed to get her mouth working to offer Miller a response. "He said... Impossible things." Rowan caught Miller's curiosity shift to impatience, and she closed her eyes again, letting out a calming breath before forcing herself to continue. "I whispered something, and he heard me. Through the glass. I could barely hear my own voice, but he heard me."

"There is a telec—"

Rowan continued over her when Miller interrupted. "He told me he could hear my heart beating." She squeezed her hands together to keep them from shaking. "He asked if I was scared, and said he could tell I was. That he could smell it."

Miller let the silence sit, tracing her jaw with a finger as she thought, going through a number of expressions. Finally, she took a deep breath. "What your saying suggests he has exceptionally enhanced hearing and smell."

Rowan nodded gravely. "It's about as impossible as him having superhuman strength, and you showed us he was capable of that."

Any note of skepticism left lingering on Miller's face dissolved away. She opened the drawer under her desk and pulled out a notepad. "Did he say anything else?" She asked while taking down a note.

Rowan didn't want to recollect more, but her mind was already deep in the memory and there was no point hiding the informa-tion. She kept telling herself as much as she wanted to avoid it, recanting the things he said was important, especially if she was quitting. She didn't want another accident to happen, even if she wasn't there to witness it.

"He didn't seem to be able to see me, so we can at least assume his vision is not that different from ours. But he was able to place where I stood just by listening. He walked over to me and stopped right in front of me on the other side of the glass. He was calm at first, but he got violent suddenly. He was obviously malnourished, and it was making him weak and irritable. He said—" She paused, panic tightening in her chest, but she pushed through it. "He said I smelled delicious."

Miller must have noticed Rowan's discomfort, trying to wrap things up to minimize her struggle. "Is that everything he said? Was there anything else?"

Rowan cringed as she remembered his violent bellow. "He yelled at me, like no one has ever yelled at me before. Demanding. He said…"

She trailed off as she remembered, the last thing he shouted at her, with his cold blue eyes burning with a scorching fire. The words that finally torn her feet up from being rooted in fear and forced her fleeing like a terrified animal. She put a hand to her mouth to muffle her sound of realization.

Blood. He had called for her blood, and when he didn't get it, he took it from someone else. He painted the walls and his face in red and he laughed like a rebellious youth, pleased with his anarchy. Perhaps his actions, made to seem like senseless violence, were actually a calculated plan concocted in a last moment of desperation. An act of starvation.

She had to be crazy, but it explained so much, and she found it hard to ignore the supporting evidence as the memories assaulted her. How on earth was she supposed to convince Miller of this wild assumption, though, when it obviously just sprung into her head? She looked up at the doctor, who sat confused and holding her breath, waiting for an explanation.

"Doctor, do we have donor blood in the infirmary?"

Miller's eyes narrowed a fraction, not following the intention of the question. "Yes, of course. We used a lot of it with William to stabilize him, but we should still have some on hand. Why—"

"There's no way I could explain without sounding absolutely insane. I'm not even sure if I believe myself right now, so I need to try something to prove whether what I'm thinking is even possible or not."

Rowan stood and went for the door, fear suddenly replaced with intense focus, directed solely on proving herself right or wrong. Miller hurried to follow, the two of them rushing to the infirmary.

Rowan was insane. This was so far-fetched, it had to be her imagination running wild again. It must have been thanks to Cameron and his conspiracy theories. She could hear the boy's yells in the back of her skull, though. Remembered him licking his fingers clean of the red fluid he stained the room in, and she couldn't fully convince herself of her madness when he had proven to defy all logic and reason previously.

Miller took the lead as they entered the infirmary, retrieving a bag of donor blood from the cold storage. She took it out of the medical fridge and held it for a moment, giving Rowan a weary expression.

"I don't trust all that easily, Miss Platts. There's something about you, though. You're acting crazy, but the look in your eyes is so level it convinces me. Don't make me regret putting my faith in you."

Rowan nodded, taking the cold pack from her. If she was wrong, she wouldn't just be letting herself down, but Miller as well. In that case, maybe she deserved to lose her career over this project. Maybe she wasn't cut out for this kind of success.

She wasn't wrong, though. As much as she wished she was crazy, wished it was impossible, that she would go to the observation room and prove her instinct false, she knew it wouldn't be so. That would simply be too reasonable, and so far nothing about this project followed any reason.

The observation room was only a stride down the hall. When they entered, the subject was leaning against the far wall in the containment room, and Rowan could tell he was pretending not to notice them, even though he probably heard them coming all the way down the corridor.

"Can you unlock it?" she asked while moving towards the security doors.

She needed to get to the food hatch: a skinny, sliding panel at the very foot of the second door, which they'd been using in their attempts to feed the subject. As she neared, he lifted his blue gaze towards her, the look freezing her to her spot briefly. She managed to shake out of the fear when the automated latch unlocked itself, though.

Rowan dragged open the first heavy door and entered towards the second. With trembling limbs, she dropped to her knees, as far from the food hatch as possible. She worried he might be desperate enough to reach through it and grab her. She hesitated again but managed to force herself to lean forward and slide the hatch open, tossing the bag of blood into the containment room. She was on her feet again immediately, hurrying out to Miller's side.

Beyond the bloodied glass, the subject had yet to move, but Rowan could see his gaze locked onto the blood like a predator. She stepped closer, changing her angle to see him better, and his blue eyes flicked to the sound of her feet. His pupils were wide and black like the day before, and earlier, when he attacked William. He looked possessed, far more animal than human.

He didn't want to move. He pushed his back into the wall as if trying to hold himself there, but whatever force consumed him was too much to restrain. Rowan blinked, and he was across the room on his knees. He clutched the blood packet tight in his bony fingers, tore into the plastic with his teeth, and drank the liquid inside. He swallowed it down until the bag was dry, refreshing the red stains on his lips.

CHAPTER NINE

SUCCESSFULLY FEEDING the subject was a big breakthrough in the project, and Miller was not the only one to think so. When she shared the news with the rest of the doctors, their somber emotions over William's accident shifted to curiosity. The discovery of a blood-based diet bypassed their previous, legitimate concerns.

It was hard for Rowan to not get infected by the new fire of enthusiasm in her colleagues also. After all, she had been filled with wide-eyed wonder just the day before, when this world of underground laboratories and secret government projects were still new and amazing to her. As quickly as her apprehensions came, they disappeared again.

Unease lingered in the pit of her stomach and weighed her down, but something else bloomed in her chest as she listened in on the questions buzzing among the other doctors. When Miller cited Rowan as the one who deciphered the mystery of the subject's diet, there was a round of applause, and Rowan couldn't help her prideful smile.

Very briefly, she forgot about the fear and anxiety, about the way the subject was able to look at her without seeing her, or even how he taunted her with blood on his face. The success was addictive, and the approval of her peers and Miller, was euphoric. Her motivation returned with a vengeance, and she was sure it showed.

Which was why when Miller stopped her before going home that day, Rowan wasn't expecting the proposal she made.

"Miss Platts, I understand how difficult this experience has been for you so far. It's only been two days, and already you've experienced personally the subject's violent nature on two separate occasions. Just a little while ago you were shaken enough to consider giving up on this project altogether."

Rowan opened her mouth to interrupt, to insist she had been thinking foolishly, that she was revived with a new drive now, but Miller insisted on continuing.

"It's clear you are not in the right state of mind to make this decision. A lot has happened today. So, instead of answering now, I want you to go home and think about what you really want. If you want to stay on this project, then I will expect you here tomorrow at the usual time. But..." She paused, considering her words carefully. She put on a stern expression as she finished. "If you think that your commitment for this project will ever waver again like it did today, don't come back tomorrow."

Shocked, Rowan found her breath catch. Dr. Miller's words felt like rejection, and after all the praise, the harshness came like a slap across the face. "Doctor, I—"

Miller let her shoulders slack and tried to warm her expression. "Please don't take this negatively. I simply want to give you an out if you wanted it. You have potential, Miss Platts, but this kind of work isn't for everyone, and I wouldn't want to be the one responsible for stealing away your career just because you ended up being more of a... *Phelps*."

She reached out to put her hand on Rowan's shoulder, an

encouraging gesture, perhaps to soften the blow of her words. After everything though, being compared to Phelps felt more like an insult, especially now that it was being used to point out how she might not be as much like Miller as she originally thought.

"If you choose to leave now, while I'll certainly be disappointed, you have my promise that you will be allowed to continue your research here at ECBS without interruption, as if this project never happened. I trust you to keep what has happened so far to yourself, because out of anyone I think you clearly understand what is at stake if there's a leak of information." Miller smiled carefully, going for a hard and fair approach as she concluded her proposal with a final warning. "If you choose to stay though, this offer won't be made again. If you come to work tomorrow, I expect you to be in this for the long run. I need to know that I can rely on the people next to me, through anything."

Rowan was sure Miller's proposition was meant to make her slow down and really consider what she was getting herself into, consider her emotions and reactions and everything else that happened in the last forty-eight hours, but the ultimatum presented had quite the opposite effect on her. Instead of reflecting, Rowan simply felt more driven to prove Miller's doubts wrong.

She allowed her fear to cloud her desires too much lately. She knew what she wanted. She wanted success, she wanted recognition, she wanted the outstanding career that Miller had committed her life to, and Rowan was ready to commit herself in the same way. No more letting her emotions get the better of her, dragging her away from her ambitions.

Miller wanted Rowan by her side, that much was clear, and Rowan wasn't about to disappoint either of them by giving into something foolishly primal like fear.

After all, he couldn't hurt her as long as she stayed out of that room.

This determination made it easy for Rowan to convince herself to return to the ECBS the following day, even though she slept restlessly and couldn't shake the smell of blood. That was easily forgotten however, when she imagined Miller's delight once she showed up, and this psyched herself up even further for the start of a new day.

She didn't get the greeting she expected when she arrived, though. Miller was too engrossed in a conversation with Phelps, which had both their faces engraved with concern. Rowan shook off her disappointment and snaked her way into the conversation instead, taking a spot next to Miller to politely listen in.

"I'm not sure I agree with the direction you want to head, Margot. It's obvious that this boy is highly disturbed. Is it in our best interest to indulge his behavior through bribes?" Phelps' voice was colored with judgement, purple bags under his eyes suggesting he also experienced a long night.

"We haven't got a single word out of him since his arrival. I see no reason why we shouldn't at least try. And it's not a bribe, Robert. It's cooperation." Dr. Miller could tell that Phelps was not convinced. She sighed, and signaled to Rowan, the first acknowledgement of the day. "Tell me what you think, Dr. Platts?"

Rowan stared, blank-faced for a moment, taken aback by the title she had just been given so inconspicuously. Miller never called her 'doctor' before, and just like that, it slipped into her speech as if it had always been there. The way she placed it was too deliberate, suggesting something else entirely to Rowan. This is what it could be like from now on.

All Rowan had to do was be on Miller's side.

"We can't allow the subject to die, and blood is the only substance he's ingested so far. Denying it to him would be starving him."

Rowan hadn't thought about how agreeing with Miller also

meant opposing Phelps, and she only realized afterwards, when Phelps' expression dropped to disappointment. Miller seemed perfectly pleased by the response though, like she was well aware that she forced Rowan to pick favorites and overjoyed to come out on top.

"It's settled then. Blood bribes it is." She gave a playful smile as she placed a hand on Rowan's shoulder blade and led her along, approaching the wall that separated them from the containment room. "Let's have a chat with this little bastard, shall we?"

The shame rolling around in Rowan's stomach was eased by Miller's attention, reaffirming her decision. This is where she wanted to be: at Miller's side, involved first hand with everything. If she had to step on a few toes to get there, so be it. Phelps would understand the situation she was in. Besides, she could apologize later for hurt feelings along the way.

Rowan was not allowed any further time to dwell. Miller signalled to the technician, and as the folding wall slowly parted, the buzzing around the room hushed.

Blood still painted the floor and glass, although it was further smudged from when she last saw it. The pattern suggested he used his hands to try and gather up a midnight snack. On the floor was the blood packet, now completely ripped opened and licked clean. Anyone who had not seen him drink from it directly would wonder if there had ever been liquid in it at all.

The boy reclined on the mattress, now removed from its bent, bed frame and placed on the floor in the corner of the room. Dried blood flaked off his skin overnight, but the color absorbed into his pores, staining his fingers and around his mouth so they looked flushed. He pretended he didn't know they were watching, but Rowan could see he had already focused his hearing. His neck straightened just slightly, his sharp gaze going blank as he listened. It was hard not to see what he was doing now that she witnessed it before.

Miller received a ear piece, which she set in place. Once snug, she tapped it twice and spoke.

"Good morning. My name is Dr. Margot Miller. I'm a biologist for The Centers for Disease Control and Prevention of the United States of America." Miller folded her arms across her chest while she spoke, her voice casual and collected as it echoed through the telecom. "My normal research would usually be working on finding that pesky cure for cancer, but considering my knowledge for human biology, I've been assigned to this case in hopes I can figure you out. Since, as we all have seen, you're a bit of a medical mystery, aren't you?"

In the other room, the boy blinked, but gave no reaction to her words.

Miller continued, determined not let the subject's silence rub her wrong. "You're being held in the Eureka Center for Biological Studies, in Eureka, California. We took you into our custody on Monday morning after authorities were called with a report of five dead and one unconscious at a hospital in the next town over. Your handy work, we're assuming?"

This statement produced a reaction, the smallest smirk twitching onto the boy's lips. It was only there for a moment, and if Rowan hadn't seen it before, she would have wondered if it had even been there at all. It sent a chill along her spine, knowing he was laughing to himself over his murders.

He didn't say a word, though.

"Let's not play hard to get now. We know you speak and understand the English language, so you're not fooling anyone by playing dumb." Miller's tone lowered a fraction from irritation.

Once again, the subject didn't even blink in their direction.

Miller scoffed beside Rowan, impatient with the subject's

failure to comply. She glared behind her rimless lenses. "We want to ask you some questions, so we can find out a little more about you. But we can't ask you questions if you're not going to answer." Miller paused, and when she once again received no response from the stubborn boy on the other side of the glass, she added the bribe. "Cooperate with us, and we'll make sure your dietary needs are met."

Finally, a full acknowledgement. With Miller's offer on the table, the boy flicked his gaze in their direction. The blacks of his eyes shined sinister entertainment, knotting up Rowan's throat. Then, the boy stood, taking a few casual steps towards them, falling in and out of Rowan's line of sight behind the blood stains swiped across the glass.

From the look of it, his feast the day before greatly improved his health. In fact, he could have been mistaken for a different person entirely. With his strength back, he held his spine straight, increasing his perceived height by a few inches. His skin regained its color and moisture back, and the deep, black circles under his eyes shallowed.

If he was able to throw a bed across the room before, when he seemed weak and feeble, now he could likely throw a house with little effort. That prospect made Rowan nervous, and the tension sat on the back of her neck. The ease he had in his pacing didn't help. It seemed as though he could be through the glass at any moment if he so pleased. If that was the case though, wouldn't he have already done it?

He halted in front of the glass, facing Miller, because Rowan was sure he knew all along where each and every one of them stood. Rowan retreated involuntarily at his closeness, but Miller stood unmoved, not caving to the boy's scare tactics.

He let the silence linger a long time, soaking it up and enjoying the palpable tension in the room. Then, to everyone's surprise, he opened his mouth and replied.

"I'll cooperate, Dr. Miller. I'll answer any questions you have, but I have conditions of my own." He stopped briefly, just to enjoy the stunned silence of the room, before finishing. "I'll speak to the doctor who fed me. Face to face, no hiding behind walls. If you send anyone else in, I'll kill them."

CHAPTER TEN

THE ROOM ERUPTED IN OBJECTIONS, filling the air with a loud buzz of concern. For Rowan, it was ambiance, though. Her heart pounded in her ears far louder.

On the other side of the glass, the boy smiled, the same dare in his eyes as the day before, only she knew what it meant now. When she delivered the blood to him, she'd started something. She solved a piece of him, revealed she knew one of his secrets. She went from just another victim to an opponent in a game, that look in his eyes saying *your turn*.

His first move was as good as a checkmate, though, and he knew it. Despite her newfound resolve to stick with the project, she refused to go anywhere near those security doors again. He already scared her stiff with the glass wall separating them; she'd never survive entering that room, especially after the last ones to enter left bloodied and nearly dead.

If he didn't kill her, her palpitating heart would.

If she refused? No one would blame her, but the project would be at a standstill once again. The praise she so quickly became addicted to would disappear, along with the promise of success this project offered. Worst of all though, her questions wouldn't have answers.

Beside her, Phelps and Miller bickered again, bits of their heated debate working its way past Rowan's considerations.

"You are not sending that girl in there. She's barely started her life, and you're going to give her a death sentence."

"Don't be stupid, Robert. No one is making anyone do anything. Of course we're not going to send her in there, but what else do you suggest we do from here?"

"We need to sedate him so we can take some samples. If we have samples, we don't need to hear anything coming out of his mouth."

"And how do you suggest we sedate him? It took an excessive dose of morphine just to slow him down enough for us to get him here. And he took five others with him. He won't be letting anyone else near him with a needle again."

"It doesn't matter. Whatever we do, we don't need to be sending any more innocent people to their deaths. William barely survived your first suicide mission."

"We got him out, and he's stable."

"He'll be scarred for the rest of his life!"

The undercurrent of panic in their argument spread around the room like wildfire. People's awe turned to fearful mutters, and weary glances in Rowan's direction, waiting with bated breath for her reaction.

This is what he wanted. Chaos. Fear. Not just her own now, but everyone's around her. Watching him through the dirtied glass, she saw glee dancing in his eyes like flames. It entertained him to have so much control when he was locked up in isolation. It became clear to Rowan that he had every intention now to make this investigation as painful as possible for everyone involved.

After all, how else was he suppose to rebel against his containment? All he had was their fear. Beyond it, he was nothing but an animal in a cage, puffing up his fur and trying to look big to keep them all scared.

He was bluffing.

At least, Rowan hoped he was, because she was about to do something extremely stupid.

"I'll do it."

The room silenced in shock at her words, then immediately erupted into outraged murmurs. It wasn't the reaction of the other doctors she was waiting on, though.

Rowan followed the boy inside the containment room as his eyebrow lifted, the smirk on his lips spreading even wider. She didn't know what to make of the expression, but she hoped it was positive. She hoped she was playing his game to his satisfaction; if she amused him enough, maybe she'd live a few extra turns.

Or just long enough to find out something useful.

"What are you talking about, Rowan?" It was Phelps who voiced outrage first, bewildered by her idiotic resolve.

Then Miller. "Please, Dr. Platts. Don't feel like you have to do this. This is not your responsibility. We'll think of something else. This is just too dangerous."

"I said I'll do it."

Rowan looked at her mentors with fire in her eyes. Where she found that heat, she wasn't sure. Only moments ago she was stone cold with terror, but now, she was hot with new resolve, much like when she banged on the glass in attempt to wipe the boy's wicked laugh off his face after attacking William. Perhaps she just couldn't stand him enjoying himself so much.

"But why, Rowan?" Miller's concern was palpable.

"We have those bracelets right?" she asked, seeking out Miller for confirmation.

The doctor raised her brow and sighed with disbelief. "Sure we do. If you wear one, theoretically he should be unable to touch you without triggering a shock, and that seems to be effectively disabling him so far."

Something about the way she worded her explanation was less than convincing, though. The subject had defied their expectations numerous times before, so there was no guarantee. Phelps lifted a hand to point out this flaw, but she interrupted before he could offer it.

"I know the risks, doctors, but the bracelet is not my only safety net in this situation." Rowan glanced into the containment room again, wanting to be sure that the fear-inducing maniac on the other side was listening. His gaze was sharp, focused on the spot that her rapid heart was beating. "I'm his only chance of getting out of here."

Those blue eyes narrowed a fraction, confirming she had his attention.

"If I go in there, he could very well kill me... But that won't get him anywhere. If I'm killed, the project will be at a standstill again. At least by speaking to me, by leaving me alive, he has some chance left of no longer being a prisoner here."

Her logic was sound, but it was yet to be proven whether their contained subject followed logic and reason. Nevertheless, Rowan swayed a few people around her, including Dr. Miller.

"You really want to do this?" She was still concerned, but behind it was that excitement she had trouble concealing. Even though Miller feared for Rowan's safety, she couldn't help but be curious for the outcome.

Just as Rowan was.

Phelps silently urged her to reconsider, but she pretended not to notice. It hurt to go against his wishes. Instead, Rowan nodded once to Miller, confirming this was her final decision. A few gasps circled the room, but otherwise, her colleagues stayed as quiet as ghosts.

"I'm glad you decided to stay with us, Dr. Platts." Miller's praise was too sugary, but it helped Rowan swallow the sour truth.

She was absolutely terrified.

* * *

THE SOUND of the security door shutting behind her was solid. Final. The bracelet, clamped snug around her wrist like a handcuff, offered no comfort. Somewhere outside her shallow breathing, she heard Miller speaking through the telecom again.

"We are sending in a doctor. You are to stay two yards away from her at all times. If you touch her, or do not cooperate, you will be immobilized. Do you understand, Subject?"

The bloodied boy did not reply. Instead, there was an unsettling silence, then Rowan heard the loud, mechanical locks on the doors. Once behind her, shutting her in, and then in front, allowing access to the monster on the other side. Rowan swallowed down the sick feeling that rose in her throat, letting out a long exhale to try and calm herself.

There was a low chuckle, then, dragging fingernails, lightly across the metal door in front of her.

"Come out of your hole, little mouse. The cat wants to play."

His tone implied he was joking, but something sinister was also laced in it. It made the air catch in her throat, escaping in a hiss across a quivering lip. She twisted the cuff on her wrist with shaking fingers, trying to find her resolve again. She must have forgotten it in the previous room.

Rowan closed her eyes, shaking off the fear that clung to her ankles like chains, and took a heavy step towards the door. Like Pandora, opening her box of chaos, Rowan reached for the heavy handle with a timid hand. She was damned, regardless of what happened after the door opened. It was the choice to open it that condemned her.

She pushed the handle down and the latch gave, the door cracking a sliver from its frame. The pungent, metallic smell of blood assaulted her senses. She tasted it in the back of her throat, and it made her gag. Throwing a hand to her mouth, her small breakfast threatened to make a reappearance.

There was no sign of him in the white line of light, so she pressed her palm flat against the metal and urged it open further, watching cautiously as the containment room came into view. A few careful steps brought her inside, until finally she caught sight of his shape and froze like a scared deer.

He leaned against the wall opposite of her, allowing much more space between them than required, as if attempting to make her less uncomfortable. Unfortunately, he followed her with a predatory precision, which negated any ease his distance provided.

Rowan swallow down another large lump in her throat and threw her gaze to the ground, hoping that if she didn't see him, she could pretend he simply wasn't there. Bloody footprints littered the tile she stood on; she resisted a yelp as she retreated a step, and her shoulderblades hit the wall beside the entrance.

Attempting to gain some control, she reached into her white jacket and pulled out the tablet she'd been provided, opening up some notes with shaking fingers. All Rowan had to do was stand there and ask some of the questions listed on the device. It would not be difficult. Just keep her eyes down.

They betrayed her almost immediately, sensing his burning stare on her skin and looking back up at him in reflex. She felt her heart stop briefly, stabbed by the frigid chill of his unblinking stare. She saw his lip twitch up a fraction, and she inhaled hard and forced her attention back to the tablet.

"My name is Dr. Rowan Platts, and—"

"Doctor?" He had been utterly silent so far, almost painfully so, but the moment Rowan began to speak he interrupted. A well-executed disruption tactic forced her bit of bravery to tangle up in her throat. "You seem young to be a doctor, *Miss Platts.*" His voice wrapped around her name smoothly, like how a lover might say it, making Rowan feel dirty and defiled.

"I'm finishing my dissertation." She managed a sharpness back.

His eyes flashed with a silent laugh. "So you're not a doctor. Yet."

"As far as you're concerned, I'm a doctor." Rowan was surprised at the levelness of her words. It seemed offense distracted her from her fear, however briefly.

His eyebrow raised a fraction, then he lowered his gaze, breaking his stare finally. Surrender? "Very well, *doctor.*" His sarcasm suggested otherwise.

"Dr. Miller has already explained the situation, so I think we should just get down to the questi—"

"You're not what I expected." Another interruption. He could tell it was breaking her focus and was definitely doing it for that reason. With her tongue twisted again, he pushed off from the wall to stand, and continued the thought. "I imagined someone older. Dark hair."

"Thank you. You've just confirmed that you at least don't have super vision and can't see through the one-way glass." Rowan grabbed the tablet pen and marked in the note, pretending not to be painfully aware of the step towards her he had taken. "Have anything else you'd like to tell us?"

He stretched out the silence, as though he was going to let

Rowan get away with that overconfident retort. He was just stewing in the moment, though.

"I have a preference for A negative."

Rowan's shoulders tensed, but she tried to not let the sick joke jostle her. It was what he wanted. Still, she could see the smug grin on his face from her peripherals, his response kicking her heart into overdrive.

"We already knew of your heightened sense of smell." But was it so precise that he could place her blood type, or was that just an extremely lucky shot in the dark? She pretended his comment hadn't shaken her as badly as it did, even though it seemed frivolous to hide her physical reactions.

"You're a doctor, so tell me. What's the average heartbeats per minute for a young woman like yourself? Seventy? You should consider getting checked out." He looked like a cat in cream, so pleased with himself that if the fear wasn't already making Rowan sick to her stomach, his arrogance would. "Yours is going a lot faster than that."

"Congratulations. You've brought attention to the obvious fact that you're terrifying. Now, if you're finished playing games with me, how about you tell us something we don't already know. Like a name, maybe."

The fear and frustration cracked her shell, and she spilled defensive words before she had time to think about the consequences of her tone. She kept her eyes glued to the tablet, because even though she found the stupidity to talk back to him, she had not yet come across the bravery to stand behind those words and look him in the eye.

Somehow, she got away with this response unscathed. In fact, Rowan thought that perhaps she heard a breathy chuckle from across the room, but she couldn't be sure. She wasn't allowed time to confirm the foreign noise.

"I don't have a name," he said, like it was the simplest thing.

Rowan scoffed. "Everyone has a name."

"I've been alone for a very long time. I've never needed a name." The joking from before seemed to have disappeared, his tone inching toward boredom instead.

"But when you were born. You must have been given one."

"I've long forgotten my family name." He paused, taking another step away from the wall as he spoke. "My first name, though. Lyall."

Rowan wrote it down on the tablet, trying to ignore his movements. The five-yard distance he started with was closer to three now. With every step her pulse raced a beat faster.

"Do you know what it means?" he asked, continuing when Rowan forced a neutral reaction. "It comes from old norse. Wolf. Fits, don't you think?" He smiled with the side of his mouth, a toothy grin that resembled the animal he cited.

Rowan simply glanced back down to the tablet, refusing to acknowledge his feralness. "Your age?"

"How old do I look?" he fired back the question immediately. His tone was the most innocent so far, like he was honestly curious. It was perhaps even more unsettling than when he was playing mind games.

Rowan dared a glance up at him, dashing over his unblemished skin and full head of blood-matted, dark brown hair. "No older than twenty."

His lip twitched up, but otherwise, he gave no further explanation.

She recorded the number, if only to distract her from how uncomfortable the silence was. Whenever the conversation lulled, Rowan heard her heart pounding in her ears, like the persistent ticking of a clock, reminding her of the time going by. Every second, a moment longer in that room with him. Every second, another violent slam against her rib cage, her fear trying to force its way out through her chest.

Was the inside of her head really this loud, or was the silence just playing tricks?

"Might I make a request?"

Finally, he broke through the beating drum in her head with his words, although this time there was something off about his tone. The mocking had been laid on thick so far, but this question rang with soft sincerity.

Rowan lifted her gaze from her tablet, inhaling sharp and pushing herself further back into the wall immediately.

He was staring again, steady and unblinking, but it was not with the purpose to make her uncomfortable this time. His pupils dilated wide, the black almost completely taking over the blue. He did not look her in the eye, either. Rather, his gaze directed lower, and when Rowan swallowed down her thick fear, she watched his lips part slightly in reaction. The pieces put themselves together, and she threw her hand up around her bare neck.

He blinked, like coming out of a trance. "Could you perhaps wear your hair down while we speak?" With his focus off her neck now, the black receded slightly.

Rowan sighed, relieved when he was no longer locked onto her neck. Removing her hand, she pulled the tie out of her hair and adjusted what she could of her thin, blonde strands forward so the skin of her neck and jaw were in shadows.

"Sorry." An apology slipped out by reflex before she could stop herself.

He didn't seem to hear. Instead, he'd shut his eyes and took in a smooth, calming breath, exhaling slowly. His shoulder relaxed a fraction. Rowan expected him to open them and see the sarcasm dancing across his expression again, the blood-thirsty animal banished, but she was mistaken. His pupils stayed dilated, black and possessed, as he returned his gaze to her.

"It would probably be best if we wrapped this up for today, doctor." His voice was steady, too steady. The kind that suggested tight control.

She didn't have to be told twice. Rowan stepped towards the exit, but offered a question while retreating. "Will you speak with me again?"

Something felt unfinished between them. Even though she wanted nothing but to get out of that room and never come back in, she also felt like there was more here that needed to be said, the curiosity that encouraged her to enter the containment room aching with dissatisfaction.

He was clearly surprised by the question, his expression flashing interest beyond the haze in his eyes. "Why?"

"We need samples. Blood, DNA, a biopsy maybe. Would you consent?" She took another backstep to the door, her fingers wrapping the handle.

"What do I get in return?"

Rowan gaped, completely at a loss of what to even offer him other than more blood. She managed to stutter out a response. "Whatever you want, within reason."

The corner of his mouth twitched up, and she saw his pupils widen further before he forced his gaze to the ground to offer a nod. "Ok."

Rowan didn't wait for anything further. The details could be ironed out when he wasn't ready to rip out her throat. She knew not to push a cornered animal, and she was beginning to shake so badly now that she worried her legs wouldn't hold out if she waited any longer.

Opening the metal door swiftly, she exited the containment room and shut it hard behind her. The automated locks latched themselves, and Rowan released a shuddered sigh, a wave of overwhelming relief engulfing her body. She was still alive.

With the fear-induced adrenaline now diluting in her veins, Rowan collapsed onto her weak knees. The door into the observation room opened, and Miller immediately crouched beside her, grabbing her elbow and helping her back to her feet. Beyond the sudden lightheadedness, she heard the doctor's praise in her ear while being led off to the infirmary to recover.

CHAPTER ELEVEN

Rowan was released from ECBS after recuperating from her journey into the monster's lair. When Phelps escorted her outside, Cameron was waiting with his old pick-up truck, and Rowan felt both relieved and guilty to see him.

She'd been ignoring his calls for two days.

"I contacted him for you, since I thought it was good that you had someone to at least get you home safe," Phelps explained. "It's important you take care of yourself. Make sure she does, will you, Cameron?"

"Will do, boss!" Cameron replied playfully before engulfing Rowan in a smothering hug and muttering under his breath to her ear, "Right after I kill you for not returning my calls."

After allowing Rowan her lungs back, she turned to Phelps, letting her eyes go to the ground. "Thank you for calling him. I really appreciate it. I was worried you were upset with me for agreeing with Miller today."

Phelps expression became slightly more guarded, but as usual, he couldn't stay sour.

"Of course it's hard to be the odd man out, but I'm not

someone to be as petty as getting angry over someone disagreeing with me. Just... Just make sure your decisions are yours, and you're not letting Miller influence you in any way. Ok, Miss Platts?"

Rowan smiled and nodded, although it felt forced with her name attached to Miss again instead of doctor.

Once in the passenger seat of Cameron's truck, the thoughtful moment between her and Phelps faded off as her guilt settled in. Rowan gave Cameron a sheepish grin when he glared at her.

"You've got some 'splainin to do."

The words were hardly out of his mouth before his bad impression had Rowan snorting as she held down a laugh. Trying her best to stay serious, she pouted and whined through her giggles, "I know. I'm so sorry, Cam. Things just got really crazy really fast."

"No kidding. Nearly had a heart attack when I got a call from Phelps."

Cameron turned on the vehicle's engine as he responded, offering a smile even though the look was obviously strained.

Rowan groaned, ashamed that she made him worry. "I'm an idiot. I'm so sorry."

"So you're alright then, at least?"

"I'm alright. Just a little shaken up. A lot has happened." It was an understatement.

Truthfully, Rowan felt completely out of control the last few days and was only now starting to gain some of it back. She didn't want Cameron to know what had been going on. He worried about her far too much. If he found out about her almost quitting the project the previous day, he wouldn't shut up for the next month.

Besides, no matter how much he teasingly pressed for details during the drive into town, it wasn't like she could reveal any even if she wanted to.

When Cameron admitted defeat and suggested they grab take-out, she enthusiastically agreed. She was not interested in making dinner that night, and fatty food was great for generating some feel-good vibes, which she desperately needed. They picked up Chinese and drove to her place, where Cameron flipped through the channels while Rowan gathered some cutlery. They settled on a bad horror movie to watch with dinner, but he set the volume on low, suggesting he intended to talk.

A silence hung between them as they ate, and she could tell that he was trying to figure out the best way to ask what was on his mind.

"So, you're sure you're alright. Like, physically. Right, Row? Because when Phelps called he said something about you being in the infirmary. I didn't even know we had an infirmary at ECBS." He shoved a bunch of rice into his mouth with his conclusion.

Rowan smiled to try and ease his nerves. "I'm fine. Just felt a little tired, lightheaded. They gave me some saline to perk me up."

"Miller also said you've been through a lot the last few days. Rumors around the halls is that someone got hurt?"

"For someone who's not supposed to know anything about what's going on, you sure seem to know a lot." Rowan smirked when he shrugged and made a faux innocent face. "Someone got hurt. Yeah. He's alright, but... It was a close call."

"Just an accident?" His question was hopeful.

Cameron must have been expecting her to confirm that William had perhaps dropped a bottle of nasty chemicals or wasn't careful around dangerous machinery.

Rowan lowered her eyes to her food and played with it before answering, "No, it wasn't really an accident. More like, results of an on-the-job hazard." She hated being so cryptic with him, but she was already saying too much.

He frowned, nodding, even though he was likely understanding even less than what Rowan felt she was revealing. He stayed silent again for a moment, but couldn't help asking more, despite knowing he wasn't supposed to.

"So, was it a body?"

Rowan swallowed a mouthful of noodles before humming to herself, sliding into a teasing tone. "Maybe." He wasn't completely wrong, after all. It was a body. Just not a dead one.

"Someone famous?"

Rowan rolled her eyes and shook her head.

"Was it an alien?" His hopefulness was too obvious.

She gave a sympathetic look for having to let him down. "No. Sorry, Cam." At least, she didn't think the boy was an alien. He certainly seemed human enough, even with his superhuman powers.

"Well, that's a downer. I'm not nearly as interested anymore." Cameron gave a cheeky grin when Rowan scoffed. "How about those nicely dressed men that were following you around?"

Rowan had seen more of the security since that day. A number of people worked to keep what was down in that basement a secret. "Government agents, I think. It would make the most sense."

They spent a few more minutes in comfortable silence, finishing up their meals and watching the movie. It was about a demon dog, hunting down the main characters. There wasn't much more context.

"You're taking care of yourself, aren't you, Row?" Cameron asked, while the black dog on the screen chased a screaming girl down a dark alley.

Rowan put down the bite she had been moving to her mouth. "Yeah. I'm ok."

"I just get a weird vibe." Cameron tried to laugh off the

comment, but it was obvious he was shaken by whatever feeling he had.

"You have no reason to be worried, Cam."

"If you say so." He saw right through her but was too kind to argue. His disappointment felt like a stab in Rowan's gut regardless.

The comfortable silence soured because of her, and they finished their food with awkwardness lingering between them. When Cameron finished, he checked his phone for the time.

"Getting late. Phelps said you should focus on getting some rest, so maybe I should leave you to go to bed."

Panic struck at the idea of his departure, not realizing how unsettled she still felt until he suggested leaving her alone with the memories of everything that happened.

"I hate to be a bother, but... Do you think you could stay tonight? I'd sleep so much better knowing someone else is in the house."

Cameron, who had stood to gather up their leftovers, stopped to consider. "I guess I could do that. I work evening tomorrow though, so try not to wake me when you get up, early bird."

"Thanks, Cam." Rowan rose, moving over to give a thank-you hug.

"Don't mention it." He hooked his elbow around her head, pulling it towards his chest and pressing his lips to her hair.

She wrapped her arms around his torso tightly, humming at the comfort the gesture provided. Rowan hadn't realized how badly she'd needed someone to simply hold her, and it led to her lingering in his arms a moment longer than usual. She sighed, some tension loosening from her shoulders, and his hold around her tightened a little more.

"Rowan..." His voice resonated in his chest as he said her

name, clearly sensing her reluctance to withdraw. "If something was wrong, you'd tell me, right?"

She hesitated with her response. He had no idea how badly she wanted to recount every detail for him so he'd know what was going on. She wanted his reassurance, because there was a small, nagging voice in her head that wondered if she was crazy for agreeing to enter the containment room that day, or if her career was worth endangering herself like this. She wanted him to tell her whether or not she was simply indulging her curiosity, or if her selfishness would get her killed this time. After all, he'd been there for her through everything; he knew her better than she knew herself. She trusted him.

She couldn't share these details with him though, not just because it was against her contract, but also because a part of her wished someone had been there to protect her from the things she now knew.

In hindsight, she never wanted to know what true terror felt like. She never wanted to see someone almost killed in a brutal attack. She didn't want to be forced to make the difficult decisions she had been faced with over the last few days. If she could, she would keep this secret from Cameron forever, because no matter how much he asked, he didn't want to know, and she knew that.

"Like I said, you don't have to worry," Rowan replied, finally pulling out of his arms.

Cameron deflated, a little more convinced, and messed a hand over her head. "Get some rest, Dr. Platts. I'll be here if you need me." He gestured for her to go, then sat himself back down on the couch and snatched up the remote.

The next morning Rowan left as quietly as she could to avoid waking him, knowing she wouldn't be able to stand the guilt of lying to him once again.

CHAPTER TWELVE

"Yesterday, you consented to the donation of various samples, so we can proceed into the research of your condition." Dr. Miller spoke firm and confident over the telecom, and on the other side of the glass, the subject paced his small, stark room, remaining unresponsive as usual.

"We will be sending Dr. Platts back into the containment room today to retrieve these samples. Upon cooperation, we will discuss your compensation. Do you understand, Subject?"

When Miller finished, the boy glanced towards the glass, but once again gave no further response. She somehow held herself together, despite his stubbornness clearly getting on her last nerve. Letting out a controlled sigh, Miller gave her attention to Rowan instead.

"You know, part of taking these samples means you will have to remove the safety bracelet and have direct physical contact with him? You will be vulnerable for the entire time you have the cuff off." Miller was very good at sounding concerned despite her obvious excitement.

"I told you, I'm his only chance of getting out of here. He won't hurt me. That wouldn't make any sense."

In the other room, the subject gave a breathy chuckle. "You're assuming that I act based on logic and reason. And you know what they say about assuming." His sarcasm was so thick it could have easily smothered Rowan if she let it.

"We can send someone else in with you. They could have a cuff on. That way if something happens, you'll have someone to help get you out." Miller offered an alternative, the subject's tactics working to make the older woman nervous instead.

Rowan stared through glass wall for a moment, trying to read his blue gaze, looking for a tell that suggested he was lying, but his facial expression was as controlled as ever. She could only bluff back.

"He said no one else. Just me. I'll be fine, doctor." Her pulse picked up a beat with the fib, and she watched the subject's lips twist up at the corner in response.

Rowan received a steel cart, topped with the equipment necessary to collect the samples. Clamped around her wrist, she wore the protective bracelet again, even though she knew it would have to come off soon. It still offered her the smallest bit of security, even if it was false comfort.

Miller ushered her through the first door of the security entrance, and before she could completely gather herself, the lock secured behind her, and she was once again faced with nothing but an unlatched door between herself and the monster on the other side. Rowan tried not to linger in her dread this time, reaching forward and pulling the door open, entering the room with her equipment in front of her.

The subject sat on his mattress in the corner of the room, as if completely uninterested in even greeting her this time. Perhaps he was already bored with the concept of having her around. She hoped that wasn't the case, since boring him could result in being disposed of if he decided.

"Good morning." Her voice shook when she spoke, so she cleared her throat to try and cover it. The crack had been too obvious, though.

"Morning, is it? I wouldn't know. You doctors don't shut off the lights in this fucking room. I've completely lost track of time. It's maddening, actually."

Clearly, he was much more irritated than the day before. It was not a promising start.

"You say that as if you're normally sane."

The reply slipped from her lips without her consent, the result of her nerves lubricating her tongue. Rowan immediately turned to fiddle with her equipment, biting at her tongue to punish herself for that bit of snark. She was sure sarcasm would not be the best approach at the moment.

A silence lulled, and then, to Rowan's surprise, she heard the boy let out something that sounded like a laugh. A relieved breath she hadn't realized she'd been holding escaped her lungs. Somehow, she managed to come out of that unscathed.

"You cleaned up," Rowan commented, extra polite this time, gesturing towards the now spotless floors and glass. His red-stained sheets had been collected and stored in the corner of the room. He even attempted to scrub his face, and his hair, although stringy, was no longer matted with dried blood. Unfortunately, there wasn't much he could do about the stains on his clothes, so he still looked horrifying.

"I thought it would make everyone a bit more comfortable."

"Considerate of you." She couldn't help but let her surprise come out on her tone. This slip caused him to make that almost-laugh noise again. Rowan continued talking, jittery with how unsettling it was to hear him chuckling. "Maybe we could provide a change of clothes if you cooperate today?" Hopefully it wouldn't hurt to bribe him. Perhaps he'd let her earlier snarkiness slide?

"How about we skip the sweet talk and just get started with the poking and prodding."

He seemed less inclined to banter today, and the chip on his shoulder made Rowan increasingly uncomfortable.

She fisted her fingers to cease her shaking hands. "It won't be nearly that unpleasant, I promise."

"That's too bad, I like unpleasant."

His gaze gleamed when Rowan failed to find a response in her stress. Instead, she pulled her cart closer to him, fiddling again with the items to buy herself some time. Taking a few deep breaths through her nose, she contemplated which of the three processes would be the least intrusive to start with.

The biopsy would have to be last; it was the most painful, and she was most concerned of what his reaction would be to pain. It was also the least important compared to a DNA and blood sample, which would give them more of the information they needed.

The blood sample was perhaps the most important, but it also included penetrating his skin, and she was unsure if the sight of blood, even his own, would trigger another relapse into monster-mode like the day before. If just the sight of her veins set him off, it concerned her what actual blood would do.

That left only the DNA sample to start with. It wasn't so bad. Just a quick swipe of the cotton swab inside his mouth. Rowan was not looking forward to getting anywhere near his face, though. She grabbed a pair of latex gloves and slipped them on carefully, putting off the inevitable.

He caught her red-handed in her procrastination. Taunting, he smirked and said, "I'm not really a patient person, doctor."

Rowan resisted staring at him, attempting to shut him out a moment longer to help level herself instead. She knew the longer she stood there the longer she'd have to stay in that room, so despite her uneven breathing and trembling fingers, Rowan pressed her finger against the cuff locked around her wrist. Reading her fingerprint, the cuff chimed in confirmation and opened.

The subject moved in a flash, so fast he was just a blur in her peripherals. Before she could react he grabbed her wrist and pulled her around. Rowan used the momentum though, slashing her arm down in reflex, silver gleaming.

He took a quick intake of air, immediately recoiling a step and releasing her, the hand going up to his face instead. Touching his cheek, a line of blood bloomed across the skin, his fingertips collecting the rich red color. His sharp eyes searched for the culprit, finding the scalpel in Rowan's hand. His pupils widened, an animal locked onto a target, but then he smirked and his eyes stretched back into blue. Letting himself fall back down onto the mattress, he chuckled a little, amused.

"I was only messing with you," he offered, wiping at his cheek when the blood began to drip down his skin, licking it from his finger.

Rowan stared, the blood pooling up in his cut again, a much darker red than her own. When he caught her looking, she forced her gaze to the floor.

"Sorry," she offered, but her hand still held a death grip around the scalpel. When she finally shook herself out of the crippling panic he induced, she put the makeshift weapon down and grabbed an alcohol swab instead. "I'll clean that up for you."

He waved her away when she got down on her knees next to

him. "No need." To explain himself, he thumbed away the excess blood again, and Rowan fell back on the balls of her feet, bewildered.

There was no wound.

"What happened?" She couldn't logic it. In her amazement, she almost reached out to inspect the unblemished skin, but managed to contain her eager hands. "I cut you. You were bleeding. It's like, you just, healed."

"If you're a scientist, why are you so slow?" He tried to be cruel, but his words didn't quite reach the sharpness he was attempting.

Rowan ignored him regardless, hypothesizing to herself. "It's like, some sort of rapid regeneration?"

"Congrats, genius. But if you would mind not slashing me with a scalpel next time... I heal, but that doesn't mean I don't feel it." He rubbed over the spot again, nursing the residual pain.

She sent him a nasty glare. "Don't touch me, and I won't have to defend myself."

"Where's the fun?" He shot back, his gaze dancing with dark humor. "You're so jumpy. It's like you think I'm going to kill you or something."

Scowling, she chose not to comment on his intentionally disturbing words, and instead stood to return to her cart.

"I'm taking a DNA sample first. Just have to rub this swab on the inside of your cheek. So, open. Please."

Rowan explained flatly, trying to distance herself from what she had to do, since thinking about it was scaring her stiff. Opening up the long cotton swab from its sterile packaging, she went back to her knees next to the mattress he sat on, waiting.

"I've decided what I want, in return for cooperating," he said, before opening his mouth obediently.

"Have you?"

Rowan's response was distracted as she caught a glimpse of his straight, white teeth and remembered them tearing through the flesh on William's neck. She wasn't sure what she expected. There was absolutely nothing unusual about them. His canines were possibly a bit sharper than the average person, but besides that, his teeth looked entirely human. It only disturbed Rowan more, because that meant it had taken a huge amount of pressure to break skin as easily as he had.

She swallowed down the knot in her throat and leaned forward, setting a firm hand under his chin and wiping the swab thoroughly against the inside of his cheek. She was careful to make sure she did it correctly, not keen on a redo. When she finished, she withdrew quickly, putting the swab in a test tube and sealing it with a cork.

The boy ran his tongue over the inside of his cheek before elaborating. "As much as I appreciate the meals you've been providing so far, I wanted to request something a little fresher."

Rowan moved to prepare the needle for drawing blood, but paused with his request. She hoped she was wrong, but it sounded like he was asking for a *live* meal. Another live meal.

He scoffed with humor, like he'd read her mind, and perhaps even made the request knowing it'd garner her exact reaction. "You assume the worst of me," he said, as if he was offended, but his blue eyes laughed. When Rowan glared, he explained further. "I just meant, a fresh donation. One of you doctors sit down and put some of your blood in a bag for me."

She turned back to the cart, unpackaging the vacutainer, her back too straight. "Is there something wrong with what we're providing?"

"The preservatives make me feel sick. And it's strange drinking it cold when I'm used to... *body temperature*." He punctuated with another wolfish grin.

Once again, Rowan pretended to be unaffected by his games

despite her throat knotting. "I'll see what I can do," she answered finally, then returned to her knees, holding out a hand to receive his arm. "I need to draw some blood next."

He sighed, like being accommodating was a bother, but moved closer to her and offered his limb. When she reached to meet him, he jerked, causing her to flinch.

He smirked playfully.

Growing frustrated with his toying, and more than ready to leave that room, Rowan hurried forward with her job, placing the tourniquet and tying it around his upper arm.

"The blood is not going to bother you?" She cupped her hand around his to direct his fingers into a fist.

"You just had me bleeding. A little bit more won't make a difference."

It slipped her mind, or perhaps she had purposely forgotten how he'd wiped his own blood from his face and licked it from his fingers mere moments ago. While massaging the skin at the bend of his arm with her thumb to find a good vein, she asked timidly, "Is it just other's blood that, you know. *Affects* you?" She didn't know how to phrase it without sounding ridiculous.

"It would be problematic if I went crazy over my own blood, wouldn't it?"

She hadn't thought of that, and found herself flush from embarrassment with her ignorant question. "It sounds terribly problematic, your condition." With the comment, she pushed the tip of the needle against his skin until it punctured.

"It has its perks, though." He added with a breathy chuckle, and she felt it on her ear, causing her to shoot her eyes up.

He sat close now, nothing but her curtain of thin, blonde hair between her neck and his teeth. Rowan tried to act unbothered and unaware, but she was holding her breath now, worried he might get a whiff of something that would stir his appetite if she exhaled. When she let the air carefully out through her nose, she saw his lip turn up out of the corner of her eye.

Rowan retrieved the vacutainer, attaching it and watching as the blood pulled from his vein into the small vial. Dark and rich like from the wound on his face, she wondered what kind of secrets it held.

He read her fascination with different intentions. When he spoke again it was under his breath. "You could enjoy those perks too, *Dr. Platts*." He said her name like a sigh, right to her ear, Rowan's muscles seizing up in reaction. He was sitting just right, angled so her head sheltered his lips from the view of the other doctors in the observation room. An enticing secret intended just for her slithered from his lips. "You could be just like me. Right now if you wanted. Just a little taste is all it would take. Aren't you tired of being so *human?* I can show you what it feels like to be a god, instead."

Distracted by his words exhaled hot across her neck, Rowan let the vacutainer fill to the brim. She swore when she noticed, removing it messily and cleaning up the blood that dripped down his arm. Her hands shaking fiercely, she tried to still them by putting pressure on his wound until it healed.

"Last thing I need is a biopsy," she said after pulling herself together again, moving on as if she hadn't heard his whispers. It was impossible to hide the quiver of her voice though, especially with him watching her fumble, his expression cool and calm, lips tilted up at the corner like a comma.

She collected the last instruments needed, and positioned herself by his shoulder, determined to do the biopsy as quickly as possible so she could get out of that room, away from the sick, blood-hungry monster currently whispering his version of sweet nothings into her ear.

"This will hurt. I have to take a muscle sample with this

needle, so it will go deep, past the skin and fat." She primed the tip on his skin, puncturing through with little warning. His brows furrowed at her aggressiveness, but his eyes gleamed with humor. He got pleasure from disturbing her, and even more from the punishment.

"I have a further request about my compensation," he said, pausing to wait for her reaction. Rowan stopped her work briefly to glare at him, and he took that as invitation to elaborate. He smiled and leaned closer again. "I'd like *your* blood."

She shoved the needle deep, until it hit muscle, then pulled it out in a swift motion. The boy swore at her, putting a hand over the spot to nurse the pain, his eyes laughing wildly.

"Why?" Rowan asked, short and sharp, collecting the muscle sample into a vial and beginning to gather up her cart to leave. In her panic, she almost forgot to put her cuff back on, fumbling to clasp it around her wrist again when she realized.

He was busy inspecting his shoulder, making sure the needle hole disappeared before standing along with her. "I told you. I have a preference for A negative." He smirked when he received another dirty look. "And having a certain smell around makes the craving for a particular flavor more, intolerable. I thought if I got a little taste, maybe I wouldn't want to bury my teeth into your neck so badly."

The imagery made Rowan shudder as her hand subconsciously jumped up to her throat. "And what if it just makes it worse?" Rowan didn't like the idea of him having a taste for her. It felt disturbingly intimate. Thinking about it made her skin crawl.

"If it makes it worse, then I'll let you know."

Rowan stayed silent, considering, but was unable to give him an answer. Her brain wasn't working correctly. All she could think about was his breath on her ear, and his laughing blue eyes driving her mad. Instead, she moved her cart to the door, opting to leave the request open-ended.

"You're welcome back any time, doctor." His tone mocked cheerfulness as she closed the metal door behind herself, the lock latching tightly.

CHAPTER THIRTEEN

"WE'RE GOING to make such amazing headway with the samples you've collected, Dr. Platts."

Miller's gushing was little more than background noise to Rowan's preoccupied mind, blending in with the rest of the praise she received after leaving the containment room. None of it was quite enough to distract her from the unsettling thoughts this time, though. Problems piled up: While the attention from Miller and her colleagues was addictive, Rowan was now gaining unwanted attention from the subject as well, a result she hadn't planned for and didn't know how to handle.

Miller didn't seem to notice Rowan's distraction, gleaming in excitement while escorting her to the infirmary, an enthusiasm that Rowan tried to mirror but struggled to emulate.

"His cooperation means everything to this project. I'm really grateful that you've agreed to his requests. We all are."

Rowan nodded away Miller's thanks, not wanting to dwell on the uncomfortable topic. The subject said he wanted her blood, and she hadn't known if she wanted to give it to him. Perhaps something about her apprehension was selfish, but the idea of him drinking her blood, even out of a plastic bag, made her itch under her skin like there were bugs in her veins.

It was only fair though, since they made a deal to give him what he wanted for his cooperation. Rowan had more blood than she needed; she donated regularly to help keep other human beings alive, so donating to satiate his appetite shouldn't be a far stretch. Keeping him satisfied would hopefully mean further cooperation, as well, which was vital. She definitely didn't want to be on his bad side. When Miller started to beat around the bush for an answer, Rowan agreed to donate without much of a fuss.

If she was being honest, it wasn't even this request that truly weighed on her mind. It was there, prodding at her brain like an annoying child, but lingering on it was an excuse to ignore the real discomfort that consumed her, put there by the words he'd given just to her.

They still turned goosebumps up on her neck as she remembered, leaving a cold chill along her spine. According to his suggestion, whatever made him the way he was, it could be shared. There was a secret in his blood, a secret he knew about, tried to share with her, and perhaps the most disturbing part, seemed like he wanted her to accept.

It was obvious he saw himself as privileged despite being made into a monster by his own hunger, and it seemed like he wanted to share that with her. Rowan didn't know if she should take it as a sincere gesture or just another game.

She couldn't just ignore information like this, though. It was important dant to consider. It would be in her best interest to take everything he said seriously. Yet, just like the first day he spoke to her, something crippled Rowan. An uncertainty that she couldn't place, that kept her lips tightly sealed.

It wasn't that she was afraid of being wrong. At this point, if she told Miller this information and it turned out to be false, it would be written off as the boy messing with them, and she would simply be praised further if it ended up being true. Her fear was not about personal repercussions of being right or wrong, but rather, the prospect of what his words being true meant.

Just a small taste of his blood, and someone could crush metal with their bare hands and hear heartbeats through walls, just like him? The idea of being so powerful so effortlessly, it was easy to overlook the possible downsides. A part of Rowan had even been tempted, if only for a brief moment of primal curiosity, so who's to say someone else wouldn't be, also? They had a vial of his blood now, stored away in a research lab, where anyone could take it.

It was a foolish notion. The rest of the doctors on this project were professionals, just like Rowan, and wouldn't cave to simple temptation. Whatever games the subject was trying to play, they wouldn't be foolish enough to fall for them. Rowan had no reason to keep this to herself.

When given the opportunity though, the information hung on her tongue.

"Dr. Miller!" Reaching the infirmary, Rowan called to stop the older woman before she returned to the group to analyze the samples. Miller paused, and so did Rowan, before shaking her head and offering Miller a reassuring smile. "I just wanted to say, I know how important it is to keep our word to him. I'll do what it takes to have his cooperation."

Miller blinked, then beamed. "Phelps will come by in a moment to take the sample."

Rowan didn't get enough time to react before Miller strode down the hall, leaving her alone with yet another dilemma: What would she say facing Phelps, alone, for the first time in days?

PHELPS WAS gentle with the needle as he punctured her skin, humming a little tune to himself as he worked, making the awkward silence between them much more painful on Rowan's end. She thought to just remain silent if he would let her, but before he even began drawing blood, she tried to break the tension.

"You didn't have to do this. One of the nurses could have. I'm sure there are more important things you could be doing right now."

He smiled and waved the comment away. "I volunteered. How else was I supposed to get a moment alone with the outstanding Dr. Rowan Platts?" His words were teasing but there was just enough pointedness in them to make Rowan lower her gaze in shame.

"I'm hardly outstanding. I'm just doing my job, sir," Rowan muttered, keeping her eyes on her blood as it pooled in the plastic bag. When the silence became thick again, she had to fill it once more. "I'm sorry about... Disagreeing with you the other day."

Phelps chuckled. "Rowan. We're all adults here. You, also a perfectly capable doctor yourself, just like the rest of us. I'm not going to judge you for coming to your own conclusions based on given evidence. While having a minion on my side is certainly easy on the ego, I didn't bring you onto this project because I thought you'd be my little lackie the whole time."

Rowan sighed heavily, nodding but still feeling weighted. "I guess I was just worried that you'd think I was... Picking sides."

Mostly because that's what it felt like it was, and it made her feel dirty doing so. However playful, there was a clearly established rivalry between Miller and Phelps that she felt like she had gotten in the middle of.

He laughed again. "You don't have to apologize. I knew that you were going to take a liking to Miller. Besides being well aware of how much of a fan you are, you and Miller are also both very similar, so of course some of your opinions will line up better with hers than mine. I don't take that personally. In fact, it pleases me, that you didn't just side with me to suck up."

No, instead she sided with Miller to suck up.

Phelps seemed to have heard her thoughts, perhaps seeing negativity on her expression, and put a hand on her unoccupied arm to bring her eyes up to his finally. "Listen. I know the affect that Miller has on people. I've been watching her woo everyone around her for her whole career. She can leave most a little... Starstruck, to say the least. But trust me, we've worked together for a while now too, and I haven't been the least bit surprised by any of your decisions so far. Whether I agree with them or not is another story. But, you've always had a strong will and sense of self. You know what you want and how to get it, and that hasn't changed just because you're starry-eyed." His gaze glinted when Rowan offered a weak smile of appreciation.

She'd be lying if she said the thought hadn't been swimming around in her head, especially now as Rowan dwelled on why exactly she was donating blood when the idea of what it was for turned her stomach. Was she really doing it because *she* wanted to, or was she getting caught up in the desires of someone else? Cameron would usually have reassured her by now, but unfortunately, he couldn't know enough details to give her what she needed to feel secure in her own decisions.

Luckily, it seemed like Phelps was ready to step up in his place. Offering one last gentle smile, Phelps let the look sink to something more somber, adding, "Just promise me one thing."

Rowan nodded earnestly. "Of course, doctor."

Lifting his hand from her arm, he pointed a finger to his temple. "Keep that hard-head of yours. Miller has one of her own, and it would be good for her to have someone to butt heads with, if necessary."

Rowan couldn't help but chuckle. Butting heads with Miller sounded... Undesirable.

"Is this one of those situations where you think Miller would respect me more in the long run if I have the guts to disagree with her?"

Phelps snorted, holding down his laughter. "Oh no, Miller hates when people disagree with her." This concept was apparently hilarious to him. After reigning in his humor, he continued, "But if anyone can in this case, it's you. You've proven yourself to Miller. She respects you more than she'll let on. So keep following your gut, and don't let Miller persuade you into simply going along without question."

Rowan smiled, nodding again in a silent promise.

"Good." Dipping his head curtly, he returned to her arm to extract the needle now that the bag had filled with her blood. "We'll take this to the subject so you don't have to worry about it. In the meantime, I've been informed that Miller will be working with her team through the night on the samples you collected. Perhaps you would like to stay the night in the infirmary, as well. I imagine a mild sedative would be appreciated at the moment, help you get some proper shut eye? You've had a busy few days."

Rowan's relief must have been palpable in the air because he laughed again after she responded with a weighted exhale. "That sounds like heaven."

WITH A LITTLE CHEMICAL HELP, Rowan fell into the first restful sleep she had in days, waking a few hours later as the ticking clock on the wall neared six. The infirmary nurse asked if she'd like to sleep longer, but Rowan decided against it. She felt stiff and wanted to move around, opting for a walk after getting a glass of water instead.

The halls of the laboratory were eerily quiet that late in the evening. Miller and the other doctors were in the research wing tending to the samples, so the rest of the floor was empty of life; except for one creature, of course.

Her curiosity pulled her feet in the direction of the observation room even though she felt like she'd regret it. Nothing good happened when she was there alone; he liked to say terrible things when it was only her listening. Rowan reminded herself that he could only do so much from the other side of the glass, and the temptation to speak with him was insatiable. She wanted to know what other terrifying, mysterious secrets he would share if she listened long enough.

"You keep surprising me, little mouse. I was sure our earlier interaction was going to be our last. After all, you got what you wanted from me, didn't you?" He heard her before she even took a step into the observation room, and it was unsettling, which was most likely the intention.

In the containment room, the subject was lying on his mattress like a lazy cat, stretched out and content, an empty bag of blood on the floor not far from his hanging hand. He didn't bother moving, even as Rowan approached the glass. His only reaction was a deep intake a breath.

"The fragrance doesn't do the taste justice."

Rowan swallowed down her disgust, wrapping her arms around herself defensively to try to keep the discomfort from getting under her skin. A coldness still managed its way into her bones.

"I take my donation was satisfying, then?"

He chuckled as he sat up, glinting eyes finally glancing towards her voice. "I was not expecting you to agree to it. It was an inappropriate request. Purposely so." A cheshire grin spread his lips, proud of his intentionally abusive behavior.

"You make a lot of inappropriate requests," Rowan noted under her breath. Whether she intended for him to hear or not, she wasn't sure.

He did regardless, the mischief in his eyes growing a color darker as she reminded him. "Why didn't you tell anyone about my other offer? Given your previous behavior, I thought you wouldn't be able to wait to share with the boss lady any juicy details about me." The question seemed genuine, his tone ringing curiosity.

Rowan scoffed, annoyed by the fact that he felt he knew her well enough to predict her behavior. "You told me drinking your blood would make me like you. Forgive me if I was skeptical about your reliability."

He grinned slick. "Solid evidence didn't stop you before. You had no proof I drank blood, but that didn't get in the way of you testing the theory. You are a scientist, after all. No, I think I know the real reason you didn't tell anyone." His voice taunted, winding around her like a snake, tightening. "You didn't tell anyone because you were tempted, weren't you? A part of you was considering it. And maybe still is."

Rowan felt the anger burn in her belly and the embarrassment flare up on her face, but she caught herself before saying something regrettable. The anger was what he wanted, and she wouldn't get anywhere with it. She was looking for answers, and answers were only given to questions.

"Was that why you made the offer then? To prove something to me about myself?" She paused for a moment, probing deeper into her suggestion. "Maybe you think I'm not so different from you?" Or maybe... he hoped?

Something kept her from adding to the consideration further.

He rose to his feet and approached the glass, stopping just in front of her, his blue eyes dancing. Tilting his head, he imitated deep thought for a brief moment before responding. "Maybe I just wanted to see what kind of monster is creeping under your skin, *Rowan*."

For the first time, he said her name, and he said it with possession, like he owned a bit of it. Owned a bit of her. As though he planted something inside of her, branded it with his mark, and was now calling out to it by a name he had given. It answered, a hot stirring in her gut somewhere between anticipation and anxiety.

Rowan uprooted her feet and stepped away from the glass. Her pulse pounded hard in her head now, a painful distraction. "Obviously, whatever monster I am, it's not the type that would willingly choose to be like you." Her voice failed her. She meant for those words to come out strong and confident, but instead, they were broken and timid. She wasn't sure he entirely believed her.

If he doubted her resolve he didn't comment on it, choosing for once to not use her weakness against her. She was thankful until he spoke again.

"What about the other doctors? What darkness is lurking in them, do you think?"

Rowan took in a sharp breath. The question already crossed her mind, but the realization that came along with it surprised her. He knew what he offered her was a dangerously tempting opportunity, for anyone. He also must have assumed they'd figure it out, once having his samples under a microscope.

"You expect the others to be unable to resist the temptation?"

His lips tilted up with her conclusion. "I have the habit of bringing out the worst in people."

So he expected chaos. She could see it in his eyes, like fire in the wide blacks of his pupils. If it was what he thought of them, mindless monsters who couldn't resist the draw to such a powerful prospect, what did it mean, that he'd offered it to her first?

Attempting to snuff out her silent question, Rowan gave a small, dismissive laugh. "We're not the monsters you think we are."

To her surprise, he chuckled as well. The tone was tainted with irony, like he knew something she failed to realize. "That's where you're wrong, *doctor*. Humans are the worst kind of monsters."

There was something in the way he said it. A sad wisdom flickered just briefly in his eyes and brought a dreadful sickness to her stomach. She wanted desperately to brush off his words like they meant nothing, but she couldn't. They lingered in the corners of her mind, tangled up with all the questions, even after going back to the infirmary to accept another dose of sedatives.

CHAPTER FOURTEEN

Rowan woke early the next morning courtesy of the infirmary nurse, informing her that Miller wanted to see her once she was ready. The sedatives had done wonders, so she wouldn't have minded staying in bed for another few hours, but she knew Miller and her team worked through the night, so if she wanted to talk, it likely meant they uncovered something.

The thought turned Rowan's stomach as she collected a coffee for herself and headed to the research wing. The subject's comments from the previous evening repeated in her head, leaving her apprehensive about what discoveries had been made. It was the first time in a long time that she felt like maybe she was better off not knowing the answer to all her questions.

Miller hid a pair of puffy eyes behind her glasses when she greeted Rowan. Her obvious tiredness did not impede her excitement though, as she hurried over to drag Rowan with her through the room. "There's so much to tell you, Dr. Platts. It's truly amazing." While talking and walking, Miller gathered up folders as she passed, shuffling through them until she found what she wanted to share.

Immediately, Rowan identified the microscopic images as Miller flipped through them. After working in the field for so long, human blood cells were hard to miss. There was something off about them, though. She wasn't allowed enough time to figure it out before Miller continued to the next image.

"So, he's not an alien, then?" Rowan asked casually, but her joke seemed to have missed Miller entirely, either because of her exhaustion or her distraction.

Luckily, Phelps joined them, picking up her comment. "Your friend Mr. Davis will be disappointed." He chuckled when Rowan smiled appreciatively. She clearly couldn't tell Cameron exactly what was going on, but it was comforting to hear Phelps include him in a joke, regardless.

Finding what she was looking for while they chatted, Miller finally butted back into the conversation, presenting Rowan with a folder. "He's certainly biologically human, making the explanation for his abilities all the more fascinating, in my opinion." She paused to let Rowan survey the papers, watching to see if the young doctor could figure out what she was seeing for herself.

Rowan recognized the new image. "That looks like, the HIV virus?"

The comment came out timidly, because she didn't see the connection yet, but with her words Miller's tired eyes glimmered as she nodded.

"You're absolutely right. We found this virus in his blood. While it looks like HIV, it's acting distinctly different than we would expect from a virus, though." She flipped through pages again, past reports and observation write ups, to blown-up microscopic photos. "Instead of weakening him, this virus is making him stronger."

Rowan gaped, shaking her head when the information didn't

work itself out in her brain. She was still slightly inebriated from the sedatives, unable to come to an explanation.

Miller didn't seem to mind Rowan's speechlessness though, continuing with a fervor she shouldn't have after staying up all night. "The virus works just as most viruses do, entering the bloodstream and reprogramming the host cells. This is usually a destructive process, but in this case the virus is improving cellular functions."

She flipped pages again, showing examples briefly as she touched on them before moving onto the next.

"It's increased oxygen capacity in his red blood cells, leading to better circulatory efficiency, easily explaining his increased muscle strength and dexterity, heightening his physical endurance and lowering his blood pressure. It's also increasing the white blood cells' immunity, making him stronger against infections. The virus is also cloning other cells along with itself. At the moment, the subject has triple the blood cell count of a normal human being."

Rowan exhaled, completely baffled with the flood of information. She took the folder from Miller, going back to take a second glance at the photos. "All that oxygen moving around his body, where is he getting the energy from?" She mused aloud while flipping through the folder.

Miller was about to answer, but Phelps interrupted with a scoff. "Come now, Rowan. You must know that one yourself. Multiplied cells means multiplied hemoglobin. And what do hemoglobin need to transport all the oxygen?"

If her hands weren't full, Rowan would have hit her own skull with her palm. "Iron. Of course."

Miller continued off Phelps' thought, directing Rowan to a page of numbers for her to look at. "His hemoglobin have a huge demand for iron, so we can only assume this is why he naturally craves blood."

"Amazing..." Rowan sighed the word, skimming the report while taking a drink of her coffee. "What about all the other nutrients he would need as a human, though?"

"You're asking all the same questions we had to ask ourselves about two hours ago," Phelps chuckled, impressed that Rowan was covering all the same bases.

"That's one we can only really hypothesize about at the moment." Miller said, offering a more concrete answer than Phelps. "We don't know for how long he's had this virus, if he contracted it or if he was born with it. Our best guess though, is blood became his main source of nutrients so early on, so his body was forced to adjust to the virus' needs. Similar to how certain drugs can alter body chemistry, it's very possible the virus altered his to provide only for what the virus needs."

Her explanation became slightly somber as she spoke, and Phelps translated the tone of her voice with his conclusion. "It's safe to say, if this is the case, the virus isn't just making him super human, but it's possibly the only thing keeping him alive."

For some reason, that sentiment caught Rowan off guard. The subject was so powerful, it had never crossed her mind he was capable of dying like any one of them.

She swallowed down her discomfort to probe the other doctors further. "Dr. Miller... You said he may have contracted the virus?"

Rowan's ill feeling must have shown on her face, causing Miller to misread its intention, smiling and offering a dismissive chuckle. "Oh, don't worry, doctor. It's not airborne. Much like the HIV virus, body fluids would have to be exchanged to risk any sort of infection. So, as long as you can keep from falling victim to his irresistible charm, you'll be totally safe."

The lewd undertone of her comment had clearly been meant to be sarcastic, and Rowan tried to fake a laugh while forcing her fingers not to shake. She convinced herself so thoroughly that he was just messing with her, so the reality was hitting her in the gut like a bag of bricks.

"What about something like... Ingesting infected blood? Would it likely result in infection?"

Miller stopped to consider for a moment before tilting her head into a nod. "Most likely, yes."

"Not getting cravings now, are we, Rowan?" Phelps chuckled with his joke to lighten the mood again. Rowan gave a weak smile but it was obviously colored by her discomfort.

Attempting again to distract herself, Rowan pressed for more. "So, what's on the agenda now that we have all this information?"

Miller opened her mouth to reply, but Phelps cut her off, excited to give some of his own ideas. "I'd love to keep a team on the samples to further research what we have."

"You read my mind, Robert," Miller replied, grinning. "We are also interested in finding out the origins of the virus, if you were up for another meeting with the subject, Dr. Platts?"

Rowan's throat tightened up again. "O-of course. I'm sure he would be interested in some of the information we've learned, as well."

"Fabulous!" Miller exclaimed, practically hopping in place. "It will be so fascinating to see what further things we can find. Maybe we can mutate the virus in some ways, make it provide the necessary iron for the hemoglobins, eradicating the need for the excess iron consumption? Don't you think, Miss Platts?"

Phelps scoffed, but what was supposed to be a laugh didn't quite reach the proper tenor. "Careful, Margot. You're entering the realm of talking about creating superhumans." There was too much warning in his voice.

Miller turned on her heels, her eyes going dark a moment before she smiled playful. "Don't be foolish, Robert." Something thick lingered in the air though, causing an awkward lull to happen.

Rowan filled it with a final question. "If this is a virus, will you two be working on a cure for it?"

Phelps gave Miller another knowing look that Rowan had a feeling she wasn't supposed to see. This time Miller's smile was taut as she responded, "Of course. It's our responsibility as doctors to do what we can to eliminate the virus and help our subject recuperate into a healthy, functioning human being again. Working next to another viral expert like Phelps, it shouldn't take us long to manufacture a treatment for his condition."

AS SHE HAD DONE BEFORE, Rowan entered the security door and listened to the automatic latch grind into place behind her, trapping her with a monster. There was something different this time, though. Discomfort still lingered in her stomach, and her shoulders were stiff from nerves, but the fear that usually shook her bones was strangely absent.

Perhaps she was simply accustomed to being in fear now, or perhaps she was just realizing that the monster locked up in this room was no more terrifying than other prospects that had recently been presented.

Rowan reassured herself that she was letting her thoughts get carried away, tangled up with the subjects patronizing words from the night before. She trusted her fellow doctors. She trusted Miller. Any doubts she had were ones he put in her head, ones he wanted there to play with her, and she refused to let them stick under her skin.

The door in front of her unlocked, and Rowan focused herself on the task ahead. She had been told to tell him about the virus and find out about his past, so she hoped *The Wolf* was feeling chatty. She adjusted her grip on the pair of folding chairs she held, then pulled open the door.

He was standing just on the other side, waiting. With his shoulder leaned against the wall, he looked so casual he could have been mistaken for innocent. As he saw her, he tilted his head a fraction and smirked. Despite his unintimidating facade, Rowan had to stop herself from taking a startled step away from him.

"Good morning, doctor." He obviously enjoyed Rowan's apprehension, trained eyes following her as she fidgeted with the cuff on her wrist. With a voice a fraction lower in tone, he taunted, "Are you going to come out of your hole, little mouse?"

Rowan glared, frustrated that he was keeping up with his antics and that they were continuing to affect her. She huffed and picked up the folding chairs, moving towards him to enter the room with determination.

When she neared him, he stood straight, blocking her path so she was forced pass uncomfortably close to him. While slipping by, she sensed him lean closer to her, hearing him inhale. Her skin crawled, and she felt a moment of panic, hurrying passed and forcing her back to a wall again.

There was something already unsettling about being *smelled* by someone, but when that someone was smelling her because she'd make a good lunch, it was a whole different type of unpleasant.

He chuckled under his breath, the laugh turning into a toothy grin, pleased by the reaction he'd gotten with his behavior. "You smell particularly tempting today."

Rowan tried not to react, although she was sure her discomfort was already visible. She cleared her throat, setting her shoulders straight to try and find some confidence. Her concern made the hairs on the back of her neck stand up though, and she had to ask, "Are you hungry?"

"Are you offering?" With his question the subject's gaze flashed with sick humor, and Rowan threw her empty hand up around her neck, hiding the pulsing veins safe from his devouring eyes. He gave her another smile that was all teeth and danger. "If I behave myself, do I get to taste you again?"

His words made her skin crawl a second time, a hot flush pricking up her neck and onto her cheeks. Rowan flinched when he reached out towards her, but he simply took hold of one of the folding chairs and pulled it from her grip.

She tried to force herself to relax. With her back glued to the wall, she watched as he dragged the chair with him to the center of the room, unfolding it and sitting down lazily. It took Rowan a moment longer to compose herself and follow his lead.

"Always," he said, while she settled across from him.

Rowan stumbled on her tongue briefly. "Pardon?"

"The answer to your question. Am I hungry. I'm always hungry." He had a smirk on his lips, but the look didn't quite reach his eyes. "But at least you doctors are feeding me enough that killing someone seems... *Counter-productive.*"

Rowan didn't like the way he'd chosen to phrase that, but she at least appreciated the honesty. It seemed that maybe she'd get a conversation out of him, after all.

She cleared her throat, twisting her hands in her lap. "Well, why I'm here might make you slightly more inclined to curb the appetite a little longer."

He seemed to appreciate her attempts at informality, but obviously for the wrong reasons. It was a challenge to him: what did he have to say to scare her? Tilting his head to the side, his teeth peeked out from behind his lips.

"It couldn't hurt. I won't lie, since having your blood yesterday,

I've been debating whether dying in here would be worth finishing you off." His words were delivered purposefully, making sure she wouldn't be able to keep up the almost-civil banter.

They were effective, draining the color from Rowan's face. "You said having my blood would help."

More wolf teeth. "I guess I was wrong."

Rowan fidgeted in her chair, feeling hyper aware of the bare skin at her collarbone and wrists. She pushed her shoulders up, discreetly adjusting her sleeves, trying to hide her veins like an addict hiding track marks. He was not giving her any physical signals to be scared, but there was always a part of him that looked at her like something to devour, and it was that look that made her so nervous.

His effect on her showed in the weakness of her voice as she tried to change the subject. "Thanks to the samples I took yesterday, we've managed to learn quite a bit about your condition."

"My condition? Am I sick, doctor?" This was the biggest he'd grinned since the day she first saw him, obviously self-satisfied with his joke.

"In more ways than one." Rowan fired back the retort without thinking, her nerves getting the better of her. She shot her eyes to his in mild horror, but luckily she was greeted with the gleam of a laugh. She resisted a relieved sigh, and continued. "You have a virus. We expect you've had it for a very long time, and it's the root cause of basically everything different about you."

He tilted of his head as he repeated her words. "A virus?"

Rowan bit her lip, unsure what to make of his neutral reaction. She continued cautiously. "Yes. In your blood. It's complicated, we still don't know everything about it, but to put it simply, it seems to be enhancing your body's natural biology. It's improving your blood cells, and as a result, the rest of your body is also improving."

He stood during her explanation, starting a slow pace towards the back wall of the room. His expression turned a fraction more curious, holding his arm out in front of him and pumping his fingers so the veins of his wrist bulged up, dark blue against his pale skin. "In my blood?"

She wasn't really sure why, but when he wandered away from her, Rowan got up to follow. She took a step towards him, nodding in response. "That's where the virus started, at least. It's been in you for so long now that it has influenced the chemistry of your entire body."

He glanced over his shoulder, the animal momentarily gone from his features. Rowan stared back, surprised by the innocent wonder in his ice blue eyes. "So that explains my senses? And my strength?"

She was so wrapped up in his infectious excitement that she didn't even flinch when he moved quickly towards her, holding out his wrists like they were trophies. She tried to keep the grin from spreading too far across her face as she elaborated.

"We're not completely sure about everything, but we are fairly confident that this virus is the root cause of every single one of your biological differences."

"And, my... Diet?"

"We have a theory. The virus demands an influx of iron, and human blood would be a direct source to a high concentration of iron. It's possible that if you've had this virus for most of your life, then it's changed your body chemistry to only need the nutrients you get from blood. How long have you been like this?"

Her question triggered something. Almost instantaneously, his elation disappeared, and the spark in his eyes went cold again. With the changed mood, Rowan became extremely aware of how close he was and took an involuntary step back.

"I've been this way for a long time." His answer was monotone as he put his hands back down by his sides and turned away from her to stride across the room again.

His reaction caught Rowan's curiosity, and despite the cold chill creeping up her back, she followed his pacing. "It doesn't have to be like this any longer, though. We've made a lot of breakthroughs with viruses in the last decade. We could find a cure. We could completely eliminate the virus from your blood. You would be a normal human being again."

She wasn't sure exactly what she had done. Maybe it was their proximity, or the way she leaned closer to catch his downcast gaze, attempting to make some sort of connection with the human she knew existed somewhere inside him that she had just seen written all over his face. Whatever she had done wrong, it was obvious immediately. Rowan watched the blank expression on his face going dark, like storm clouds rolling in.

"A cure? To *fix* me?"

She regretted the eye contact immediately. His gaze cut through her like her scalpel had his skin, leaving her shocked and tongue twisted. She tried for words, but they rolled around in her mouth, and nothing close to comprehensible escaped.

"Because there's something wrong with me? Because I'm not *normal*, like you?" With his question he took a purposeful step towards her, forcing Rowan to retreat, her body stiffening defensively with the sudden spike of nerves. She had started to become accustomed to his scare tactics, to his sly grins and perfectly placed suggestions that made her heart race and kept her uncomfortable. She had even gotten used to seeing the animal in his wide, black pupils, and the way he looked at her like something he would kill one day.

Something was different this time, though. Normally his behavior was so calculated, controlled, but not this time. The way his voice shook at the end and how his gaze burned her skin like a lit cigarette: It told her this reaction was not rehearsed. This was a genuine emotion, anger, and brought back the familiar terror of the first time Rowan walked into the room with him.

"You're ill. You, you have a virus." She tried to stay calm, but her lips trembled as she spoke.

He didn't seem to care any longer that he was scaring her, though. He wasn't enjoying it like all the times before, when it had been just a game to see how far he could push her psyche. He didn't even seem to notice her wide, unblinking eyes as he tilted his head to the side and gave a small, low chuckle that sounded somewhere close to insane.

"I'm not ill. Last time I checked, sick people can't crush metal, *or your throat*, with their bare hands." With his threat, he clenched his fingers into a tight fist, adding to their intent.

Rowan held her arms straight at her sides, even though she wanted desperately to curl up and hug them around her body. She couldn't let herself be scared of him any longer. He had no power except what she gave him.

Straightening, she pushed her chin out and cleared her throat, trying to find her voice. "We want to help you be healthy again. This virus has given you a destructive and dangerous addiction. We can eradicate the virus and in turn, eradicate the addiction, and no one else has to get hurt. I thought you would be happy, to get help, to get out of here and live a normal life?"

"Why would I want to be human? To have a *normal* life? Why would I want to be a disgusting, feeble, selfish creature, spending my time clinging to life and battling my fragility just to die alone, scared, and pathetic? I have not been human for a very long time. I am a God compared to you. I am practically immortal."

He spit his venomous words like a snake, and its toxicity spread through Rowan in waves of goosebumps. Paralyzed by the neurotoxin of his words, she could do nothing but stand and stare in awe of his furor. It was ironic though: the behavior that managed to scare her again was actually his most human.

She watched him struggle to pull back his emotions. Then, as if a momentarily comforting thought crossed his mind, the corner of his mouth twisted up before speaking again.

"No, I'm not the sick one. Mortality is the disease, and I'm the cure."

If Rowan felt anything close to a human connection with him before, it was gone now. It felt like the first day in that room again, looking at a monster. His biology said he was human, but all she saw was the darkness in his eyes, black holes threatening to steal her soul if she searched too hard for something in them.

Despite herself, she still stared, letting the silence between them stew until she felt like his anger dissipated enough to not get her head bit off for speaking. Even with the time she had to collect herself, her voice came out shaking.

"It's not worth killing people. For an illness, an addiction."

"Addiction?" He laughed, and it sounded cold and distant. "I think you misunderstand what the hunger is like. The people I've killed were not victims of my starvation or uncontrolled desire. I think I've proven very well that I can control my hunger, considering you're still alive. No, I kill people because I can, and because I like it. Humans are disgusting and deserve to die, and if I ever get out of this room, I will kill every last human that had anything to do with me being stuck here."

During his speech, Rowan unknowingly withdrew, only realizing when her back hit the wall. Flashing a toothy grin, the monster stalked a few steps forward to follow her retreat. The blacks of his eyes were wide and wild, but something told her that his look had nothing to do with her blood or his hunger. She saw him as a boy with an animal behind his eyes, but perhaps he had always been just an animal.

"Are you disappointed? Did you think I was a lost soul, had a devil on my shoulder? A helpless boy needing to be saved? A victim? I'm the monster, *Rowan*. This virus, it's not what makes me monstrous. I choose to be."

Something didn't feel right, though. Watching him more closely with her wide, horrified eyes as he delivered his lines, a perfectly placed smirk on his lips to confirm his insanity, Rowan felt like it was all just another game again. Through his brief anger, she got a glimpse of the real him, seeing the chips and cracks beneath his level, calculated veneer. Now that he was back to his classic scare tactics, something felt disingenuous about them.

Rowan used to think a game of fear was all he wanted from her, but now all she saw was a defense mechanism, to keep her eyes away from what he didn't want her to see: a wounded animal.

"I can understand why you would want to kill us. Why you'd want to kill me. We've locked you up in here. To you we're just, blank faces behind mirrored glass, using you for our own benefits." Rowan tried not to let his narrowing eyes silence her already timid voice. She needed to understand, and maybe, with his anger bubbling at the surface, he would tell her something. "All the others you've killed, though. All the innocent lives you've taken—"

He interrupted with a bitter laugh. "Innocent? No one is innocent."

A fire flickered in his bottomless gaze, showing she had hit far too close to a nerve. Rowan remembered their secret discussion the night before, of darkness, selfishness, trust, and other scary thoughts.

Humans are the worst kind of monster.

She let her mouth fall open slightly, the pieces coming together into a fragmented ghost of an understanding. Scared of his reaction, but also unable to keep the question to herself, she asked in barely a whisper, "What happened to you?"

The pupils of his black-hole eyes contracted, and she saw his lips part as a breath escaped, like her question winded him. As quickly as he reacted though, his defense was back up, the side of his mouth pulling into a sly grin.

"Do you really want to know?" His voice teased, like in his position of knowledge he knew she wouldn't. He stepped towards her again, so close his bare feet almost met hers now, forcing Rowan to press further back into the wall he trapped her against. He leaned towards her to make the discomfort worse, so close she could smell that familiar sharp scent on him, making her stomach turn. Lowering his voice like she had, he offered a warm breath to her ear, another secret just for her. "Take off that cuff, and I'll tell you everything."

Rowan slid to the side, away from his whispers, escaping her spot between him and the wall. Brushing off the panic, she cleared her voice and stood tall in her new spot. "Why should I?" Once again, when she spoke, she couldn't hide how his behavior shook her.

His smirk shrank a fraction. "How am I supposed to trust you when you don't trust me?"

Rowan shook her head. "Because I haven't killed anyone."

"I don't know that." He countered, chuckling when Rowan shot him an angry glare.

"Why can't you just answer my questions? Why does it have to be a game to you? I've compromised this whole time. Too much so. I think it's the least you can do to be civil, answer my questions, and not mess with me." She wasn't sure where her confidence came from, but at that moment, it was greatly appreciated.

He laughed again, the sound knocking her down a notch. "Where's the fun?"

Rowan held back an annoyed huff, frustrated with his defiance, but trying to not let it get the best of her. Instead, she took a moment to gather her thoughts, glancing down at the cuff on her wrist. She had taken it off once before, and left the room unscathed. Actually, when she thought about it, he had done more to prove his trustworthiness than she had.

Why would he want to share anything with her? Why should he, even? From his point of view, she was just going to use it to prosper herself anyway. Was it so unreasonable for him to be asking for a level playing ground? Asking for her to do something to show him she was not just interested for her own selfish reasons?

Had that been why he offered her the secret of his blood before anyone else? A test, to see what she would do? A test, to see if she was on his side like she tried to seem?

If she wanted him to respond to her, she needed to treat him like the wounded animal he was. She had to make herself vulnerable, reach out, offer her hand but let him come to her. If she forced it, if she moved too fast or cornered him, he would lash out and bite. He'd shown that already.

"You'll answer my questions, then? That's the deal."

Rowan always got the farthest with him when she did things his way, after all. If he wanted to play games, she'd come along for the ride.

His expression was surprised at first, like he hadn't honestly expected her to agree. Quickly enough, another toothy grin spread wide across his face, too satisfied. "Of course, doctor."

Rowan gave one, short nod, trying to be casual as she turned to sit again, but feeling the anxiety weighing down her muscles. It made it hard to breathe, like a heavy force pushing on her chest so she could only take short, shallow breaths. After a lingering silence between them, the subject followed her lead and sat, long and lazy just like before. She could see him eyeing the cuff around her wrist, locked on and waiting.

She glanced briefly towards the mirrored glass, surprised that no one objected yet to her rash decision. Rowan thought that Dr. Miller would have tried to stop her, because obviously, what she was planning on doing was simply foolish. There was silence on the telecom though, and that fact alone made her even more determined. Whatever they thought would happen to her, she would prove them wrong. She'd get through to him.

Just like last time, Rowan let out a long, slow breath to calm herself, then pressed her finger to the scanner on the cuff. After the chime, it released and fell to the floor.

Surely she had lost her mind, to let herself be so vulnerable while sitting across from a killer. Surely there was another way to get what she wanted from him, but maybe it wasn't about questions or answers anymore.

Maybe it was just an excuse.

Taking off her last bit of protection had been shamefully euphoric, empowering, in the way that dangerous things often can be. A reminder of her mortality. The silence in the room was near deafening, making the hard pound of her heart even louder, beating out the rhythm of her fear and adrenaline, every pulse another successful, satisfying second without putting the cuff back on.

She stared at the subject, putting her trust in him and daring him to break it. He got his game, and now she waited for him to make his move.

It happened too fast. She watched him blink, slow and easy like a comfortable cat, a smile playing at the corner of his mouth like he was unwilling to admit how easily she just won him over. Before that expression could completely develop onto his face though, he seized in pain, curling up and falling out of his chair as he began to moan and convulse against the violent shock emitting from the cuff on his leg.

Rowan stood immediately, horror striking her face as he screamed through his clenched teeth. Her voice failed her when she tried to scream.

The telecom buzzed to life. *"Dr. Platts, you are advised to evacuate the containment room immediately."*

Rowan looked at the speaker in the corner emitting Miller's voice, then at the mirrored glass, and finally down to the boy who was fighting off the immobilizing waves of electricity pulsing through his body.

She didn't want to leave. She wanted them to stop and wanted to fall down onto her knees and tend to his pain because that's what he deserved. Not more torture.

She would have to be foolish to stay now, though. Rowan had gotten through to him, but Miller took away whatever chance at trust she obtained. When the subject got control of his body again, he definitely wouldn't be quite so tame. She was not safe in this room with him. Not anymore, and she knew that.

Rowan leaned down quickly to grab her cuff from the floor, then moved to the exit, taking one last look to the boy before leaving. He opened one tightly shut eye to watch her go, fire burning in the deep, blackness of his gaze.

The door closed behind her and locked, and she pressed her forehead to the steel, a hand to her mouth as she stifled the sobs threatening to wrack her body. Sobs of frustration, loss, and guilt of the betrayal she just inadvertently stabbed him with.

On the other side of the door, his painful yells stopped, and there was a few seconds of silence, before the steel she leaned on shook with the force of his body slamming against it. "Who's the monster now?" He bellowed, untamed and violent like the barks and snarls of an angry wolf.

Only he wasn't the animal anymore. He was just a wounded, scared boy locked up in a room, and she just run away while he suffered. She was the animal. Just as he said, she and the other doctors...

They were the monsters.

CHAPTER FIFTEEN

THE DAY of his electrocution was when everything changed for the worse.

It had been only just over a week since she first saw them bringing the subject into the facility, but meeting him seemed like a lifetime ago. When Miller suggested Rowan take the weekend off to clear her head, it felt like it might as well be a life sentence.

She didn't want to be away from the project. No, she *couldn't* be. The last meeting with the subject left her with a terrible sickness in her gut, especially how she had left. The idea of being cooped up in her house where she could do nothing to participate, to make things right, left her with a dread she couldn't shake. She wasn't locked up in a stark white room, but she felt equally as helpless to her fate.

For the whole weekend, Rowan struggled to eat, sleeping sporadically while ignoring phone calls from Cameron that she couldn't bare to answer. When Monday finally came, she arrived at the facility early, ready to make up for the wasted time in any way she could. Unfortunately, the bit of hope Rowan had left that something might be salvageable from the havoc of the previous week was quickly stifled as she met Phelps, who was leaving the facility as she arrived.

"Rowan." He seemed surprised to see her, but not in a good way, and when she gave him a curious look, he lowered his eyes and sighed. "I was hoping I wouldn't see you today. Rather, wishing you'd have the good sense not to show."

She shook her head, baffled. "Why wouldn't I show? After what happened, I have to try and do... Something. Miller... She completely destroyed any trust I had built with the subject. How are we supposed to move forward without his cooperation?"

Phelps gave a hopeless laugh. "I admire your dedication, Rowan. But... Margot is not going to allow you to see him. They've abandoned the observation room, moving onto research now. She has what she wants from the samples you collected. She doesn't need his cooperation anymore."

"No, that's... Impossible."

Rowan didn't like what his words were doing with the terrible considerations that had been lingering in her head all weekend. She talked over her own thoughts, not wanting to give them attention, not wanting to doubt anyones' intent, but the apprehension was already there, festering on her growing hopelessness.

"Miller said we would be working on a cure for the virus, so how are we supposed to give him an anti-viral treatment..."

Phelps reached out a hand, touching her shoulder in comfort when Rowan's voice cracked in her realization. "Leave with me, Miss Platts. I'll speak to Margot. Since you helped so much, she'll let you walk away from this and go back to normal. We can just, go back to our previous study, like nothing happened."

His touch had been encouraging, but at the addition of his offer, Rowan found herself withdrawing. "You're... You're leaving?"

He nodded, a grave expression sweeping him. "I can't stay. I feel like I know where this is going, and I can't take part." He sighed, unsure how to elaborate further. Instead, he added. "I know this is not what you want to hear, and I know my opinion isn't going to do much, but it would be smart for you to leave, also."

"I can't." Rowan frowned hard with her immediate response, the panic setting in around her lungs, making her breath shallow.

Phelps was already nodding, expecting her reaction. After all, he knew her so well. He knew her career was important. He knew that she would do anything to be successful, just like Miller. He knew she was stubborn and determined and never gave up, even when she probably should. Yet, when she added to her words, they seemed to take him by surprise.

"I can't just leave him."

Phelps inhaled, speechless for a moment, before giving her a weak smile. "Well. You're a brilliant woman, Dr. Platts. You'll think of something."

With that, he gave her his hand for a goodbye shake, a careful smile as he dismissed himself, leaving behind his key card in Rowan's palm.

***

ROWAN WANTED to believe Phelps was wrong, assuring herself she could convince Miller to let her see the subject again. She just needed the right leverage. It became clear very quickly she wasn't getting anywhere near the observation room anytime soon, though.

"How dare you put me in that position and expect me to go along with it?" Miller tried to keep her calm, but clearly, she was stewing in her frustration for the weekend just as Rowan had been. "You could have died, Miss Platts."

Rowan noticed immediately the sting of being called *Miss* again, instead of *doctor*. "I was trying to gain his trust."

"We don't need his *trust*. He's a murderer. All we needed was his cooperation, which we received. God, I shouldn't have even allowed you to go back in there after getting the samples."

Miller said that as if it had been Rowan's decision to do so, which left her jaw on the floor for a moment before she managed to pick it up and respond. "*You* wanted me to go back in there to learn more about his past."

Miller scoffed, the sound of it closer to a growl. "Unnecessary information. We can learn about the virus' development during trial studies."

"Trials, doctor?"

Something about that word did not sit well with Rowan, a hot wave of nerves crawling up her neck.

Almost on a dime Miller's mood switched, lighting up with wild excitement as she dove into an explanation. "That's right. We'd have to be crazy not to study this virus further. I've made a request for more funding so we can speed up our research and eventually move to human testing. If we can harness this virus' potential... Well, at the very least we could have a powerful tool for use against disease, and at best..."

The flush that teased around Rowan's collar drew cold sweat from the back of her neck. "You're talking about turning people into monsters. We can't even handle one boy with the virus. How are we supposed to handle multiple test subjects?"

Miller's gleaming eyes went dull with Rowan's disapproval. "You sound like Robert, " she said, rolling her eyes with the intended jab.

"This testing won't start for a while. We'll have the proper facilities for it, and an antiviral for anyone that becomes too much of a problem. And from now on, don't use a word like *monster*. It's so negative. We're talking about turning people into superhumans. This could be groundbreaking. You should be happy you get to be involved, Miss Platts. Not many women like us get to have something like this on their resume."

Rowan bit down on her own tongue to try and level the disgust threatening to slip from her lips. She was already walking a delicate line. If Miller wanted, she could send Rowan away, as she expected would have been done with Phelps as well if he hadn't left on his own accord. She couldn't give Miller a reason to drop her, because there was still the subject to think about.

"And what about the subject? Are we just going to let him die in there?"

Miller sighed and rubbed at her temple, like Rowan was giving her a headache. "Please, be reasonable. It's not like I'm happy about the situation either, but my hands are tied. There's nothing we can do for him without putting someone in danger. Why would we waste time and resources rehabilitating a murderer when it's not even positive it will work? What's the best we could offer him? Moving him from this containment room to a prison after he's cured? It's easier for everyone to just have him expire in a controlled environment."

Rowan put her hands in the pockets of her lab coat to hide them, her fists curled with tightly restrained frustration. Miller's callus conclusion left Rowan feeling rubbed raw.

She put her trust in this woman because she was driven and successful, and she saw so much more of herself in Miller than she'd ever seen in Phelps. Now though, she was remembering all the gentle warnings Phelps had given her, that Miller could be cold and detached, blinded by her goals, hard-headed. She hadn't seen anything wrong with those things before, but now Rowan realized where her moral line was, because letting someone "expire" certainly crossed it.

She reminded herself of how she'd look to Miller if she reacted hysterically: soft and emotional, in no state of making logical, reasonable decisions worth humoring. Misguided and infatuated with a blood hungry monster. So, instead of arguing her morals, that just leaving him was *wrong*, Rowan forced herself to nod in surrender.

"You're right, doctor. I'm being... foolish. Thank you for allowing me to continue to contribute. This is an amazing opportunity."

This wasn't defeat, though. Clearly Miller had no intention of letting Rowan anywhere near the subject again, but arguing until she gave Miller reason to throw her off the project definitely wouldn't do her any good, either. The only way she'd get back into the observation room was by playing by Miller's rules.

While she was watching, at least.

Rowan dismissed herself with a trained smile, her mind already running wild with disjointed thoughts, trying to piece together an idea as she exited Miller's office and headed down the hall to the research wing.

Just a moment was all she needed. To at least tell the subject she hadn't left. That she was trying to help. Ideally, she'd want to get some blood to him too. It had been a few days, and while she was sure he probably didn't need to eat as often as regular humans, his type of hunger was particularly unmanageable when left unattended. It was just a matter of waiting for an opportunity to present itself, which didn't take as long as she expected.

She'd forgotten that she would pass the observation room on her way to the research lab, only reminded when she turned down the familiar corridor and saw the door ahead of her. Her heart caught an extra rhythm as her thoughts went into overdrive, scrambling for a cohesive plan to execute in the few seconds she had before reaching the door.

She could slip in while she passed the room and talk to him. All she had to do was pretend she was meant to go there. No one would notice as long as she wasn't suspicious. But, then what?

It wasn't like she'd be able to feed him this moment, unless she wanted to let him take straight from the source, which was out of the question, judging by the chill running up her spine at the idea. All the good it would do going in there would be letting him know she was trying to help. Trying to do something. That she hadn't forgotten him. It was reason enough for her to feel the pull in her feet, inching closer to the side of the hallway with the observation room door.

What if someone saw her, though? If the wrong person caught her going in or leaving, she'd be dropped from the project immediately, which was the opposite of what she aimed for. Maybe she would have enough time to release him, before she was removed by Miller's security...

And what, get killed along with everyone else? A foolish idea. No, he certainly couldn't be released before getting treatment. As much as she'd like to help him out of that room as soon as possible, she needed to remember what he was still capable of. What he would certainly do given the opportunity.

Besides, that was all assuming she'd even get into the observation room. Her card key likely didn't even work, and if she tried it and the door didn't open, it would be a guaranteed cover blow. It was why Phelps had given her his. She was meant to make use of it, one way or another. If she used it now though, she likely wouldn't get another chance.

The observation room door approached, and then it passed as she continued down the hall. She wanted to stop. Wanted to go inside and grovel against the glass for him to forgive her, make promises to help, but as badly as she wanted to offer some sort of comfort now, it wouldn't do either of them any good in the long run.

She had to make a real plan. She had to be smart about it. He would have to wait, and Rowan would just have to pray he'd forgive her.

Maybe for now he was safer behind glass. Safe from himself, and from the ones on the other side of the glass that intended to use what he had for their own personal gain.

CHAPTER SIXTEEN

THREE WEEKS. That's how long it took for Rowan's last bit of hope to slip away. Three weeks of pleading with no results. Three weeks of ignored objections. Three weeks of everyone acting like the subject had disappeared, never existed, and Rowan was likely to follow him into exile if she wasn't careful.

It was difficult, though. She was so distracted, her research and work performance were slipping, putting the project and her position on it at risk. She was constantly in her head, trying to think of a way out, consumed with the regret, worried it would be too late, that she waited too long, that even if it wasn't, he still wouldn't forgive her.

The forgiving part she dwelled on far too much. After all, why should he? It was partly her fault he was in such a situation. She couldn't even imagine what it was like, to be trapped in a room, scared and alone, starving, and unsure when or if he'd ever get out.

An almost immortal, never having to worry about dying, facing the idea of death for the first time. Had he lost track of time yet? Was he in pain? If she did get to speak to him again, what state would he be in? Would he even be alive? And if he was, what would a few weeks of hunger do to him? Would he even be himself, or would she be speaking with the monster lingering in the blacks of his eyes?

Before the electrocution, Rowan wanted to know more about him for her own selfish reasons. She wanted to help him because it would be good for her, for her career, for the project. Now though, she didn't care at all about the project, about Miller's plans for the virus. She even would have left with Phelps, pushed all memories of what happened out of her mind and continued her career like nothing changed, if she didn't know she was the only one that would help him.

To help she needed a plan, though. And the longer she spent trying to figure out what to do, the longer she waited for an opportunity that never came, the more she realized she would need to do it herself if she was ever going to see the subject again. All the help she was going to get was from a handed-off key card and the one person that was always ready to follow her into a fire.

So, when Rowan knew she couldn't wait any longer, she swallowed her pride and shame from ignoring his calls, and paid Cameron an unannounced visit during his night shift.

"I brought you a midnight snack."

Cameron could never say no to mint chocolate chip ice cream. He could, however, get suspicious of her intentions. His apprehension immediately showed on his face, as well as his mild annoyance.

"If you think you can bribe your way into my good favor again..." He didn't finish his sentence because they both knew that it was entirely possible for her to do just that with how weak willed he was.

"It's your favorite," Rowan said, letting her voice take on a sing song tone as she teased him with the carton.

He rolled his eyes, trying to stay stoney. "What do you want?" He asked, snatching the ice cream and leading her along with him behind the security desk, where he pulled a spoon out of his "lunch" bag.

Rowan gave a wide, fake grin. "To apologize, of course." Cameron snorted at her innocent attempt, so she skipped the pretenses and added, "And to ask for your help."

"You've got some nerve, you know that?" he replied, his frustration still on his voice but his body language caving. He hadn't said no, so Rowan moved forward, lifting her bag up onto the desk and pulling out it's contents, all of which she had stolen over the last three weeks from the lower laboratory.

Cameron stared for a moment as she set out the tourniquet, blood bag, a needle, and gloves, along with various disinfectants. "Um, should I even ask?" he questioned, dumbfounded, but not nearly enough to keep him from shoveling a spoonful of ice cream into his mouth.

Rowan offered a forced smile. "It would probably be better for you if you didn't. Hold this." She handed off the empty blood bag, then sat in a chair next to him. Rowan was taught a long time ago how to take blood and used to practice on herself. It wasn't a necessary skill in her particular field, but she was thankful for it now that she needed a peace offering for the blood-hungry boy locked up downstairs.

She tied her upper arm off and primed the needle before Cameron clued in and turned away. "What the hell, Row!"

"I didn't know you were so squeamish," she teased, hoping to avoid explaining herself.

He took the bait, giving an offended look as he refused to look back, responding sharply. "It's not everyday I see my best friend stick herself with a needle, though." Daring a peek and seeing the worst was over, he twisted around, his expression shifting a fraction away from sour and closer to concern. "You know... You don't have to draw the blood yourself to donate to the blood bank, right? They do it for you. And you get cookies and juice after and everything."

Rowan gave a breathy laugh. "This is... A different type of donation."

"Cryptic. Anything to do with the alien?"

She shouldn't, but if Cameron was going to help her, he deserved to know *something*. "Yes," she said simply, all the answer she could bring herself to give.

Cameron lit up with curiosity, but he didn't push for more, knowing she probably already said too much. Instead, they sat in a silence together that was far less awkward than Rowan expected it to be. In fact, she found herself wishing she could stay there all night, finish off the ice cream and laugh until her sides hurt, like they used to before all this.

Being happy and normal with Cameron would have to wait a little longer, though. Hopefully, he'd still be there when she was finished...

"Was that it? You just wanted me to hold a bag for you?" Cameron seemed rightfully suspicious.

Rowan gave a sheepish smile as she removed the needle and released the tourniquet, holding the bend of her arm to stop the blood. "Not exactly. There's just one more thing."

Cameron was trying to act difficult, but it was so clear to Rowan that he'd agree to whatever she asked, it almost made her reconsider. Asking this of him would get him in trouble along with her, and as much as she wanted to help the boy locked up in the basement, it also wasn't her place to make that decision for Cameron.

When she waited too long to make her request, he gave her a pointed look, before reaching out to mess his hand in her hair.

"You know I'd do anything for you, Row. You're still my best friend, even if you're being a terrible one right now."

Rowan tried to laugh, but it came out heavy. "Thank you, Cam." She could tell him how sorry she was, for everything, when time was more on her side. For now, she could at least show her appreciation with another secret. "I need you to turn the elevators on, so I can go downstairs."

Cameron froze, his eyes immediately widening. "D-down?" When she nodded, he almost choked. "It— It exists?"

"It does. It's amazing, Cam. And one day, I'll tell you everything." If she had it her way, she'd sit there and spend the rest of the night telling him each and every detail. In fact, she needed to so badly that the words swelled up in her chest, and it was painful keeping them down. Instead, she replaced them. "But right now, that's already way more than you should know. Actually, you should probably know, if you do this for me, I can't guarantee you won't get in trouble. But... It's important I get down there. Do you trust me?"

Cameron watched her as she went somber, his gaze softening with a subtle realization. "This isn't about your career anymore, is it?"

She swallowed down the emotion that crawled up her throat at his question, positive it shined across her eyes despite herself, though. "No. It's so much more than that now."

He hummed thoughtfully, taking a moment to leave Rowan hanging, perhaps just to torture her, before nodding. "You know I always got your back, Row. No matter what. Just... Don't take too long this time, yeah?"

* * *

ROWAN ARRIVED at the observation room with her bag of blood

tucked in the bend of her arm, standing in front of the door that had remained off limits to her for three weeks now. She pulled Phelps' key card from its safekeeping spot inside her lab coat, scanning it on the doors reader. It responded with a chime of confirmation, and the glass door slid open.

She hesitated before entering, as if second guessing her rash decision to come here without permission. It was already far too late for her to back out now, though. She'd already done more than enough to warrant her removal from the project, and the subject definitely would have heard her.

If he was even still alive.

Rowan entered slowly, letting her eyes adjust to the low light. Since the room had gone "unused" all these weeks, the computers and fluorescents were powered off, along with the lights within the containment room. The only bit of brightness was the white glow coming in from the hallway behind her, making the observation room and the objects inside it nothing but shadows.

It wasn't hard to find the glass wall, though. She had grown to know the space quite well. Avoiding chairs and tables, she headed for the left wall, placing her hand on the cool glass when she found it. She put her bag down on the floor, then let her eyes wander, searching for a shape through the darkness.

If he was alive, he would already know she's there, so why hadn't she heard from him yet? With how she left him before, Rowan had been expecting a less than pleasant reunion. He was nowhere to be found in the lurking shadows of his stark white cell, though.

Standing there, her hand on the glass and her heart beginning to race, she found herself scared to call for him. What if he really was angry with her? What if he refused to speak? Or worse, what if he didn't reply at all? What if something terrible happened? She could barely bring herself to consider it, the thought putting pressure on her lungs.

Despite her nerves, Rowan untangled the knot in her throat and searched with a whisper. "Lyall."

It was the first time she used his name, and it felt strange and unfamiliar in her mouth, but at the same time it slipped out so naturally, like it had been right there, on the tip of her tongue all this time. She hoped that maybe using it would garner a reaction, but the stretched silence that followed left her disappointed.

"Please, I just want to know that you're alright."

Again, her pleads were left unanswered, the space engulfed in a deafening quiet. With no sign of life, Rowan pressed her forehead against the glass in defeat, a sigh escaping onto her lips.

On a breath, she offered one last attempt. "I'm sorry."

Something shifted, the sound of a creature unwinding itself, and she opened her eyes to watch the blackness of the containment room once more, hunting for the noise. He slipped out slowly into the low light from the shadowed, far corners of his cell, following the wall with his hand as he moved towards her. Each step brought him further into detail, but he was still mostly just a dark figure.

She moved to meet him, and as she did, her adjusting eyes found the troubling details of his state. He was malnourished again, evident in his graying skin and the way it stretched across his bones, thin like rice paper. The hand he held against the wall was most likely the only thing keeping him upright, although he did a good job at pretending otherwise. Right next to him now, with nothing but the glass separating them, Rowan could see the dark circles under his eyes, the paling color of his irises, and most troubling, the scratch wounds up and down his forearms.

"What's happened to you?"

He chuckled at her concern, but the laugh came out dry, like his lungs were arid and brittle. "I keep forgetting that when I'm not feeding I don't heal as fast." There was something bitter on his tone as he replied.

She felt her throat swell, seeing the wounds better as he neared. "Have you done this to yourself?"

"It helps me not think about the hunger. For a while, at least." He moved to rest his shoulder against the glass. Then, as if his legs could no longer stand the weight, he slid down to sit. The bones of his back seemed to grind against themselves as he settled on the floor, his spine visible ridges down his back.

Rowan followed, her knees biting the floor. "I'm so sorry, Lyall. They wouldn't let me near you. No one was feeding you?" He looked so much worse than before. He looked practically dead. "You were right, about us being monsters. It's like suddenly they all have a second face."

"I thought you left me for dead. Would have been the smartest thing you've done."

"I guess I'm stupid." She grabbed the blood bag, standing again. "Here, I have something for you."

The outer security door was unlocked, so she opened it up and entered, gliding towards the second. Like the first time she ever fed him, she kneeled down to the food hatch at the door, but hesitated with the bag in her hand.

She knew she should just slide it in across the floor like always, that she shouldn't get anywhere near the hatch with him in this state of hunger, and yet, she found herself lowering further, her hands beginning to shake as she opened the hatch.

She needed to prove that she trusted him. Prove that he could trust *her*. So, now nearly laying on the floor, Rowan reached her trembling hand holding the blood through the hatch, elbow deep, to hand the bag off to him.

She heard him move in a flash from the glass to the other side of the door, flinching with the movement and covering her mouth to silence a yelp. She expected him to snatch the bag from her grip, or something worse, so when she was still holding it after a long moment, it sent her heart beat into a wild pound in her ear as she tried to listen through it.

It took a moment before she heard movement again, like he was just as timid and unsure about reaching out as she had been putting her hand in there with him, but after a second, she heard him shift slowly closer. She flinched a second time, when her skin sensed his reaching hand, but she managed to keep from withdrawing the unsteady limb for just long enough to allow the weight of the blood to transfer to his palm, pulling quickly back to the safe side of the door. With her recoil, his fingertips grazed hers, and it left her with electricity under her skin, like the touch had shocked, even though she wasn't wearing the protective cuff.

Once the blood was in his grasp, he reacted as she'd expected, tearing into the bag immediately to quench a deep thirst. Leaned with her back against the door to try and calm down, she could hear him drinking, taking deep heavy breaths through his nose as he did. Her curiosity getting the better of her, Rowan lowered her head to peek through the hatch, and one of his hands came down onto the floor to brace himself. Blood stained his fingers.

Shaken, she stood quickly and returned to the glass wall, waiting patiently for him to finish while trying not to think about the fact that it was once again her *donation* he drank. No matter how she spun it, the thought still left her uncomfortable in her skin, so she preferred to ignore it all together.

The wounds on his arms stitched themselves together now that he had a fresh meal rejuvenating his system, and even in the darkness, Rowan could see a bit of color come back to his face. With his dire state tended to, the air between them shifted to an uneasy contemptment, a silence stretching for far longer than

Rowan would have liked. She didn't break it though, not yet. It wasn't her place. She'd let him speak first, if he even would.

He sighed, a breath filled with the anger, frustration, and hopelessness he had to have felt the last few days, then looked over his shoulder towards the glass. His gaze landed right where she sat, and Rowan wondered if those predator eyes could see her shape through the one-way glass now that all the lights were down.

"Why are you even here?"

It was obvious that he wanted to be more sour, but restrained himself in gratitude for the first decent meal in weeks. She appreciated the attempt at civility. Considering she had been expecting him to not even speak with her at all, this was going far better than she could have ever imagined.

Rowan neared the glass, her legs feeling weak with nerves and the remorse of seeing him so broken. She allowed herself to settle back down onto her knees as she considered her words.

"The first day I talked to you, I said I was your only way out of here. When I said that, it was just insurance, a way of hopefully convincing you I was of more value to you alive than dead. Now though, I realize by saying that I also made a promise. By saying I was your only way out, I promised the chance to get you out, and I don't like the idea of going back on my word."

He watched her for a long time, his shoulders rising and falling with labored breaths. When he turned away, he chuckled, although it wasn't humorous at all. "You're delusional if you think I'm ever going to leave this room." His defeat was written all over him, from his sallow cheeks to the brittleness of his bones. They had broken him.

He wasn't fighting her because his fight was already gone.

Frustration flared in Rowan. She wanted to get angry and tell him not to give up, and that she'd find a way, but she knew being upset wouldn't help anything. The hostility between them had to stop. She offered a joke instead.

"I think we've kinda proven that I'm not very sane, considering I agreed to talk to you in there in the first place."

She searched for his shadowy figure, curled up on the floor like a wounded, scared animal, and saw the small, bitter smile spread across his face. Had she won him over? She held as still as possible, scared that even moving would send him retreating back into his shell.

He reached out and used the wall to pick himself up again, shuffling closer to the glass separating them. Rowan wanted desperately to help, but she could only watch him struggle. He stopped in front of her, leaning his back against the glass and sliding down to the floor.

He sat there, his head resting on the wall between them, his expression softer than she had ever seen it. He looked weak and tired. Too tired to hold up pretenses, too tired to pretend to be anything other than trapped and dying and hopeless. He closed his eyes and took in a breath, and she wondered for a moment how she had seen anything other than the scared and wounded boy he was now. How had she ever been afraid of him?

She curled up her fingers, trying to resist the urge to reach out to him. He was a monster, a blood hungry animal who admitted to killing people for sport the last time they spoke. So when had she suddenly become so protective of the beast? When had her primal fear of him turned into something more? When had she become more scared of the people around her than of the blue-eyed demon she talked to?

When did he stop being a subject, and started being...

"Lyall."

The corner of his mouth twitched up. "No one has called me

that in a very long time. It's strange hearing it on someone else's voice."

"I'm sorry." Rowan feared she offended him, but as she said the words she realized the apology wasn't just for her using his name without permission, but for absolutely everything.

He shook his head, brushing off her remorse. "I like how it sounds," he replied, barely a whisper, like he physically wouldn't dare say it louder.

After settling the flutter of her gut, she added, "I mean, for all this."

He sighed in response. "I would have killed you if you stayed. You did what you had to."

"You must have thought I abandoned you."

"I've been abandoned before," he added, like it proved some point, a point that his heart was steel and nothing pierced it. All Rowan heard was pain, though.

"Well, I'm not leaving. I'm going to help you get out of here. Whatever it takes. I promise."

She couldn't resist anymore. Without hesitation, she flattened her fingers onto the glass.

Rowan couldn't be sure how he had known. Whether he could hear her racing pulse through her palm, or could see her ghostly shape through the glass. He knew though, and as he glanced out of the corner of his eye towards her, his expression shifted, and Rowan's heart picked up a beat.

"I'll disappoint you." He spoke, and his eyes went cold again as he directed his gaze back to the darkness. A warning. "Whatever you think will happen, whatever you want me to be, you'll be disappointed. You'd be better off letting me die in here."

She pretended like his words didn't bother her, but they crept passed her hard-headed determination and infected her with doubts. Rowan understood why he was saying it. It was the same reason he called her delusional and stupid for thinking there was any way he was leaving the cell he was trapped in. Because he had accepted that he was going to die here, a fact she was choosing to ignore.

Even though Rowan knew that the only way he would get out would be virus-free, and she knew that he would never willingly accept a cure, she didn't want to think about it. It was too hopeless, and she wasn't ready to stop fighting yet. She'd figure out a way, whatever it took.

She'd promised.

"I'm going to help you get out of here," she repeated, giving her final word. Because even though she didn't know what exactly she was committing to, she felt the vow in her bones.

CHAPTER SEVENTEEN

ROWAN FOUND herself in Miller's office again the following morning, the mood already dreadful, right where it left off three weeks previously. Back then, Rowan would have appreciated any moment she was offered to get herself closer to the woman's good side. That was before, though. Before the electrocution, before leaving Lyall to die, before Phelps was forced to leave just to avoid getting tangled up in the mess she was now neck deep in.

When Rowan sat across from Miller, she already knew she wasn't there for pleasantries. Miller confirmed the suspicion by simply turning her computer screen to reveal what she was watching: a security video of Rowan entering the observation room the night before.

"I thought you were smarter than this, Miss Platts," Miller sighed, leaning back in her chair and sending a sharp look over the edges of her glass.

This wasn't how Rowan wanted her to find out. She had accounted for the security footage ahead of time but hoped she'd have enough time to speak to the woman before she was made aware of what Rowan had done. It didn't really matter, but she would've liked to have approached the woman without her judgement already made.

"Maybe I was giving you the benefit of the doubt, but I at least thought Phelps knew better than to help you ruin your career like this." Shaking her head, genuine disappointment crossed Miller's features, and she leaned forward onto her elbows. "You do realize what you've done here is ground for termination and retraction of your doctorate? If you had one, of course. I won't even get into what this could mean for your friend on the security staff…"

Rowan lowered her eyes, locking them onto her folded hands in her lap, trying to keep herself calm. She had her words planned out. They'd been written in her head like a script that she'd been practicing for days. Miller wouldn't listen though, if Rowan came off even the slightest bit irrational.

"I understand."

She must have expected Rowan to put up a fight, to be hard-headed and argumentative like previously, because she seemed thrown off by Rowan's surrender. Miller inhaled, contemplating something difficult. When she spoke again, it was after releasing a level breath.

"You've put me in a really difficult position, Miss Platts. I should make an example of you. If I don't, my position as a leader of this team could come into question, and in a situation like this, it's important that the others trust me, and respect me. What will they think, if I get wishy washy with my rules, if I pick favorites and allow exceptions?"

It was clear Miller was trying to express some sort of appreciation for Rowan, making her remember that first day when she looked at Miller with starry-eyed amazement, so sure she found a mentor she could truly identify with. Her words, however dire and disappointed, were also almost comforting. To know she still respected Rowan so much, that at least part of the connection was real.

Miller ruined it though, by adding an afterthought. "Thank God nothing worse happened while you were in there. I can't even imagine what it would have meant for us if he injured you in some way, or something worse."

Rowan couldn't help but notice that this time Miller's concern wasn't so much about her and what could have happened, but rather the effect it would have on the dynamics of the project.

She resisted a frustrated tone as she forced a level, recited response. "I'm very sorry my actions might have caused problems, doctor, and I apologize for having to put you in a place where you have to make a difficult decision. I understand if I'm no longer allowed to participate on the project, or even this profession. If you have to make an example of me that's perfectly fine, I was prepared to accept the consequences of my actions, and I will take whatever punishment you deem acceptable without argument. I only ask your forgiveness on Cameron's behalf; he didn't know what he was helping me with."

Once again, Miller seemed taken off guard with Rowan's passiveness, clicking her pen for an extended moment as she thought. Unable to help prodding Rowan's reasoning further, she posed a question instead of making a decision. "You knew that not only could you lose everything for this, you were also putting yourself in serious danger, and still you went against me and visited the subject. Why?"

"I thought it was worth the risk," Rowan answered, continuing when Miller gave a skeptical noise in her throat. "He has value to this project. He's lived with the virus for his whole life, and he knows things about it that we will never be able to learn from just studying it under a microscope."

"When we move onto human testing, we'll know all we need to," Miller countered, unamused by the recurring argument.

Rowan insisted, though. "If you're doing human testing you'll be required to have a working antiviral completed beforehand. How will you test its effectiveness without an infected subject?"

She'd managed to catch Miller with that one a little, but as quickly as the consideration passed her expression, she was responding. "How will we test it on an uncooperative, infected subject?"

Daring to lift her gaze finally, she caught Miller from across the desk, trying to establish a connection. She grew to know Margot Miller rather well the last few weeks. She was, at the very least, not a stupid woman. Rowan had clearly pointed out a flaw in the course of the project that needed a solution before they could ever think of moving forward. A flaw she had a solution to. Now, it was just a matter of selling it, with a little embellishment.

"I went there last night to talked to him. He's tired, and hungry, and scared. He just wants to leave that room. I think... No, I know that I can get him to cooperate with us, if given the opportunity."

Miller sat back again in her seat, swaying back and forth and clicking her pen a few times once more, letting the silence stretch as she contemplated. When she spoke again, it was less like a argument than her previous additions, and more like she was just looking for confirmation to what she already predicted Rowan was offering.

"None of my doctors want anything to do with him."

Rowan didn't bother hesitating. "I'll do it. If you allow me, I'll give him the antiviral."

"A very well executed proposal, Dr. Platts." Satisfied, Miller gave a small smile, nodding, an expression close to approval on her face. "Seems like I was right. You were smarter than that. We'll discuss the details of this arrangement tomorrow, then."

She tried to keep her professionalism, but Rowan was sure her posture dropped a fraction in relief. Without further conversation, she rose to leave, but Miller stopped briefly once more.

"I just have a last question. A curiosity more than anything." When Rowan paused to invite the question, Miller gave another sly smile before continuing. "What's in this for you?"

Her mouth opened to respond, but when words didn't come, Rowan realized she hadn't prepared for that question. The answer came right away, but didn't dare say it. Miller saw the look that swept across Rowan's expression before she could conceal it though, getting all the answer she needed.

Miller hummed, adding, "You're not obligated to answer that. Perhaps it was an inappropriate question. But, I'd consider having a response ready, for next time. Otherwise, someone might see your commitment as something closer to infatuation."

Rowan nodded curtly, and left Miller's office, the outcome of their conversation successful, yet, it still left a sour taste in her mouth.

MILLER'S STIPULATIONS WERE CLEAR: Rowan was prohibited from participating in the research portion of the study anymore, nor allowed speak to any of the other doctors, and was restricted specifically to the observation room where she'd work on re-establishing trust with the subject. It was up to her alone to provide the dietary needs for the subject now, and when the day came to administer the antiviral, if she hadn't done her job at making him trust her and something happened... Well, any evidence of Rowan's involvement with the project had already been disposed of, so nobody would know any different.

On top of all that, Miller tied it all together with the threat that

Cameron's career would go along with hers if she failed to gain the subjects trust, just to ensure Rowan was much more motivated to prove herself.

Miller could keep piling on the insurance. It didn't make a difference to Rowan. She wasn't doing it to help Miller, or the project, or even herself this time. She was doing it to help Lyall. To help get him out of there. The only way to do that, was to take the virus away.

While there was still a ways to go between them after the electrocution, it wasn't trust that she needed to work on building with Lyall. It was a flickering flame between them, but it was there now, she felt it. Instead, it would be convincing him to let her help, which took a lot more than just trust. She'd have to make him see her plan, make him understand that there was only one way out of that room, and as desirable as the power the virus gave him was, he'd have to let it go for her to be able to get him his freedom.

Rowan knew she had a task ahead of her, but she also had time to worry about the details later. For now, she could be relieved that her plan worked. So far, at least.

Left by Miller to enter the observation room alone with a bag of previously collected blood, Rowan swiped her key card, which chimed confirmation now after a change in security. She walked through the sliding glass door and waited for it to shut behind her before letting out a breath she felt like she'd been holding since leaving the room last.

All the lights were still off, just as she'd left them, but Lyall had proven before that he hardly needed sight to sense her. "You just can't get enough of me, can you?"

Her shoulders loosened with the sound of his tired voice. She headed for him immediately, meeting where she'd heard his hand, sliding up, bracing him against the wall as he rose to his feet and came closer.

He leaned his forehead against the glass once he reached it, trying to get a better look into the observation room, and when Rowan stepped close enough for him to make out the shadow of her shape through the low light, he managed a weak noise of disbelief that fogged the glass between them as it escaped his lips.

She couldn't help her own breathy laugh in response, her stomach flipping in relief. His appearance had improved, but was clearly exhausted, the color lacking from his face and the whites of his eyes bloodshot. His attitude clearly reappeared, though.

"What do I have to do to get you to leave me alone to die?" Lyall managed a bit of sharpness with the words, but Rowan learned the fine line between his threats and his teasing, and responded by rolling her eyes.

"You're not getting rid of me that easy," she said simply, putting her fingertips to the glass to give him a noise to follow as she moved closer to the security door. "I said I was going to help you get out of here."

"Come to break me out?" he asked, following with his eyes, a joke burning in them despite how tired they looked.

She made a disagreeing noise, and watched the corner of his mouth turn up. "Not exactly."

Lyall mocked a yawn. "How boring. What's the plan, then?"

Rowan paused, knowing the answer to that question would put a halt to the tolerable exchange between them. She knew his place when it came to receiving an antiviral. The whole point was to change that position. Hopefully.

Not yet, though. For now, she wanted to just enjoy her moment of victory. "I brought you something."

"I was starting to wonder if you were just teasing me."

When she moved to the security door he followed to the other side, and this time Rowan found herself barely hesitating as she lowered to her knees and feed the blood bag through the hatch.

"Take it slow, there's no rush anymore."

Despite her reassuring, he was still quick to collect it from her grasp, the sound of tearing plastic and thick, heavy swallows closely following. Rowan settled in, her back against the door, far less disturbed this time by what she knew was happening on the other side of the steel she leaned on. His thirst didn't make her skin crawl in the same way it used to, his threats no longer leaving her frozen in fear. Maybe she was just getting used to it, used to him, or maybe there was just other things to be more disturbed over.

Too lost in her head, Rowan hadn't even noticed when he paused with his meal, words leaking out into the space between them, as if he heard her thoughts. "You shouldn't want to help me. You should be scared of me."

Rowan scoffed. "Scared of what?"

"I have your blood on my tongue, and you ask what you should be scared of?" he added, this time a fraction sharper, his tone accusing. When Rowan chose to let the silence hang instead of responding, he continued, so quiet she had to hold her breath to hear. "Sometimes, it feels like the hunger is something inside of me. A beast, growling in my gut, and when I feed it, it just gets more angry."

Her throat went dry with his words, making it hard to swallow. Once she did, she managed a response, trying to be reassuring. "There's a bit of a monster in all of us."

She heard him inhale, letting out something heavy from his lungs. "Other times, though... It doesn't feel like something inside of me. Sometimes, I feel like I'm the monster. I want it all so badly. The power, the hunger, the fear. I don't know where the line is. I'm not even sure there is one. I don't know who I am, without the taste of blood in my mouth. I don't... Trust myself."

Rowan sat as quietly as she could, worried she might disrupt the moment of vulnerability he shared with her if she reminded him that there was someone on the other side of the door. Instead of speaking, when the silence grew thick and heavy, Rowan had a foolish idea.

"You don't have to trust yourself." She moved her hand from fiddling in her lap, to slide it along the cold floor towards the opened hatch between them, just enough to feel with the tips of her fingers the edge where the door met with the floor on his side. "I trust you, Lyall. So just... Trust me."

He let out an unsteady breath. She heard the sound of his shoulder shifting against the door, and then, her hand twitched ever so slightly at the spark of his skin, as he carefully weaved his fingers between hers.

CHAPTER EIGHTEEN

AFTER THE FIRST DAY, Rowan's *observation duty,* as Miller called it, never went quite as smoothly as she'd like.

It was already frustrating enough not being allowed to know the research's progression or how the antiviral was coming along. Within a few days, it became clear the biggest reason Miller agreed to Rowan's proposal was simply to keep her out of the way. Being cut off from the rest of the project had not been part of the plan, but Rowan put herself between a rock and a hard place with her desperation, and Miller knew that. With Lyall's life, and both Cameron and her own livelihood in jeopardy, she had no room to argue Miller's new rules.

The actual part of the plan that Rowan had control over also wasn't going as well as she'd hoped. The moments of weakness Lyall shared with her at the beginning became few and far between once he was being fed again, and while she was happy to see him being a more familiar version of himself, at times it was also discouraging.

As the days went on, no change to his situation in sight, he became fickle and hard to read, his mood swinging on a dime, making her have to tiptoe around him with her words frequently. He'd make sure to remind her he was ready to die in that room constantly, that she was stupid for trying, that she should just give up and leave him to die. Then, moments later, he'd be whispering to her, in a tone that was too alluring.

"Let me out, Rowan. Open the door. I know you want to."

Sometimes, when he really wanted to torture her, he'd even beg.

"I can't stand it in here anymore. Please, Rowan."

She got more and more frustrated with her isolation, her lack of knowledge, her helplessness, and he'd fed her uncertainty with dangerous ideas that would linger far too long in the back of her head.

"You've been so generous, feeding me. I want to give back. We could punish them, you and me. Just a little bit of my blood is all it would take. Be a monster with me, Rowan."

He wasn't a monster, though. At least, not in the way he thought he was. There was something there in him, burning in the blacks of his eyes, a darkness in him he had trouble controlling, that bloomed violent red sometimes, but Rowan could tell it was only there out of trained necessity, out of survival. He had been alone for so long, of course he learned how to protect himself. How to keep people away or lure them in.

Rowan had a lot of time to speculate while trying to ignore his attempts at manipulating her. Being what he was, he probably spent his whole life avoiding this exact situation. He never needed to let his guard down, to open up to someone, to trust. In fact, being so vulnerable was not in the best interest of a predator. A predator kept their teeth bared even while backed into a corner.

It was clear there was a part of him that had given up, though. A part that decided this was the end. When his moods swung away from the usual smirking, manipulative manic state, he'd grown quiet and defensive, the wolf grin sliding away from his face into something less prickly.

Sometimes, the exact number being so few Rowan could count them on one hand, he'd sit next to her on the other side of the glass in a silence that would stretch into something as close to comforting as she could offer. From these moments, she could clearly see him for what he was, behind all the bluffing.

A scared, broken boy waiting for death.

As terrible and hopeless as it made her feel to see him like this, she also liked to think it made her special. That this tamer side of him was just for her, a small glimpse at the part of him that wasn't always thinking of blood. They were prisoners together in the situation, sharing a common enemy, and while she was sure the fact that she was the only one feeding him also made him more inclined to be polite, she liked to think it was more than that. They'd shifted, from victim and villain, to something almost friendly.

As friendly as the prey could be with the predator, of course.

"How much longer are you going to put me through this torture?"

He'd meant his words to be playful, sarcastic, but with the days turning closer to weeks, his little patience in her was wearing even thinner.

Rowan offered a gentle scoff as she sat down, cross-legged, her back to the glass separating them. "It's not that bad… I just need you to bear with me." She tried to downplay his complaining, but she knew he had the right to be frustrated.

She teased him with a plan to get him out, but hadn't revealed her idea yet, and could only continue to ask him to trust her when he clearly struggled to do so. It wasn't really her fault, though. There hadn't been news on the antiviral yet, and she was terrified of bringing it up with him. He wasn't ready yet. In the state he was in, he wouldn't accept her plan. If Rowan was getting a bit of cabin fever, she couldn't imagine how he must feel.

"I'm going crazy in this room," he added, as if he'd been in her head too, before joining her on the floor, on the other side of the glass, letting his temple rest against it after a disgruntled noise.

Rowan hummed, trying to offer some condolences. She could tell he was struggling. He paced a lot, and she caught him scratching at his arms again, even though the wounds never stuck now that he fed regularly. She could talk him down sometimes, but other days, he'd just blow up at her. The animal simmered just under his skin, waiting for a few wrong words to rear and snap.

He was calm today. At least, he seemed like it, so Rowan tried a gentle joke. "I'd let you out if I knew you wouldn't go on a killing spree." She watched for his reaction, noting that if there wasn't a wall between them, they'd be brushing shoulders with how close he'd placed himself.

She fully appreciated the grin when he reacted to her words, wickedness flashing across his features in his response. "What if I promise to only kill a couple people?"

Rowan hummed again, used to his humor now, and played along for a moment. "Nope," she finally said, shaking her head despite him being unable to see her.

His grin stretched as he reconsidered, pushing a step further. "What if I promise to kill only you?"

Rolling her eyes, Rowan answered, "And how will I know if you keep your promise if I'm dead?"

Sticks thrown in the cogs of his logic, he shrugged playfully, conceding for a moment and letting the silence between them roll in a little.

He wasn't finished yet, though. Third time was always the charm for him. When he spoke again, Lyall lowered his voice to the tone he used when trying to tempt her, the humor completely gone. "What if I killed everyone but you."

He didn't say it like a question, but instead, an offer.

Rowan felt the air escape from her lungs without her permission, the first time in a long time that he'd made a chill run up her spine. This time, it wasn't from discomfort or bone rattling fear. Instead, she found herself momentarily seduced by his suggestion. The monster in her that sat curled up on her frustration and helplessness, purred in satisfaction. Everyone gone, so she was no longer stuck in the middle, stuck between her career and her morals. Lyall, no longer caged.

That was the problem, though. Lyall, if allowed his freedom now, with the virus still intact, would be even less reasonable than he ever was. If she let him out, he *would* kill everyone.

On the other side of the glass, Lyall gave a frustrated noise. "Don't lie to me, Rowan." Because he already knew what she was going to say, despite her rapid heartbeat and shallow lungs.

She said it anyway, if only to banish the dark thoughts from her own mine. "Being done wrong doesn't justify doing wrong."

He chuckled, but it hid a note of bitterness. "Dog eat dog."

Rowan let her eyes drop to the floor as she countered. "You can't spend your whole life alone, Lyall."

"I already have," he said, as if it proved a point.

Snorting with the irony, she added, "Yeah, and look where it got you."

His expression shifted to annoyance, but he resisted letting his tone get too sharp when he responded. "Point taken." He followed with a defeated sigh, which she copied to try and shake off some of the negativity.

When the somber air between them became too much, Rowan tried to offer some reassurance, not wanting his decent mood to go too sour. "I'm going to get you out of here, I promise. It won't be much longer, I'm sure. Once the antiviral is finished—" She'd said to much, cutting herself off but the mistake already made. She hadn't meant for her personal mantra to leak out onto her lips, but it had, her tongue betraying her.

She cringed away from the glass, preparing for him to react violently to her plan being spilled, but the angry outburst never came. When the silence grew palpably thick, Rowan turned back to see his expression go deflated and cold.

"I should have known." Lyall lifted his knees to his chest, wrapping them in his arms and leaning his head back against the glass, shutting his eyes. "There's no other way, is there?" He said finally, but the question sounded more like it was to himself than her.

Timid to answer, Rowan fiddled her fingers in her lap for a moment before she got the words out. "They'll definitely never let you leave like this."

He huffed at her confirmation, letting the somberness of that point settle for a second before adding another question. "And you?

"What about me?" Rowan stumbled, unsure what he meant.

He'd smirked a little, but it was far from playful. "You don't want me like this either. You want me to be human."

"You *are* human," she objected, garnering a scoff from him.

"You know what I mean," he added sourly. "You want to fix me. No more virus."

Rowan sighed, pulling her legs up to her chest like him. "It's not like that..." She offered, but the response was not good enough. He made another noise, a sharp exhale full of disbelief, and Rowan forced herself to continue, her own tone picking up a defensive note. "I just don't understand. You're suffering. You can't argue that. Why wouldn't you just want to get rid of it?"

He shook his head, his lips twisting up a little, but it was just a look to cover something else that had passed his expression. Something pained and too real. "You wouldn't understand..."

"Try me," she pressed, because clearly, whatever he was holding back made all the difference in the world. If he would just tell her, maybe she could finally understand.

Lyall considered it for a moment, but instead resisted a growl and ran a stiff hand through his hair. "What difference does it make. It won't change anything."

Irritation tightened his shoulders, and this was usually the point where Rowan would keep her mouth shut until he settled again, but she found herself frustrated as well, his stubbornness bringing more words to her lips.

"You'd think the least you could do is give me a decent reason why, if you're going to make me suffer through waiting for you to die in here." She tried to be gentle with her objection, but too much of her own annoyance leaked out, making the point of her words taper to a dangerously sharp edge.

The black in Lyall's eyes sparked with something dangerous. "Make you suffer? What kind of pain do you have to go through?" He'd lifted his voice, as if her words had been a joke, but it was obviously one he hadn't found the least bit funny. "You're not the one locked up, tortured, starved. *The other doctors are mean to me, boo hoo*. You have no idea what real suffering is."

She hadn't meant to upset him. Actually, the moment his words shifted to fire, Rowan felt the burning in her own chest drowned with regret. "Maybe I don't. I just... I don't want you to suffer any longer either. Why do you insist on holding onto the virus, when all it's brought you is pain?"

She tried to backpedal, she tried to reword herself, but her thoughts came out of her nervous mouth all wrong, only making matters worse.The blacks of his eyes seemed to darken a fraction as he narrowed them in response, his anger boiling over. He stood, taking a pace away from the glass but unable to hold back his outburst.

"Who are you to tell me about pain? What do you know about suffering? Suffering is watching from under the floorboards as a mob of monsters who look and sound *just like you,* butcher your mother like an animal. Suffering is not understanding why they yelled "fiend" and "demon" as they hung her corpse up by the feet to bleed her out. Suffering is a child, alone in the cold, waiting to follow his mother to the grave. You know nothing about my suffering, *doctor.*"

There it was. The happening that made him the broken animal he was now. The pain burning like coals in his eyes when she got too close to him. The memory making him bark and snap at everyone and everything that dared to even look at him. It read on his face as a reopened wound, deep and bleeding, and Rowan felt her own heart fissure.

He was something beastly now, but once he had been just a boy. A boy who saw something red and violent, blooming a darkness within him. A boy surrounded by nightmares like *her.* What he became only seemed fitting: a monster born of blood with a taste for nothing else.

"Lyall."

She couldn't help herself. Rowan followed him to her feet, her hurting heart pushing her forward, taking a step and reaching a hand out. Her fingers never touched the wall between them, though.

He advanced in one quick step, slamming a fist against the glass. "Stop! Stop calling me that. Like you know me. You don't know me. You don't know *anything.*" He yelled, and his words were hot flames searing her skin, but Rowan stood and took her lashing, because she deserved it. Because even though she did nothing, there was blood on her hands. The blood of his murdered mother, and the blood of the boy he might have been if things had been different.

He paced the containment room until the angry, explosive layers peeled off into something else. Something fragile and scared, a fragment of what was left of the child he had been before being infected with darkness. Cautiously, Rowan took a step back towards the entrance of the observation room, watching as he listened to her retreating footsteps. He looked momentarily disappointed, as if he regretted scaring her off, but also not surprised. An expression that said he was used to scaring everyone away.

Rowan wasn't fleeing, though. She was trying to offer what she could while being separated by a glass wall. She reached the door, flipping the switches just beside the exit, the lights in both rooms powering down. With shadows engulfing them again, she stepped carefully back to the glass, seeing Lyall's eyes focus through it onto her approaching shape. It felt important, that he could see her, even if it was barely. So he knew she was still there.

"Why do you keep coming back?" His question was prickly, his defenses shelled around him, a thick wall.

"If I don't, who will?"

He looked away from her, a defeated chuckle. "Stupid mouse."

Rowan couldn't help the smile that twitched at the corner of her mouth, because something about the way he said her pet-name sounded distinctly more endearing than usual.

They both ended up sitting on the floor again, the darkness surrounding them like a thick blanket, hidden from the real darkness outside their shared, but separated prison. The silence settled his anger, until Rowan felt it was safe enough to speak again.

"Tell me. Tell me what I don't know." A barely there question, timidly presented in case it would upset the volatile balance of emotion between them.

He blinked, searching through the glass to her shadowed gaze, then to the floor. He didn't speak for a very long time, so long Rowan thought he decided to ignore her. When he did finally offer words, they were small and quiet, as if he'd reached deep inside to the child he left behind years ago.

"I wasn't always like this. Whatever made her different, I didn't have it. I was like you. I was *human*. But being human meant being helpless to save her. I could only watch." He paused, as if it hurt to continue, to remember, but he managed to find words for the things in his head that chiseled a deep line between his brows. "My mother warned me about the wolves in the woods, but when they came to make a meal of her corpse they had more pity for me than the previous predators. I was outcasted by the things that looked like me, so I decided I didn't want to be like them anyway. Instead, I ate my mother's flesh with the wolves and swore to be the monster they thought she was. Now... The darkness in me is all that's left of her."

The silence was heavy with the weight of years of pain, pushing down on Rowan until she couldn't stand it any longer. She put her forehead to the glass, holding back a sob as it crushed her chest, trying to escape. "I'm sorry," she whispered, because it was the closest thing to articulating the truth of it all.

This changed everything.

CHAPTER NINETEEN

THE TIMING COULDN'T HAVE POSSIBLY BEEN worse. The following day, after a night of restless sleep filled with too graphic recollections of a memory that wasn't hers, Miller called Rowan into her office for the third time since the electrocution.

She already knew why she was there, but her stomach filled with sick anticipation regardless as she sat across from Miller at her desk. Even while seated, the light-headedness and tunnel vision lingered, the room now associated with negativity and making Rowan feel suffocated.

Miller didn't seem to notice Rowan's discomfort, diving into things the moment she sat down. "It's been a while now since our agreement about the subject. I wanted to thank you, for being so cooperative since then, Miss Platts."

She had permanently dropped *doctor* for a while now, but it still stung every time Rowan heard her use *Miss* instead. It felt demeaning, downtalking.

It felt like disappointment.

"I wanted to speak with you because we have good news." Miller pulled open the draw at her left and retrieved a manila folder, handing it across the desk. "We're nearly done with the antiviral. We just need to work on dosage and should have it all ready for administration on Monday."

Rowan let her eyes rove over the contents of the file, but they were unfocused, leaving the words unreadable. It didn't matter. The details were unimportant. All that needed to be taken from it was that Lyall had one weekend left, before they'd steal away the last bit of who he was, and it was all her fault.

She didn't even bother pretending to be happy. It didn't matter. Miller didn't seem to notice.

"So, how has your observation duties with the subject been? Is he ready to cooperate?"

Returning the folder to Miller, Rowan shook her head slightly. "He's not as easily convinced as I'd hoped." Not a lie, but also not completely the truth. She decided to stop trying to change his mind after learning why he was willing to die to keep the virus.

Miller hummed, giving a weak frown. "Well, I'm sure you tried your best. It's no matter, we planned for such a situation."

Despite her numbness, the statement pulled Rowan back for a moment, and she gave a questioning look. "I'm sorry, Dr. Miller. Planned?"

She certainly hadn't been let in on any alternative plans. After all, convincing Lyall to take the antiviral had been her idea in the first place. She assumed the alternative would just be the original plan of letting him die.

Miller nodded. "Of course. You made a valid argument about needing to test an antiviral before starting human trials. It's important we administer the antiviral, cooperatively or not. That's what you wanted, after all, isn't it? To help him get rid of the virus?"

"Yes. That's..." Rowan swallowed down the regret threatening to rise up her throat. "What I wanted."

"Good. Then you'll help us. We'll need you to go into the

containment room on Monday to administer the antiviral. We'll have an injection prepared, as well as a sample of blood with the antiviral infused, so he can have the option of how he'd like to take it. It can be... A last chance to convince him."

Miller's previous concern about letting Rowan in the containment room seemed to have disappeared now that she needed her to go back. Rowan might have been more angry about that fact if she wasn't already doing everything just to hold herself together.

"He won't agree to either. I'm already quite sure about it, doctor." Rowan responded, as level as she could.

Another little frown, before Miller shrugged slightly. "No matter. Try what you can. If it doesn't work, we'll disable him again, and you can administer the injection before exiting the room."

Rowan had to force herself from cringing at the thought of betraying Lyall a second time. She worried the sick in her stomach was given away by the color loss in her face, but if it was noticeable, Miller didn't comment.

Giving a last try, Rowan noted an observation. "This seems dangerous. I'm worried, for my well being."

Miller blinked with her comment, then offered a dismissive smile. "No more dangerous than any previous occasion. You'll have the bracelet, so he won't be able to touch you." She seemed like she was going to leave it at that, but something crossed her mind and she added, "If you're really concerned, we can give you an injection as well. If he's so adamant about not receiving the antiviral, that should deter him enough from making a meal of you, shouldn't it? See it as a little... Extra security, so you feel better."

Sure that Miller did not miss the irony in her words at all, Rowan kept her eyes down as she nodded and rose to her feet. "I understand, doctor. If that's all, I should really go. Maybe I can try again at convincing him," She managed to wait just long enough for Miller to nod in dismissal, before hurrying out of the stifling office.

The stark hallways felt pressing and heavy, her throat tightened, the anxiety choking her. She barely made it to the observation room before it all hit her like a tidal wave, and she collapsed against one of the tables, shoving a hand over her mouth to stifle the sobs wracking her body.

When she was finally able to open her welded shut eyes, Lyall was at the glass, his expression twisted in a distinct look of concern that only made Rowan crumble more.

"They finished it. The antiviral." How she got the words out so evenly was beyond her. Her breath shook after.

He tried to hide his reaction, but she had learned his body language so well she was practically bilingual. He'd turned to the side, and his chest expanded with a single, sharp inhale. He had thought he was ready; he spent the last few weeks trying to prepare himself, but was anyone ever really ready to face death?

Had she only made it worse, by making promises she obviously couldn't keep?

Rowan stood and hurried over to the glass, stumbling on her weak limbs and dizziness until she admitted defeat and collapsed to the floor. Tears stained her face, but she somehow managed to stifle her sobs. She didn't want him to know how bad it was.

It was already too much knowing he could hear her heart breaking.

"I thought I wanted this, I really did. I thought I would be helping you. But I don't. I don't want this." Her words were a mess of sensical and nonsensical thoughts, a jumble of emotions. "I don't want this." Was the only tangible thought that she could hold onto, and each time it circled her head, it beat her further and further to the ground until her whole body felt sore and weak and broken.

On the other side of the glass, Lyall folded himself up on the floor in front of her, an arm around his knee and his forehead to the glass. He sat there, so close yet still so far away, and she sobbed until she couldn't anymore.

When she was finally able the catch her breath, using her lab coat to wipe up the last of her tears, she leaned against the glass as well. "I'm sorry," she whispered, because it was all she could think of saying that meant anything. Even though it meant nothing. His breath fogged the glass for a brief moment, disappearing as quickly as the condolences offered by her words.

He closed his eyes, his lips twitching into a sad smile. "Stupid mouse."

They sat together for a long time, two lost souls surrounded by monsters, with no words to share. The silence was more profound, so Rowan let it sit, even though her nature compelled her to fill the gaps with meaningless rambling. What could she say that would change anything? The fate they knew was coming had arrived, and she could do nothing to change it.

She had promised him, and she had failed.

She watched him for a long time as he stared at nothing, lost in thoughts Rowan couldn't even fathom. What was it like, to know your death was approaching? Was he cold and unaffected by the news, like his calculated exterior suggested, or was the lost boy behind his eyes as terrified as she was for him?

"You know my choice." He spoke finally, ages later. So long that the silence became almost deafening, and Rowan was so surprised by the sound of him speaking she barely comprehended his words. Once she did, her throat tightened, and she was unable to reply, leaving him to continue on the somber note. "If you try to give me the antiviral, I'll kill you."

Rowan had become use to his threats. At one time they scared her, but his claims of making her his last meal or tearing her open were now ineffective from sheer repetitiveness. This threat was different though, and it was because she knew it was true. It was not said to scare her, and it was not said to bring the rapid pounding of her heart that often monetarily satisfied him. In fact, it didn't even seem like he enjoyed saying it at all.

It was true though, and she knew it, and that's what made her heart stop briefly.

After hours of motionlessness, he stood, and stalked over to his mattress. "Go home now, Rowan," he said after laying down onto his back to stare up at the ceiling. Her name was a sigh on his lips, and Rowan held back a sob at the idea that it would be the last time she'd hear him say it like that.

She did as he told her because it was the least she could do, even though the dread of another lifetime-long weekend was more than she could bare. She only drove halfway home before she dialed Cameron's number, the pain far worse than her shame that it'd once again been too long since contacting him.

He answered, although she distinctly noticed that he'd let her hang on the line for two extra rings. "What do you want, Row?" He wanted to sound sharp, but a note of concern leaked into his voice over the line.

"Please come over." She tried to keep her voice from cracking, but failed miserably. "I need to tell you. Everything."

It took her most of the evening even with Cameron letting her speak without interruption, but as midnight creeped up on them, Rowan finally finished her retelling of the last few weeks. She told him about the first day in the underground labs, hearing Lyall speak for the first time, and what really happened to William after the "accident" he heard about. She told him about all the times she'd entered the containment room, the electrocution, and why she'd needed his help late that night when she couldn't explain further. She told him about Lyall, and the virus, his past and his mother, and why she wanted to help him but couldn't. Every relevant detail, she covered, up until that very afternoon, finally telling Lyall about the finished antiviral.

It took a while for Cameron to process everything, leaving her sitting in her thick anticipation. When he finally reacted, it was after a deep, heavy sigh. "Well... I guess now I know why you've been too busy to answer my calls."

Rowan offered a weak smile with his teasing. "I'm sorry, Cameron. I really am."

He shrugged away her apology. "Hey. I imagine I'd probably be a little flaky if I was tangled up in a government conspiracy."

"It's definitely not all it's cracked up to be. Sometimes I just wish I'd listened to Phelps and gone with him when he left. Or... I dunno. Wish I hadn't stayed working late that night and seen everything I did." Rowan gave a huff as she slumped down onto the couch cushion she'd been hugging in her lap.

Across from her, Cameron snorted, which garnered a dirty look. He smirked, putting up a surrendering hand towards her offense. "It's just... Hearing you pretend as if you'd done anything differently comes off as such a joke to me. Given the same opportunities, you would have made exactly the same choices, Row. You're where you are because you've been true to yourself. I'm honestly not surprised in the slightest."

She knew he meant it as a compliment, but the hopelessness of her situation felt stifling, and she was sad and bitter about it. "Maybe I need to learn how to take other people's advice." She responded, letting that sourness at herself leak out onto her tone.

Cameron chuckled. "Maybe. But then you wouldn't be so special." He let the air linger a little to allow her to accept the words reluctantly, before adding, "Speaking of, what makes alien boy so special?"

It was hard to miss the suggestion on his tone, and Rowan blushed. "It's not... It's not like *that*."

He gave a playfully skeptical look her way. "Really? Because it seems a little... *Like that*."

Rowan buried herself further into the pillow she hugged, unable to stop the mortification from showing on her face. He let up on his teasing and gave her a break though, allowing her to elaborate once the joking toned down and the flush on her face subsided.

"He doesn't have anyone on his side. He doesn't *let* anyone be on his side. He made me feel... special. Like he trusts me... and knowing I'll be letting him down is unbearable."

Cameron sighed on her behalf, a furrow coming to his brow. "I'm sorry, Row."

She nodded, then huffed to try and shake off the heavy air, but it stuck, dragging the mood down into the defeated somberness Rowan had been sitting in all day. It made her feel better to pour her heart out to Cameron about everything, but she thought for a moment that telling him would somehow make things better. Like maybe revisiting everything that happened would make her see something she'd missed, an opportunity to change things, show it wasn't too late.

Unfortunately, they'd gotten through the whole story, and now they were there, sitting together in silence, and nothing changed. Everything was still hopeless. Rowan was out of options, her and Cameron would be out of jobs, and Lyall would receive a death sentence of his own making come Monday morning.

Cameron tried to break the thick silence with a gentle offer. "Hey. How about I pick you up on Monday?"

Rowan lifted her eyes up from staring at the floor, pulled from her weighted thoughts and perking up a little with the offer. "Could you?"

"Sure. You owe me some of your time, anyway. We can pig out on comfort food. I assume you'll need it." He gave a timid smile, which spread a thankful one on Rowan's face.

"That would be really nice."

He nodded, dismissing her gratitude. "It's a date, then. And hey, if you figure out an escape plan, alien boy can come too."

CHAPTER TWENTY

SHE WASN'T ready when the day came to administer the antiviral, although it was likely she would have never been ready, regardless of how long she was given. Even so, the weekend that she expected to be painfully long actually went by too quickly, blending together into a haze of sleepless nights and numbness.

The Monday morning was no different. Miller greeted her with apprehensive concern, but Rowan barely registered what the woman had to say. She gave some spiel about making history, and how she appreciated Rowan's dedication, even though her tone suggested she was well aware Rowan's actions no longer held much enthusiasm.

She was sent to the infirmary for a donation of blood from her, and then she was given an injection of the antiviral, as previously discussed. She didn't bother putting up a fight, even though she had no way of knowing if the antiviral worked, or was even safe to be in her body. At this point, the prospect of dying didn't seem so horrible. At least she wouldn't have to face Lyall again.

She hadn't gotten a chance to go back to the observation room since telling him the antiviral was finished. He told her to leave, and it didn't feel right returning. Even though she desperately wanted to be there for him, it was obvious he wanted to face this alone. Whether for his sake, or for her own, she wasn't sure anymore.

Now she was going back to the containment room to speak with him face to face one more time, and the prospect made her feel strange. A part of her wanted one last chance to see him, to speak with him, to maybe have some sort of closure before he refused the antiviral and began his slow starvation. Another part of her felt scared though, knowing Miller and the others would be watching, meaning Lyall's mask would be back on and the boy she wanted desperately to say goodbye to would be nowhere in sight.

Beyond the numbness on her exterior, in the very deepest, darkest part of her mind, the monster inside her continued to plot as it had desperately all weekend. Schemes and plans to somehow save him, from escape missions to accepting his offer to be like him and going on a rampant killing spree together. None of it was logical, most of it was foolish and flawed and dangerous, but just thinking about it settled an angry, growling part of herself that threatened to erupt from her chest if not tended to. Perhaps this was what his hunger was like, itching and crawling under her skin, unsatisfied but not quite uncontrollable.

Rowan received the cuff for around her wrist, and another cart, like the day she took his samples. This time, only two objects laid on it. To the left, the blood donation she made only briefly before, with a dose of the antiviral added. To the right, a syringe filled with the same substance they injected in her. Rowan herself made three doses in total, three separate choices he could make, although she already knew Lyall would refuse all of them. The virus was too important to him.

Regardless of knowing the inevitable outcome, she followed her given directions, entering into the containment room with her cart like she had done many times before. With the steel door locking behind her, anxiety flared in her chest, although it wasn't for the usual reasons. She didn't fear him anymore, in fact, joining him in the containment room relieved something tense in her shoulder, considering how out of place she felt while surrounded by the other doctors. Instead, the anxiety was from the looming dread crawling in like storm clouds, of this being the last time she would ever be allowed to see him.

He didn't taunt her through the door. He wasn't even within sight when she pulled the second door open. She wheeled her cart all the way into the room before seeing him, leaned up against the far wall, as much space between them as possible. His positioning disconcerted her because she wasn't sure what it meant. Rowan felt so close to him lately that the inches he put between them felt like miles.

Before she analyzed it too much, he tilted his head and moved his icy eyes to her. "Good morning, doctor." On his voice was a teasing tone, and his lips pulled into a taunting smirk, but there was something insincere about it. No one else would notice, but Rowan saw through the act immediately.

She glanced at the glass wall briefly, reminding herself of their audience, of the character he played for them, and tried not to take the mask he had on too personally. This was just a skit they would recite off for the crowd. It was just pretend. It was a fantasy where he was cold and calculated and not actually a beaten and broken animal, and she was not hopeless and sad and misguided.

"Good morning," Rowan replied, looking back at him with her squared, stiff shoulders and determined gaze. She'd play her part, if only for now, so the two of them wouldn't have to feel anything for the moment.

"I appreciate you delivering my meal for the day, but I have to say, lately I've been feeling positively stuffed."

His sarcasm was almost unbearable, wickedness in the blacks of his eyes; Rowan pretended to not see the red and purple painting the skin around them, telling her stories of his actual state. However hungry he was, he never even glanced at the blood on the cart she stood beside. It was like he knew if he did, he wouldn't be able to resist.

"I'm not here to deliver a meal, but rather the antiviral we promised, to help cure you of the virus you're currently carrying." She held the most professional tone she could, but when her voice shook a little she had to look at the ground to collect herself.

She couldn't pretend as well as he could.

Noticing, Lyall offered a helping hand. Across the room, he hummed in his throat, pushing off from the wall and taking a step closer. "I thought we already discussed how I felt about being cured." His voice lowered to a dangerous tone, and even though she knew it was all an act, she couldn't help but feel her back stiffen with a tremor of fear. He would scare any sort of lingering empathy right out of her at this rate, and maybe that was his goal.

She nodded, keeping her eyes on the floor. "*We* thought I might be able to convince you." Rowan was particular with her words, emphasizing her powerlessness in the matter.

He stepped closer again, and his feet came into her lowered vision. She was tempted to retreat as she used to, but somehow, she stayed rooted to her spot. Her hand tightened around the cart she stood next to.

"Did you tell *them* I said I would kill you if you tried?" Again, the viciousness of his voice was chilling. Rowan lifted her gaze to meet his, but his eyes casted to the side, glaring at the glass wall, his threat not only for her.

"No," she breathed.

He locked back onto her with a sharp, predatory gaze. "Imagine if you had. We might have never gotten to enjoy each other's company again." His lip twitched when he said this, dangerous suggestion in his words.

Rowan shifted on her feet, his behavior getting to her even though she kept reminding herself it was just a game. She put her hand up and rubbed the back of her neck to try and fend off the nerves, and when she did his gaze caught the cuff on her wrist.

"Still wearing that thing I see." He barely reacted, and she wasn't able to read the expression that passed. He added a word that made the air bitter. "Shame."

The silence stretched until it was thick and uncomfortable, so Rowan filled it by speaking, clearing her voice to present the items on her cart. "We have a bag of blood that you can drink, it's been infused with the antiviral. And we have a single dose in a syringe, if you'd rather just have it directly injected."

"You forgot my third option." His smile stretched into a wolfish grin as he approached further, circling around the cart to stand in front of her, leaning close to invade her personal space. "You take that cuff off and I have a last, fresh meal before starving in here."

"Actually..." Rowan trailed off, looking down at the cuff, and then forced herself to catch his gaze again, even though his proximity made her heart jump into her throat and was now pounding away at her ears. "I don't need it, really." Without hesitation, she pressed her finger to the cuff. It read her print and unlatched, like all the previous times. She set it down on the cart with the bag of blood and syringe.

Lyall raised an eyebrow, but didn't move, obviously knowing there was a catch to her flippant concern for her safety. After his threat, and knowing his state of hunger, she wouldn't just leave herself vulnerable. Not in front of the other doctors, at least.

"I've been given the antiviral also." She trusted him, but there was always some doubt, lingering worry that there would be one time his hunger would get the best of him. Even with the antiviral, that nagging voice screamed at her, making her hands shake with nerves despite trying desperately to keep up her professional act. "So, if neither of the previous options satisfy, you can have your last meal, but it will cost you."

He stared at her for a painfully long moment, as if trying to decide whether she was bluffing or not, and Rowan held her breath under his gaze. She worried that he'd think she had done this to try and lure him into some sort of trap, a trick, a last attempt at making him what he thought she wanted.

When he did react, it was a tilt of his head and a smile. His eyes slid to the side, towards the glass, and tsked, his tongue against his teeth. "Now, that's just unfair. How am I supposed to refuse an offer like that?"

He figured it out, understanding completely that the antiviral in her blood had not been her idea, and Rowan felt herself deflate as she released the air from her lungs.

"You doctors are more clever than I give you credit for," Lyall chuckled, stepping to circle around Rowan. She didn't have the opportunity to notice before, but he had very little care for personal space, and since there was nothing keeping him from invading hers, he took it as an invitation. Brushing his shoulder passed hers as he moved, once behind her, he leaned close and inhaled her scent.

She withdrew from him and fumbled with her hair to cover her neck. He made a face close to offense. "How unfortunate. It even ruins the smell." Just to torture her more with his unnecessary contact, he looped a blonde strand around his thumb and slid it through his fingertips, eyes dancing mischievously as he did so.

"Have you made a decision?" Rowan asked, freeing her hair from his grip by combing her fingers through it to tuck behind her ear. She only wanted to fill the air again, try to drown out the rapid race of her heart rather than to encourage him to decide. She would rather him focus on anything other than toying with her, at least.

Her question killed his fun though, and his expression turned sour. He looked down at the cart they both stood next to, and his eyes narrowed a fraction.

"I haven't been much a fan of needles since you started sticking me with them." He grabbed the syringe with his joke, and held it up under the light to inspect it. He pulled the plastic cover off the top, the steel tip glinting like his eyes. Before Rowan could react, he pushed the plunger down, and the dose of antiviral sprayed out onto the cart. When it was empty, he flicked the syringe across the room.

His eyes moved onto the bag of blood for the first time since she entered the room. Despite his steady expression, Rowan saw his pupils grow a fraction wider, like the shudder of a camera stretching.

"And to be honest, I'm growing a bit sick of bagged lunches." Pun delivered, he reached forward and grabbed the packet, tossing it in his grip once before clenching it tight with both hands and ripping it open like a snack bag. The blood bursted out onto his hands and arms, splattering her as she retreated a step from him to try and avoid the splash.

With his two options destroyed, Rowan began to feel that dread again, this time hitting her hard in the chest when he took a deep breath, smiled, and looked at her. The blackness of his eyes was wider yet again, and her heart pounded so hard against her chest she thought it might explode through her ribs. She tried to remind herself there was no way he intended to actually hurt her, but his tightly-controlled act suggested otherwise.

"I guess this just leaves you. You forgot, I don't have to drink your blood to kill you."

It all happened too fast. His words had been a trigger for

Rowan, encouraging her to uproot her feet and escape from him, but before she could even take a single step away, he reached out and grabbed her by the elbow.

She attempted to resist but he was so much stronger than her. In comparison, she was a ragdoll, twisted around, bent to his will. He pulled her into him, then with a smooth waltz-like turn, she was pinned between him and the wall.

"Lyall, please." Terrified was an understatement. Rowan was in shock, and surprised she could even manage the words to beg him to stop. They stumbled from her mouth on a broken, cracked whimper.

His eyes burned with something unrecognizable as he put a bloodied hand over her mouth to quiet her. When she silenced, the hand slid away to her throat, fingers gripping, leaving behind a trail of red that she could taste on her teeth, sharp like metal.

He tsked again while watching her, like a thought he just had was disappointing. "I wish you had taken my offer that day, Rowan. You look so much more appropriate in red." His grip on her neck loosened, but she still found it hard to breathe.

Her heart was beating so hard she was sure he felt it through her skin. It could have been just her own skull shaking from the pounding blood, but the blacks of his eyes seemed like they were pulsing wider and wider at each rib-shattering slam of her heart. He wasn't watching her throat or the veins in her collarbone or even the blood that he swiped across her face, though.

His eyes were trained on her lips, his thumb sliding slick over her jaw, painting her skin with blood, and when she opened her mouth to let out a shaken exhale with his name on it, he pulled air in sharp through his teeth, as if she had stabbed him.

She heard something, beyond the deafening rhythm of her heart and the drowning blackness of his eyes. She didn't recognize the electronic buzz of the telecom though, not until after the shock came.

Rowan felt it on her skin where he touched her, recoiling from the pain immediately. Her neck pulsed with a lingering ache, but she barely noticed, distracted instead by the blood-stained boy who collapsed to the floor beside her.

She followed to her knees, reaching out to touch him but realizing quickly she would get another shock if she did. Helpless to do anything else, she screamed. "What are you doing? He wasn't going to hurt me! Stop this!"

"His threats to kill you are being taken seriously. If he will not feed from you, then this is over. Please leave the room, Miss Platts." Miller's voice was disgustingly monotone over the telecom, level and unemotional while Lyall screamed and convulsed.

"I won't leave him this time! Stop hurting him! Please!"

Her begging fell on deaf ears though, and her yells dissolved into panicked sobs, desperate to stop his pain however she could. He had curled up on the floor against the constant wave of electricity, shaking and groaning.

She tried to calm herself, to help her think rationally, and an idea came to mind like a shock of her own. She hurried over to the cart, snatching up her cuff and putting it back on her wrist. According to Miller, this cuff would create it's own electrical shock, administered instead to whoever touched the wearer. She hoped it would be enough to short circuit the cuff he was wearing, if she focused the electricity.

Rowan stumbled back onto the floor next to Lyall, who trembled now. She paused, giving herself another moment to calm down her racing heart and pray to whoever would listen. Then, in a swift movement, she reached out and grabbed his ankle, and the cuff that circled it.

She wanted to hold it for longer to make sure it did it's job, but the shock she received from touching him felt like being punched hard in the chest, and she had to pull away after just a second. Winded and blinded momentarily by the pain, Rowan took a second to recover, nursing her hand against her chest, struggling for air. She pulled off her own cuff, which was mangled, burnt, and scalding against the skin of her wrist. Taking this as a hopeful sign, she looked back to Lyall.

He laid limp on the floor, no more shaking or sounds of pain, and the cuff on his ankle seemed in the same state as her own. Rowan sighed in relief, then leaned forward and let her forehead rest against the cold floor, holding her arm to her stomach as the limb shot with afterpain.

A few deep breaths, and she heard Lyall move, groaning as he tried to lift himself to his hands and knees. His shoulders shook in effort, and Rowan noted how terribly beat up the both of them must look, covered in her blood and shocked into submission. She didn't care, though. She helped him this time. She hadn't run away.

"Lyall."

She called for him but he didn't react, only semi-conscious. He managed to sit back on his feet, inhaling deep and heavy, his head hanging low in his hands. His back to her, she couldn't tell if he was ok or not.

Rowan shifted closer to him, concerned for his well being but also shaking with nerves. "Lyall... I'm so sorry." She hoped using his name one more time would garner a reaction, but he once again was silent. No other option left, she reached a hand out timidly to touch his shoulder, like reaching out to pet a scared animal. She paused, almost recoiling, but scolded herself for her fear and followed through. Her fingers barely grazed his arm when he reacted.

She was pinned to the floor before she could even blink, his hand gripped tight around her throat, and his knee holding down one of her arms. He sat perched on his other foot, straddled above her like a predator who had just taken down it's prey. His eyes wild and black, more like an animal than Rowan had ever seen him. He squeezed his fingers.

Rowan shut her eyes tight against the pressure, choking out a plead. "Stop, please."

He blinked, and his expression shifted. He relaxed his grip, and Rowan got a gulp of air. Lyall raised his head a fraction, looking over his shoulder at the glass wall, then at his ankle where the broken cuff still hung, then back to her. She watched as he put the pieces together.

Then, he leaned down to whisper a breath to her ear. "I'm sorry also."

Rowan didn't have time to question his apology. He stood, pulling her up by the neck.

She was too weak to resist, but attempted to anyway, grabbing at his wrist to fight. He twisted them both around to face the glass, wrapping his forearm across her stomach and pulling her into him so her back leaned flush against his body. Her legs shook, barely able to hold up her own weight, and the grip she had around his wrist became more to keep herself from collapsing than to struggle against him.

"Rowan," his voice adopted a teasing tone, as if he found her fright amusing. "Why don't you stop fighting and instead show those doctors your pretty face."

She gave one last twist of her body before admitting defeat. When she stopped, he loosened his grip on her, making her heavy, labored breaths less of a struggle. She did as she was told, looking at the mirrored glass in front of them.

Lyall's eyes burned again, angry, violent black holes that threatened to suck up her soul. Considering her position, with his cheek against her hair and her skin covered in her own blood, it was a miracle she was still alive. The hungry fire in his gaze was not for her blood, though.

She had saved him, and he knew it. This anger that made him appear a wild, monstrous creature, was for the blank faces on the other side of the glass. She could see it, feel it clearly in his careful grip around her. She worried though, that she'd end up as collateral in the war between Lyall and the monsters that caged him.

"Now, tell them to open up those doors for us, or I'll make them watch as I tear your pretty face from your skull."

CHAPTER TWENTY-ONE

Rowan saw herself through the mirrored glass as the fear spread across her stained features, the blood swept over her mouth accentuating the terror in her eyes. She shut them tight and let her head fall, not wanting to see her trembling lips and his murderous expression.

Lyall refused to let her off so easily, though, moving the hand on her neck to cup her chin and direct her face back up. She opened her eyes, and he was watching her now through their reflection, but nothing about the way he looked at her was hostile. His arm around her stomach tightened just barely, and he tilted his head to speak in her ear, his gaze locked on hers.

"Don't let them use you anymore. You're better than that. Get angry with me."

His words stirred something in her. Hot lava rolled in her stomach, burning up her throat, and her expression shifted from horror to frustration and anger. The emotions that curled inside her all weekend, festering on her helplessness and despair, desperate and dangerous, roared for release.

He added one last whisper on a breath, securing the fire in her glossy eyes. "You promised to help me, remember? Let the monster come out and play, *Rowan*."

With his words, her gut purred. Yes, she promised to help him, and she would.

They would escape this white cell together, as monsters.

Rowan knew only one person held the power to let them out of this room, though, and appealing to Miller's sensibilities would be difficult since she seemed to have less and less recently. She had to try something, though.

And then, amongst the tangle of frustration and hopelessness, Rowan had an idea.

"Are you really going to let me die in here, doctor?" Her call was timid, not knowing what she was supposed to say, the plan forming in bits and pieces. Knowing Miller was listening even though she couldn't see her face helped to fuel Rowan's nervous words. "After everything I've done for this project? This project wouldn't exist without me. I figured out that he drank blood, I came to talk to him over and over again, and I put my life on the line for this project."

Anger bloomed in her chest, because as she said it, she knew Miller was debating with herself. What should be done with Phelps' problematic assistant, who just couldn't play by the rules? Tears of betrayal and frustration welled in Rowan's eyes, so she used her own emotions to her advantage, shutting them tight and letting the salty drops slide down her face.

"After what happened to William, you promised no one else would get hurt."

She hoped this would do it. She prayed this would be enough to convince Miller, because she wanted to trust the woman, and she wanted her to be the mentor Rowan had been searching for. She wanted to believe Miller was still reasonable.

The woman said so herself though, she had responsibilities as a leader that could not be compromised, and Rowan had broken all of her rules. Even ones that Miller didn't know about yet.

Trapped in the arms of her accomplice as he stared at their reflections with fury in his wide pupils, she offered a last plea. "Open the door, please. Don't let him just kill me."

All she could do was wait, and Miller made her wait forever. Her body ached all over from the electrocution. Her neck throbbed with pain where Lyall held her, even though he was trying to be gentle. She could barely hold herself on her own two feet, grasping at his wrists to keep standing. With every second her anger and frustration grew thick and suffocating, turning the hopelessness on her face hard.

Miller wouldn't open the doors. She decided it was too risky. It was easier to just let them both disappear in this room, something else Miller had already implied. After all, no matter how much control Lyall had, once he starved enough, he would eventually tear her apart, if Rowan didn't die of starvation first, and then he would starve as well. They'd both be forgotten. An admirable, but futile attempt on Rowan's part.

She wasn't finished fighting, though.

"Phelps is not going to let you do this." Rowan added after the long lack of response, her weak voice finding a new fervour. "He knows I'm still working on this project with you. Do you think he's just going to keep his mouth shut if I disappear?"

Finally, this garnered a reaction, and Rowan heard the telecom click on, Miller's voice ringing through the room. "It would be his words against mine." The response was cold, not in a way that suggested tightly trained emotions, but rather no emotions at all.

Against her stomach, Rowan felt Lyall's hand curl into an angry fist around the fabric of her lab coat, but she allowed a sharp smirk to lift the corner of her lips instead as response. "Not just his word."

Because Phelps wasn't the only one who knew anymore. Rowan broke the last of Miller's rules that weekend and told someone everything. Cameron, who now knew about Lyall and the project and the virus, knew what Rowan was being forced to do, and what would happen if she failed. Cameron, who now waited upstairs for Rowan's safe return and who she'd warned what to think if she didn't.

A long, steady silence followed, and Rowan knew it was the sound of Miller piecing together her words. And then, beyond the deafening slam of her heart in her skull, she heard the familiar sound of the automated latch as it slid open.

On the back of her neck, she felt Lyall exhale sharp, as if he had given up somewhere along the way, but unlike Rowan, who stood gaping in shock that her plan worked, he dealt with his surprise far quicker. Forcing her out of her motionlessness, he let go of her neck and took her elbow in his grip instead, ushering her along as he went for the door.

Finally moving, everything hit her all at once, and her already pounding heart went into overdrive with a rush of adrenaline. They were doing this. They were getting out of there, together, with his virus intact.

All this time, she ignored and stifled the itching desire to just free him and run, knowing it was selfish and stupid and impossible, but now that it was happening, she couldn't keep the dark part of her from blooming. It was scary, but it was also powerful and thrilling and addictive. She let her thoughts run wild with it.

Cameron was waiting for her. It would be easy. They could just get in his truck and take off, together. A grand escape fit for such a long and weary fight.

She was ripped from her fantasy when Lyall walked her closer to the unlocked door between them and the observation room. Rowan paused to look at him, and she was sure he understood because he must have saw the wicked in her gaze and smelled the adrenaline in her blood.

As if daring her to embrace the excitement she was considering, he nodded towards their escape and said, "Are you going to let me out, Rowan?"

The corner of her mouth going up, and she pulled open the door. So what if he killed everyone? They were all monsters anyway. As long as he didn't kill her. And he wouldn't. Because she was special. She was *his* monster. As if confirming that delicious thought, Lyall grabbed her upper arm gently and nudged her forward, following close behind as the two of them exited the containment room.

Her colleagues all stood still as statues, the pure horror written on each and every face, except for Miller. She found the other woman across the room, and their eyes locked. The look she gave covered something else, as if she was congratulating Rowan on her momentary win but had a trick up her sleeve.

Lyall paused for a moment next to her, and his dark eyes scanned the room, stopping briefly on every face as he wrote them into his mind. Finally he reached Miller, who he smirked at. "It's a pleasure to finally see all your faces. Hope you all sleep well tonight." Leaving the room in a perpetual state of terror with his threat, Lyall's hand trailed down Rowan's arm to her wrist, yanking her after him into the hall.

Upon leaving the observation room, the emergency alarm went off, signalling a floor lockdown, and Rowan swore out loud. She was so lost in the thrill, she hadn't thought things through clearly and didn't consider the fact that the entire laboratory had the back-up security feature.

"The elevator will be disabled. There's no other way to get out of these labs. It's designed that way for this exact reason."

Lyall slowed for only a brief moment to glance at her and

smirk, like he took her words as a challenge, then picked up his pace into an almost jog. Her limb still tight in his grasp, Rowan practically ran to keep up with him. Her heart raced, thrashing in her chest like a caged animal, the loud sirens blaring around them only making her anxiety more overwhelming. And yet, a grin lingered on the corner of her mouth, tugging at her cheeks until they ached.

As they took the corner to the elevators, she remembered the security guard they were approaching. She opened her mouth to say something, but it was already far too late. She pulled her wrist from Lyall's grasp and retreated back around the corner, covering her ears as the sound of assault rifle fire broke through the screaming emergency sirens.

The shots lasted forever it seemed, and when they finally stopped, Rowan opened her eyes to see the wall across from her littered with countless bullet holes. She stared in horror as she realized: Lyall was superhuman, but certainly not bulletproof.

She turned quickly to peek around the corner where Lyall had been, where she failed to warn him of the danger, expecting to see him dead, or at least bleeding profusely on the floor, but to her shock, he was standing.

His shoulders rose and fell with labored breaths, but otherwise he seemed completely untouched. At the other end of the hall, the security guard stood frozen, his eyes wide with horror, his gun still aimed and pulling the trigger even though he already emptied it.

Rowan moved to reach out to Lyall, but he acted, using his speed to appear in front of the guard before she could reach him. He took hold of the gun by its barrel with one hand and forced it back so the butt hit hard against the guard's shoulder. Then, in a swift motion, he jerked the gun to the side so its stock slammed square across the guard's face, flooring him.

She approached as Lyall used the gun for support to lower

himself over the guard. He grabbed the man by the front of his hair and lifted him up to inspect the bloody, broken nose he created. With the sight of the blood, Rowan watched Lyall's face slide into a familiar, dark expression. He discarded the gun and grabbed the guard by the collar, his heavy head falling back to expose his neck.

Instantly, she felt like she was hit in the gut, her regret resurfacing and killing the excited high from before. All those thoughts about not caring who he killed, the monster inside her could growl the idea all she wanted, but the fact was, she did care. It was why she kept that dark part of herself stifled, because that wasn't who she was. She didn't want anyone to die. No one deserved to die.

"Lyall, no!" She cried out her objection when he opened his mouth, staring with nervous horror as he stopped and turned his wild eyes to look at her.

"He tried to kill me," Lyall argued, his grip around the man's collar tightening.

Rowan swallowed hard, her voice breaking as she begged. "Please..."

Lyall stared at her for a moment longer before closing his eyes and sighing heavily. He rolled his shoulders, and when he opened his eyes again, it was as if he eased the animal back, his expression settled. He shoved the guard back down to the floor, then got up and stepped over him towards the elevators.

Rowan didn't follow this time, unsure if he wanted her to, now that she had shown him that she couldn't be the monster he wanted her to be. She could never accept this darkness that he lived by. It wasn't her.

He got five steps before he stopped to glance back at her. "Are you coming?"

CHAPTER TWENTY-TWO

THEY ARRIVED AT THE ELEVATOR, their next obstacle since it was the only way out of the underground. Lyall moved to tear the doors open like a pair of window shutters, but Rowan stopped him.

"I might be able to override the lockdown. Let me try first." She wasn't supposed to know about these details of the security system, but Cameron had a big mouth. With a key card that had high enough access, it was possible to use it and an emergency code to get things working again. And she still had Phelps'.

She scanned the card and tried a few different codes, her fingers shaking with panic and adrenaline. She glanced over her shoulder every now and then, even though she knew none of the doctors would take the risk to try and stop them. This likely meant though, that if they were stopped, it would be once they reached the upper floor, after reinforcements were sent for.

Lyall, who seemed less concerned about being interrupted, leaned his shoulder against the wall next to her to wait casually. Something resembling amusement played in his eyes as he watched her fiddle with the touchpad.

"If you can't slow your heart a little, I'll have to do it for you."

Suddenly aware of the painful pounding in her chest, Rowan lifted her gaze to see his fall to the line of her neck. She scowled slightly, pulling her hair over her shoulder and turning back to her work.

"You can't, yet. There's the antiviral in my blood."

She realized immediately what she said, flushing as the look in Lyall's eyes spread into a wolfish grin in her peripherals.

"Yet?" He pushed off the wall, and she tried to ignore him as he leaned towards her to whisper, "Does that mean the offer stands later?"

Rowan pretended to not be bothered, but goosebumps flared over her skin at the touch of his breath on her ear. She wanted to taunt back, to indulge finally in the fact that they were alone again, without an audience, and without a wall between them. They didn't have time for his particular form of pleasantries, though. The touchpad chimed as she landed on the correct set of numbers, recalled from the back corners of her memory, and she snaked away from him, entering the now opened elevator.

"Cameron is waiting, but... They're going to be waiting for us up there also, so... I don't know how you want to do this." Rowan warned, the doors closing behind them, silencing the ambient wailing of the alarm.

"I can kill them all without a problem." Lyall tested, his lips curled at the end.

"I don't think that's the best solution." She glared, stepping forward to scan her keycard. "Where should we go after this?"

Behind her, Lyall sighed, sounding sour that she ruined the fun. He leaned back against the far wall of the elevator, staying silent until Rowan purposefully caught his gaze.

"We're not going anywhere, Rowan."

She frowned, confused. "What do you mean?"

Rowan watched him, his expression forced from disappointed

to cold. His blue eyes like ice now, he said, "I mean, you and I, we're not going anywhere. This ends here."

Her eyebrows sunk further down, her chest beginning to tighten but refusing to accept the panic setting in. "I don't understand." She did though. She just didn't want to.

Lyall seemed to soften. "What did you think was going to happen?" The question was sharp, but its intent was genuine.

When Rowan tried to answer it though, her mouth came up empty and dry. She had no idea what she thought. She didn't think that far, considering this whole thing had just been a dark, illogical desire sprouted from the shadows of her heart. There was no after-plan, but she definitely hadn't expected it to end like this.

Or perhaps she had, and simply refused to acknowledge that the only thing left for Lyall to do after escaping was to disappear. Maybe Rowan thought she would disappear with him. Maybe it was why she didn't care about the consequences she would have to face for helping him.

"I don't know," she whispered, feeling her throat constrict as the pain stung at her nose. Her eyes threatened tears, but she fought them back as hard as she could.

"It can't be any other way." Even though he was right, something about the way he said it was bitter. She tasted the flavor in her mouth, sharp like the smell of the blood, and it made her feel ill.

Rowan gnawed hard at her lip as she nodded, fending off her crumbling heart. "What should I do then? After this."

Lyall stayed silent for a brief moment as he thought, then pushed off from the wall and approached her and the touchpad. He reached around her to select the ground floor, and the elevator came to life.

"When I tell you, you're going to close your eyes, and before you open them again, I'll be gone. It will be like I was never even here. They'll find you alone, and you'll answer the questions they'll have for you. You'll tell them you had no choice but to help me, I threatened to kill you if you didn't, you were just trying to stay alive. You'll tell them I manipulated you this whole time, because that's what I did. You were nothing but a tool to me. I was using you this whole time. Do you understand, Rowan?"

Rowan gasped, the tears brimming her eyes now, but she refused to let them fall. She swallowed down the lump in her throat, shaking off her reluctance, and nodded. She didn't want to agree with him, because agreeing meant letting go. She understood what she had to do, though. She had to play her part just as he did all this time. She had to pretend to not care, pretend to be a victim, so perhaps she wouldn't have to feel the pain of the truth.

"Are you angry?" he asked.

Rowan was sad, upset, hopeless. She was anything but angry. Anger was what she had to feel, though. Anger was what would help her forget him. So she thought about all the things she had done for him. She thought about how she'd risked her career, her life, her friendships, how she'd given herself to him in every sense of the word. She thought about how she'd considered herself special, and how naive she had been, how she'd been ready to be a monster for him, and how he was leaving her with that darkness.

"Yes," she said finally, gritting her teeth to feel the frustration in her bones. She stifled the part of her that knew the truth, down into her gut with her monstrousness, and repeated the story to herself. He lied, deceived, manipulated. None of it was real. He used her, all this time, he had just used her.

"Good," he said, another bitter note on his tongue. "Now close your eyes."

Rowan did as she was told, shutting them tight. She felt him step closer to her, not quite touching but able to feel the warmth of his body. She resisted reaching out, her fingers twitching at her sides. The elevator slowed, and she felt a sigh pass her lips that was not her own. A chime sounded to signal they arrived on the ground floor, and as the doors opened, suddenly it was quiet and cold.

Rowan opened her watering eyes and put her hands up in surrender, alone in front of a mass of armed gunmen.

THE SUITED MEN escorted her down a long hall to a windowless room, where Miller waited inside. Although no one was in handcuffs or restrained, the whole ordeal felt like detainment. Rowan wondered if she had her right to a lawyer, but decided against asking. It didn't matter anyway, she had her story, it was already leaking doubt into her bones.

They asked a series of questions, and she answered while staring straight ahead, unfocused and barely there. She told them Lyall manipulated her into caring for him, used her to help him escape. He promised not to kill her as long as she cooperated and threatened to harm everyone if she rebelled. She told them she didn't know where he went. Rowan played the victim better than she expected, perhaps because a part of her was starting to wonder what really was the truth and what was a lie.

Miller stared at her the entire time over her rimless lenses. She worried briefly that the woman would call her on her lies somehow, that she would pull out evidence of Rowan's dedication to Lyall. How would Miller prove such a thing though, if Rowan herself wasn't even sure anymore what had been her own actions and what had been Lyall's influence. What had been real, and what was just fantasy.

Despite her concerns, Miller never interrupted, never spoke a word. When the suited men finished questioning her, the woman simply nodded and left the room along with them.

Cameron was just outside waiting, also detained by the suited men. They were both put into protective custody, which meant house arrest, so the suited men drove them to Rowan's tiny bungalow, where they were told they would stay for the rest of the night. Out on the curb, the men set up their lookout from inside their car, to either make sure Rowan and Cameron didn't take off, or to keep a watchful eye for a visitor.

Their effort was futile. If he was smart, Lyall would be long gone now and wouldn't be returning.

It was when they were inside, the door closed, the bolt locked, that Rowan could breathe. She inhaled shakily, and the feeling in her limbs came back, the crushing pain of everything hitting her in the chest and suffocating her all over again. She didn't make a sound, but the sobs wracked her body hard, and Cameron caught her as her legs gave out.

He held her to his chest and rocked her for what felt like eternity, until the sun went down, and the sobs stopped, and she went numb again. Then, he led her upstairs to the bathroom, ran a hot shower for her, and left her alone to wash away the stains of the day.

Rowan turned the lights off and lit some candles, hoping the honey and cinnamon would bring back comforting memories of her mother's hair and sunny summers rather than the current emptiness she felt. She shed her clothes slow and deliberate, letting them fall to the floor in a dirty, blood-stained pile. Her t-shirt stuck to her, and she had to peel it away from her flesh like a second skin. Her blood-soaked hair tangled and matted together, and her face was still painted in red; she looked like a victim, and she was beginning to feel like one.

Rowan considered herself a strong person, someone who knew

what she wanted and how to get it. She didn't see herself as someone susceptible to lies and manipulation, but Miller pulled the wool over her eyes for longer than she was proud of, so couldn't it mean that Lyall was capable of doing the same?

The more she considered, wondered on the details of what happened, the more she started questioning every moment.

Things she thought had been her own actions, she started wondering if she was somehow convinced to behave and feel the way she had. The things she said, felt, had they just been her own creations? The moments where they shared something close to tenderness, were they just fantasy, hopeful wishes, her mind bending the truth to help her face the necessity of brushing shoulders with a monster every day?

Lyall had proven from the start that he was capable of controlling her. He did so with fear at first, but had he decided to switch his tactics midway? Had her dark thoughts about helping him escape been planted there somewhere along the lines? He certainly lured her with the idea enough times. Was this just his plan, all this time? For how long? The sympathy she felt, the infatuation, the affection, where had it started? Was any of it true?

She stepped under the shower, the water at her feet turning red. Still feeling numb, Rowan blasted the heat until it scalded her, then let the beating droplets pound her skin raw. She forced her face under the burning bullets of water, scrubbing away the last bit of the bloody brands he'd left on her. The water washed away all the dirt and blood and tears, but there was no way for it to get into her skull and rinse away her doubts.

Maybe none of it was real. Maybe she really had just been infatuated, like she knew Miller thought. It didn't change anything. He was gone, and he wasn't coming back. Maybe it was easier, to accept that it had all been a ruse. That he'd never cared.

That he used her. This, a pool of anger in her gut, hurt less than the thought that he'd left her behind.

She'd hoped entering the cool air after leaving the hot, steamy bathroom would be refreshing, but instead, it settled as a heavy chill in her bones. She forced herself to ignore it, pushing through, and discarded her bloody clothes in the laundry bin. She threw on her oversized, university tee over a pair of boyshorts, the worn cotton offering some much-needed comfort, but she longed for more.

She returned downstairs, and Cameron was set up at the living room table with a box of pizza. When she gave him a curious expression, he smiled sheepishly. "I told the suits if they were gonna keep us locked up, they would have to feed us, so they ordered takeout."

Rowan managed a tiny laugh, sitting down and looking over her selection. Cameron flicked on a movie, then grabbed a cheesy slice as he flopped down next to her.

They ate in a comfortable silence for a while, commenting on the film and the food, Cameron teasing when Rowan hogged all the garlic bread. The relaxed feeling dissipated after a while, though. It always did. Food and a movie was how Cameron got Rowan talking.

Usually, Rowan was a willing participant in their serious conversation, but this time, a part wished there was a way to just wipe it all from her brain and pretend none of it happened. She didn't want to think about all the things she said, last time they were together on this couch. It mortified her.

"So…" Cameron initiated the conversation delicately, staring down at his food with his question. "He's gone?"

Rowan had already stopped eating, playing with a pizza crust as she nodded. "Yeah. He's gone."

Cameron hummed. "You sure he's not coming back?"

"He'd be stupid to," she replied, swallowing down the ache the answer left in her throat. After a moment, she added bitterly, "Besides, what would he come back for?"

Shrugging, he continued. "I dunno. From what you said…"

Rowan couldn't stand to hear it, so she interrupted, her voice going a fraction sharper even though she didn't mean for it. "Well, I was wrong. He used me. I was just… A way out. What I thought wasn't… Nothing was real."

It didn't matter what she said before. It didn't matter that he told her secrets, shared vulnerable parts of himself with her, had tangled his fingers with hers for a brief moment through the darkness. It didn't matter that she secretly gave herself to him. It was a lie. It had to be a lie. Because if it wasn't…

"It's okay if you cared about him, Row," Cameron commented, triggering a flush on her cheeks, red and hot from shame and embarrassment. He had tricked her into caring, though. That was all. Her feelings, they were based on lies. This pain in her chest. It couldn't be real. Like Cameron heard her inner struggle, he added, "Just because some things weren't true, doesn't make your emotions any less real."

His words were gentle but stabbed at her regardless. She tried to nod through the pain, but she couldn't fight the emotions as they welled in her throat and filled her eyes with tears. Rowan shifted closer to Cameron, and buried herself in his collar when he reached out for her, pulling her into a messy hug and kissing her wet hair.

"I don't know what I was thinking would happen. I'm so stupid…"

Cameron shook his head. "You're not stupid. You're human."

That was an ironic comment. She let a bitter scoff leave her lips, pushing deeper into his comfort before muttering, "Maybe being human isn't all it's cracked up to be."

After all, it was certainly the only reason she was still there, crying, hurting, sulking. Maybe if she'd just accepted Lyall's offer to be like him... If she had just said yes...

"Don't say that," Cameron scolded, nudging his nose into her hair, faux pouting against her temple. "If you weren't so human, you wouldn't be Rowan. And I like her. I'd miss her a hell of a lot if she went somewhere."

She felt her forehead contort, before giving a defeated breath and nodding to his shirt. "I'd miss you, too."

She felt him smile and hug her closer. "I guess that just means you gotta stay here and be human with me. I know it's kinda lame sometimes, but I'll get you through the boring parts."

Her pained smile turned into a tiny laugh as she sighed and deflated in his arms. "Thank you, Cameron."

They laid on the couch and finished the movie, Rowan tucked under Cameron's arm, feeling safe for the first time in what seemed like forever. They stayed there for a long time, actually, well after the movie stopped playing and a silence engulfed the room. They laid together until Cameron's hand, rubbing over her shoulder comfortingly, stilled eventually, and his breathing became shallow and slow.

Rowan considered waking him, but she knew his day had been hard as well and thought it best to let him rest. She stood carefully and retrieved a quilt off the back of her living room armchair, laying it over him gently before shutting off the lights and returning upstairs. She should probably try to get some sleep herself. If her thoughts would let her, at least.

With evening approaching, the natural light flooded her room in fiery red and orange, casting warmth across her bare skin as she moved to shut her curtains. While she did, she checked on the suited men below, still in their car on the road outside. Annoyed, she shut the thick fabric forcefully to block them out, but then peeked back through, unable to resist spying on them. They did nothing, just sitting and watching, and Rowan scowled to herself, frustrated she needed babysitting.

She was the last one who wanted it to be true, but Lyall was gone. None of them would ever see him again. That was how he wanted it. That was the smart thing to do. He was a predator, and predators followed their instincts, not their hearts.

"You boys are wasting your time," Rowan muttered under her breath, although the words felt more like they were for her own sake. A reminder to get him out of her head. She gnawed at her lip, closing the blinds and scolding herself. "Stupid mouse."

"That's my line."

CHAPTER TWENTY-THREE_

SHE SCREAMED, but Lyall silenced her with a firm hand around her mouth before even the faintest sound could actually escape her. She grabbed for the curtains but he dragged her away, holding her tight around the stomach as she wrestled and kicked.

Rowan continued to yell against his palm, and he chuckled, the sound somewhere close to her ear. "With how loud you're being, it's almost like you want to get me caught." He twisted around and pushed her against the wall next to her window, one hand pinning her arm down, the other held tight over her lips. "If you can promise me you'll stop yelling, I'll let you go."

She managed to take a breath through her nose to calm herself, her eyes tightly shut. It took her a moment to will her heart down from palpitations, but when she settled her breathing a little, he kept to his word and removed himself, taking a step back to give her space.

Released, Rowan finally opened her eyes, and her shoulder blade hit the wall as she retreated. She hadn't been willing to believe he was there when she heard his voice; it was foolish, but a part of her would have preferred it being just the phantom of his memory haunting her. She couldn't pretend otherwise now though, as he stood there, the burning ice of his eyes staring her down through the low light of her bedroom.

"I'm sorry if I scared you." The apology seemed genuine, gentle, but the animal was in his gaze. She'd noticed immediately, even through the shadows. His pupils dilated wide and black, possessed. It had been a long time since he looked at her quite like that.

"What are you doing here?"

She voiced her first thought, then as the shock dissipated her mind ran wild with the possible answers. What was the only reason he would still be around? What would matter to him enough to risk coming back? And then she remembered, his threat to the others before leaving. The bitterness that never failed to leave him, even when he was starving and broken and had given up. He had unfinished business with those doctors. With her.

"Are you here to kill me?"

Lyall raised an eyebrow, legitimately surprised by her first reaction. Then, his expression slid into something playful, even though it looked more sinister than anything with his eyes so black.

"Give me some credit, Rowan. I don't play with my food."

He stepped forward, and in reaction, she flinched, pressing herself into the wall further. He stop sharply, like her fear wounded him, and leaned away again, onto his heels. With the silence stretching between him, his eyes dragged down to her collarbone. "Your heart is racing."

It was. It pounded so hard Rowan felt like she was having a heart attack, the silence only amplified the beats, deafening in her ears. She knew she had to settle it, that it was dangerous to keep letting it pulse violently out of control in her chest, but she couldn't focus on slow breathing or calming mantras anymore. All there was were questions.

"How did you even find me?"

"It wasn't hard when I was still covered in your blood," he explained, forcing his eyes to the ground to avoid staring at her, maybe to keep her from being even more frightened. Despite his wild, black eyes, he seemed calm, tamed, and under control. But Rowan couldn't be sure. His shoulders were tense, like he was holding something back. "I saw the men outside, so I went to your neighbor's first. I thought it would be smart to clean myself up, get some fresh clothes, be a little less conspicuous."

Her mouth dropped open as she thought about the family next door, the mother and father, and their teenage son who was taller than Lyall, fresh faced and friendly. She looked over him for the first time since he arrived, seeing the jeans and black long sleeve shirt he now wore instead of scrubs. The oversized waistband hung too low on his hips, and the wide shoulders of the shirt didn't quite fit right on his thin frame; minor details that others might overlook, but Rowan recognized immediately as signs the clothes didn't belong to him. Where did he take them from though? The boy's closet, or off his body?

"Did you—"

"No one was home." At first, he sounded like he was almost offended she would even think he'd do something so horrible, but then pulled the defensiveness back as he realized his previous behavior didn't suggest any other outcome. "I cleaned myself up, took what I needed, and left."

"How did you get in my house?"

Lyall chuckled. "You really shouldn't leave your back door unlocked, you have no idea what kind of psychos could just waltz right in." He carded his hands through his damp hair awkwardly as he glanced up with his joke, smiling a little at first then letting it fall when he saw it had done nothing to her horrified expression. "Bad joke. Sorry."

Rowan stared for a while longer, her back forced against the wall as far from him as possible. In normal clothes, with clean hair, and no blood on his face or under his nails, he seemed almost normal. His smile was less wicked when his skin was not stained in red, but no amount of normalness could distract her from the predatory look that possessed his vision. She didn't want to know the answer to the next question, but she had to, because the possible answers were what immobilized her.

"Why are you here?"

He closed his eyes, and Rowan watched as he clenched his fingers into a fist by his side. He didn't speak. He didn't have to.

Her exhale was unsteady, her heart in her throat, choking her as she forced out her trembling reply to his silence. "If you're going to kill me, I wish you would just do it."

"I'm not here to kill you."

His voice was strained as he ran a hand through his hair again, his body language too stiff, too controlled. He seemed genuine though, despite the hunger possessing his eyes. Actually, the way he responded, sounded almost like her suspicion was wounding.

"Then why are you here? Why would you leave me like you did just to come back? I don't understand. Is this another one of your games? Are you just torturing me?" Her confusion and anger came out in her tone, shaking and rising in volume with each word.

"Please... Lower your voice." Lyall warned, his eyes darting around as he listened to the men outside, and Cameron downstairs, to make sure they hadn't heard.

Rowan took in a deep breath to level her shaking words. She spoke again, volume lowered but still pained. "I sacrificed everything to help you. And you just left, like it was nothing."

"I thought it would be easier if I gave you a reason to hate me," he countered in a quiet voice, his being far less confronting. It was almost timid, as if he was nervous that speaking would make her blow up.

It did.

"So why are you back? You got what you wanted from me. You're free. Why couldn't you stay gone with your stupid virus and let me hate you?"

She stepped away from the wall, towards him, forgetting all together why she was even scared of him in the first place. She didn't see the hunger in his eyes, didn't remember him tearing open William and drinking down his blood like water. All she knew was she'd let him hurt her, and now she wanted him to hurt also.

She advanced on him, a terrifying one hundred and ten pounds of feeble human being, but there was a ferocity behind her that made her feel powerful despite her disadvantage. The angry tears in her eyes blurred her vision just enough to make him look like the monster she needed him to be, a demon that used her up and left her alone, left her behind. She hit him as hard as she could, on his chest, and then his stomach and collar, knowing it was doing nothing but needing desperately to feel something after going so numb.

When Rowan finally did feel something, it was all at once. Her explosive anger dissolved into stifled sobs as her chest swelled in pain, tears escaping from her angry eyes and running down her face, muttering incoherently about how much she hated him. Hated him for all the times he scared her breathless, messed with her head, fed her lies. Hated him for making her care.

She hit him until her punches became weak shoves, sending her wobbling on her feet rather than moving him. She hit him until she couldn't see through the tears in her eyes anymore, and she swung at the air as much as she was at him. She hit him until he stopped her, grabbing her thin wrist and fending off her struggling until she couldn't fight anymore, collapsing into his hold on her, her fisted fingers now curled around his shirt instead.

"I don't know what I'm supposed to think anymore. I don't know what was real. You weren't supposed to come back. Coming back means... It means..."

It was the feeling of his heart that made Rowan realize how close they were. They'd never been so close for her to have noticed. Not like this at least. Without anyone spying from behind a glass wall. Just the two of them, in the dark, her own heart pounding wildly in her chest, mimicking the rhythm of his as it raced in his ribcage, under her palm. It was his fingers, electric digits loosening from her wrist and trailing slow up the skin of her arm, that made her realize they'd never touched like this. Not without it being part of a show. A mask.

Except for once, his hand tangled with hers on the floor, making her realize for the first time how tangible he was. How real he was. How real *this* was. The touch that made her think maybe he was more than just the hunger in his eyes.

His touch, trailing static up her neck, thumbs swiping at the tears on her face, pulling her head back from his chest. Rowan let out the breath she had been holding, her shoulders sinking in relieved tension, not realizing how badly she'd been aching for this. Letting her eyes open again to finally look up at him, she admitted defeat to the words she tried so hard to keep out of her head all night.

If he came back, maybe it meant he came back for her.

Through the gleam of her wet lashes, she met his possessed, black-hole pupils, sucking her exhale from her lungs, instant panic washing over her like ice cold water. She was wrong. He hadn't come back for her. He'd come back for a last meal. The look in his eyes said so.

She stiffened, and so did he, pushing closer so she found the wall again, the fingers cradled around her jaw reaching up into her hair and pulling her head back further, stretching her neck long. Rowan gasped, finding strength again to grip at his wrists, her voice shaking as she managed out a whispered beg.

"Lyall, pleas—"

But he interrupted with his lips, taking hers with hungry intention, and the grip in her hair that Rowan had been resisting ending up being the only thing keeping her on her feet.

Catching herself on his shirt after her knees buckled, Rowan attempted a noise of protest, but it dissolved in her throat and came out as something much closer to pleasure, sagging her eyes shut in surrender.

Rowan wasn't sure when things begun building to this moment. When her fear turned into desire. When the uncomfortable crawl under her skin had shifted to a burn. How long had she ached with this need? Was it when he first whispered in her ear and brought a chill instead of a tremor of fear? Was it in the dark, a glass wall between them, when all she wanted to do was reach out and for once touch his warm flesh and not the cold barrier between them?

Whenever it started, Rowan didn't have the sense to stop it now. Lyall pushed to part her lips, a desperate exhale to her mouth that breathed life back into her shocked body, intoxicating her with the taste of his tongue; metallic and pain and a certain indescribable wildness, leaving her hungry for more. So she reached, leaned closer, begged for some grounding for her suddenly spinning head, and instead of steadying her, he took her legs away completely, leading them up around his hips to pin her between himself and the wall, deepening his kiss when she gasped at the new closeness of their bodies.

This was foolish. Dangerous. Selfish. She knew it, and was

only reminded when he parted from her lips to catch a breath, and it was clear in his roving eyes, still wide and black with the same starvation he arrived with as they jumped over the details of her face. Her instinct told her to push him away, but her fingers gripped at the fabric of the sweater that wasn't his.

"You're too hungry..." she said, unable to manage more than a weak, whispered protest.

He gave a breathy laugh, countering her words by pushing closer, punishing her for letting some sense filter through her foggy brain. "I'm hungry, but not for your blood." She felt the words against her lips before he took them again.

She didn't question it anymore. Because his fingers — the ones he strangled her with, painted blood across her face, tangled in hers — they traced fire along her bare skin now. At her thighs, along her hips, up under her shirt. His lips — stained red more often than not — whispered along the length of her throat, teasing the tender flesh with the same teeth she'd watched tear open a man, causing a hot assault of goosebumps down her arms. Those wide, black pupils, that had only ever looked at her like something he would eventually devour, begged her permission to do just that.

Is this what the virus was like? Ravenous, insatiable, primal. Rowan imagined in that moment she had an idea of what it was like to be him. To be starved of something she hadn't realized she needed. To lose herself to the dangerous and demanding thing twisting hot and hungry inside of her. To give in.

Rowan's fingers fumbled with the fever in her belly, with the need to be closer, pushing those too-loose jeans from his hips as he dared to unwrap her too. He shoved her freshly stripped spine flush to the frigid wall in another kiss, steady hands snaking across newly exposed skin, stealing her breath, setting a fire in her as he pressed their bodies tight together, closer, *closer*, until he smothered her cry with searing lips.

CHAPTER TWENTY-FOUR

THEY FOUND THEIR SENSES AGAIN. Eventually. Cleared their weighted, cotton-filled heads with hungry, panting breaths after collapsing together on Rowan's mattress, tangled limbs and tired, heavy eyes. It was another million seconds before they spoke, though, Rowan preferring to listen to the steady, echoing pound of her heart in her ears as it came down from its peak.

When she finally broke the silence, with a moan in her throat that sounded more like a purr of pleasure, Lyall let his lips curl up into an exhausted, but noticeably wicked grin.

"Who exactly did you say was too hungry?" he asked, peeking at her from the corner of his eye with a pointed look, his pupils still dilated in the low light but significantly less possessed.

She gave a sheepish laugh in response, rolling over to her side to bury her flushed face into her sheets as she responded. "If that's all you came back for, why didn't you just say so?"

Rowan bit at her lip when he responded with a playfully dangerous noise in his throat, rolling over also to bring his nose to her hair. "*That* wasn't part of the plan." He paused for a moment, humming lips at her hairline when she shift closer, then added on a slightly more somber note, "None of this was really part of the plan. Coming back."

The angry ache in her heart drowned out by her desire came raging back. She tried to not let it take over though, and the sound of his smooth breathing helped a little. She waited a moment before responding, "Why... why did you come back?" She would have been alright, left behind to hate him.

Now though, the thought of him leaving again pressed down on her chest, heavy and suffocating.

He didn't answer right away. Instead, Lyall stretched the silence until Rowan shifted to gaze up at him, catching a flash of shame across his face as he finally answered. "I didn't know where else to go. I was so hungry."

Rowan frowned hard, replying with a tone sharper than she intended. "Did you only come back for my blo—"

Immediately he protested, shaking his head and bringing hands up to circle her jaw, leading her eyes up to his. "No, that wasn't it." Still, the answer seemed weak, like there was something more he wasn't saying, leaving Rowan with her throat tight.

"Why didn't you just kil—" She stopped, that word sticking in her throat and forcing her to think of one less terrible to say. "Why didn't you just *feed* on someone?"

He'd sighed at her question, shifting closer so his forehead met hers, and she felt it contort in struggle, trying to find the words. Instead, he kissed her first, smooth and sultry, nearly making her forget what they were talking about all together. It was only when he offered a response to her lips that she remembered they'd been having a conversation.

"I didn't want to. I knew I didn't want blood."

Rowan sighed to his lips, trying to understand, the heat he left in her skull making it more difficult. "You're starving, Lyall. You need to eat."

He kissed her again to silence her, before giving a firm growl against her lips, like a warning not to argue again. "I am starving. But it feels good to refuse the hunger."

She didn't speak again, instead shaking her head to beg for elaboration. He sighed, raising himself up to sit and run a hand through his hair. Rowan shifted to follow, leaning her shoulder to his but staying quiet as he took a moment to sort through his thoughts.

"Being locked up in that room was the first time in my life I've been forced to control the hunger. I thought I was choosing to kill people, because it was always so satisfying, because I always wanted to. I just, accepted that as my truth. But in that room, for once I wanted something else more than I wanted to feed the hunger. I just wanted out, and you gave me an opportunity to get out. I just had to do the one thing I'd never had to do before. *Control* my hunger."

He'd gotten somber with his explanation, the air thickening between them, so Rowan tried to tease to lighten the topic. She brushed her shoulder against his, her lips to his skin in a tender gesture before joking, "It didn't seem very difficult. You played with me the moment I walked into that room the first time. I felt like a mouse being batted around by a cat."

Lyall laughed a little, denial on his tone even as his lips curled up. Perhaps deciding it had been too long since he'd instilled a little terror in her bones, he leaned closer to sigh to her ear, "I was still so hungry that day, I had every intention of making you my last meal if I wanted it badly enough."

His lips stretched into a wicked grin when Rowan exhaled, fighting her hand away when she went to shove him, catching her around the nape of her neck and teasing his lips away from her ear and along her jaw until her sharpened edges softened. If she thought he was persuasive when there was glass between them, now she was like putty in his fingers.

He continued when Rowan settled again thanks to his wordless cohersion. "I refused myself the satisfaction of killing for once, though. And it made me feel... More powerful than ever. Every time you visited, I pushed myself a little further, at your expense. I didn't lie when I said I used you, for my own personal experiment, and I'm sorry. But I also learned so much about myself. How it felt to be that hungry, to really experience it for the first time, and control it. The more I was able to control it, the less consuming the hunger felt. I mean, I had a guard right there in my hands, completely ready to give in, but I managed to stop. And it felt amazing to stop. It felt like I was completely in control finally, not the virus.

"But then after escaping today, the hunger hit me so hard. It was all I could think about. I could take anyone, anywhere, anytime, and no one could stop me, and I was starving. I didn't want to give in again so soon, but it felt like it was taking over."

Rowan hummed with understanding, banishing his need to continue, and offer a reluctant surrender. "You have to eat sometime, Lyall, or else it will take over eventually. I can give yo—"

"No!" This time, his tone was a little more than just teasing after his outburst, immediately cutting Rowan's words short in her throat. His sharp eyes lowered right away though, softening in regret as he added. "I'm sorry. I just... I don't want to. Not yet. I didn't come back for your blood, Rowan. I just knew I needed something... A distraction. It was always so easy to control the hunger around you."

She let the silence sit for a moment to allow the tension to simmer off the air, before giving another little noise in her throat, trying to bring some playfulness back into the moment.

"I distract you?" she asked, while shifting a little closer so she could return his earlier teasing, bringing her lips to the tender skin under his ear, grinning when he leaned his head ever so slightly to encourage her to continue. She paused instead, to add another consideration. "I'm not entirely sure what it was about me you found so distracting."

The pleasant noise she could sense building in his throat turned into another warning growl. "I can think of a few things," he said, letting her taunt for a moment longer before being unable to keep himself from retaliating.

She fought, but Lyall had her pinned under him without much effort, Rowan covering her mouth to stifle a uncharacteristically feminine fit of giggles. Once on her back, he replaced her hand with his lips, tasting, tugging, teasing her laughter down, until it dissolved into begging, mercy noises against his teeth.

Finally giving her some air by roaming his torture down to her neck instead, Rowan offered some taunting of her own through her breathless lungs. "How's the appetite now?" If it wasn't for her pounding heart and hot, foggy head, she'd maybe be slightly more concerned about his grinning lips against her throat.

"I'm not sure," he whispered wickedly, and when she stifled a giggle he held her down more firmly and buried his face deeper into her neck and inhaling, forcing her to bite her tongue to keep the laughter at bay. Tickling her ear with another breath, he added, "I might need a little more distracting, you smell terribly tempting right now."

"That's just what you say to all your *snacks*." Rowan joked, squirming under his roaming hands, forcing him to pin hers down above her head to settle her wrestling. Continuing his torture, Lyall returned his lips to her skin, down from her neck to her collarbone, only making the rise and fall of her chest even more difficult to settle.

When he inhaled her scent again, it was after Rowan had been wooed away from her wild giggles and dragged down into hot desire again. He hummed with the draw of her scent, but instead of a teasing comment, he groaned against her skin this time.

"Seriously, why do you smell like that?"

The words did not completely filter through the fog in her head at first, lost in the wonderful fire of his lips on her flesh. It was his fingers tangled with hers, gripping tighter, nearing the point of uncomfortable, that finally had her giving a curious noise. "Smell like what?"

He released her hands and instead wrapped an arm around her waist firmly as she questioned him, arching her up off the bed to hold her against him, her heavy, dizzy head falling back and exposing her neck further. Rowan heard him give a pleasurable groan, like he was extremely satisfied with the sight he'd just presented himself, but the sound of it soured as a note of frustration slipped in when he inhaled again.

When he answered her, his voice dropped noticeably from tauntingly husky to breathy and strained. "Like... Like you'd taste as good as the sex felt."

Something about his tone and his hand gripping the fabric of her shirt at her spine sobered Rowan up a little, and she tried to work through her lingering afterglow to figure out what would be driving him so crazy. A plausible answer hit her immediately, as she reminded herself of all the other things he could smell on her, like the adrenaline during the escape, the antiviral when it dirtied her veins, pinpointing her blood type itself by the particular fragrance. It remained very possible that if he could smell all those things, he could probably also smell hormones, like the ones produced during certain *pleasurable* activities.

"It's... It's the endorphins. Lyall."

Rowan twisted in his grasp, putting her hands on his shoulders, up into his hair to try and drag his eyes up to hers. The concern that started seeping into her hit hard as she saw his eyes, wide and dark again as they had been when he arrived. There was no mistaking that this time the look was blood-lust.

Rowan swallowed, careful to try and keep the panic from consuming her. "Lyall, you have to let go of me, okay?" She moved her hands to push firmly on his chest, encouraging him away, but knowing her resistance would do nothing if he didn't cooperate.

He did as he was told, removing his arm from around her and pulling away a fraction, letting his eyes shut tightly, trying to shake off the hunger threatening him like he'd done several times before. Rowan thought to slip away from under him, but she also worried that moving would distract him, make it difficult to focus on pulling the hunger back, so she held as still as she could, willing her heart to rest for just a moment so he could get through his second of weakness. He'd get it under control again. He always did.

He exhaled when he opened his eyes again, like a sigh of relief, and Rowan allowed herself to breathe again too, only to have the air stolen from her lungs when his dark gaze locked on her, Lyall completely gone from his eyes and replaced with something ravenous.

Rowan's instincts reacted immediately, rushing to get herself away, but he was so much faster, pinning her down with little effort. She didn't want to scream, but the fear boiled up inside and came out in a panicked yell, which was silenced with a firm hand over her mouth before it even broke the air. Lyall put a finger to his lips to shush her, the wicked blood-lust reading clearly in his wide, glossy stare. Even though she knew no one would hear, she screamed against his hand, tears filling her eyes.

She twisted her body and threw out her arms, doing whatever she could to keep that dark gaze from locking onto her exposed neck. She knew that, much like the predator he often resembled, the moment he found a target it would be his.

He snarled at her struggle, causing her to sob soundlessly, but she continued to shove and hit him until he grabbed one of her wrists with his free hand to cease her fight. Unfortunately, in her panic to save her throat, Rowan forgot that it wasn't the only part of her body currently exposed and filled with acceptable veins. Now, with a vice grip around her wrist, there was nothing she could do but surrender as he found his target: the smooth, white plane of her forearm.

CHAPTER TWENTY-FIVE

IT WAS FAR MORE painful than she ever imagined.

Rowan watched for as long as she could, eyes wide with horror as he gripped her limb firmly with his thin fingers and brought his teeth to her skin. When he bit down, she couldn't help shutting the sight away though; it hurt too much, and he hadn't even broken the skin yet. When she screamed in agony, it was muffled by his palm, the tears drowning the image and the sobs wracking her chest as her flesh finally gave into the pressure and tore apart under his teeth.

There was too much blood for him to drink it all, and through her blurred vision, she saw the red escape from under his lips and down her arm. Her shirt and hair began to soak it up, the rest creating a stain on the comforter beneath them. The smell made her feel ill: thick and metallic, heavy in the air, pushing down on her lungs.

He made fast work of her; she felt a particular weakness already overcoming her limbs. She tried to struggle again, but he had her held down firmly, her attempts just a waste of energy that made her heart beat faster, forcing the blood more quickly from her wound.

Maybe he would stop once he got his fill. Maybe he just needed a little, to feed the hunger that consumed him, and he would stop as soon as it was under control again. Rowan tried to comfort herself with the thought, but a part of her knew this was not just an innocent snack, and she couldn't keep her chest from convulsing with uncontrollable sobs. He never stopped.

He'd never let anyone live.

Rowan's screams silenced, no longer capable of drawing in enough breath passed her crying to yell. He removed the hand around her mouth as a result, using it instead to get a better hold on the limb he drained her from. With her lips free, she tried to speak to him, even though the darkness of his eyes was so deep she didn't see Lyall anywhere in them.

"Lyall, you have to stop."

With her free hand, she reached up and grabbed his wrist, gripping, tugging, until her arm grew too weak and her fingers fell away. "Please." She could feel the numbness setting in. He was taking too much. "You'll kill me," she whispered, staring into his dark gaze, begging through her tears.

He wasn't there, though. He was so far away. Lyall didn't hear her, and the hunger didn't care, closing his eyes to savor the taste as he pulled more blood from her veins.

Rowan began to shake, feeling a chill setting into her bones. She had no fight left, no chance left, no ideas left. She was going to die here. She looked away from Lyall, hoping she could forget, at least for a moment, how she was being killed. Soon enough, she would have lost so much blood that the wound wouldn't even hurt anymore. Hopefully, she would just get too weak and tired to hold her eyes open, and she'd just fall asleep as he took the last bits of her.

She let a soft breath out, ready to go, and was surprised by a thought she had in her last moments. She hoped he wouldn't feel too bad about what he had done to her when he finally regained control. She would hate to become a regret to him.

Rowan didn't notice at first when Lyall removed his lips from the wound on her arm. It was only when he let go of her, putting one of his bloody hands up to his own throat, that she regained some consciousness and turned back to watch him.

He gripped at his neck like he was choking, until he fell forward onto his hands and coughed up some of the blood he drank. He pulled a few sharp breaths through his gritted teeth, stained red, then collapsed onto his side, holding his stomach and clawing at his throat and chest.

Rowan dragged her mangled limb across the bed and pulled a case off one of her pillows, using the fabric as a makeshift bandage and wrapping it tightly around her arm. The blood soaked through almost immediately despite her best efforts. She sat upright, leaning over to press her injured arm between her thighs and her stomach to make some pressure. It was all she could think to do to help slow the bleeding for now.

On the other side of the bed, Lyall tossed and writhed, overwhelmed with pain. He gripped at the comforter, pulling and scratching at his skin and hair. Eventually, another coughing fit hit him, and more of her blood came up. This seemed to settle the pain a little, long enough for him to get out a few words.

"What's happening? It feels like my throat is raw."

It sounded like it too. Every breath he took was ragged and broken, like his throat was seared with holes that his lungs were trying to get air passed.

Rowan was as baffled as he was, staring at him helplessly as he fended off the pain, fighting as hard as she could to not let her own aching arm get the best of her. She closed her eyes, trying to understand what was happening.

"The antiviral."

Lyall gazed up at her. The skin around his eyes looked dark and bruised, purple veins stretching. The whites were blood-shot, but luckily, his pupils contracted back to normal.

"It was likely still in my blood. You drank so much, you must have gotten the dose you needed."

With her words, Lyall's gaze instantly fell, his forehead furrowing against the pain. He curled up into himself, suddenly looking so small and helpless. It took everything for Rowan to keep her distance, because he had just almost killed her, and she would have left the room entirely if she knew she wouldn't pass out from blood loss. Yet, she still wanted to comfort him through the pain he was enduring.

After a little while, the coughing fits seemed to settle, and he was able to breathe easier. With his shoulders rising and falling slowly, his gaze staring off, unfocused and glossy, he asked on a whisper.

"Is it gone now? The virus?"

Rowan exhaled heavy, trying to shake her head but only getting dizzy when she did. "It won't work that quickly. In a few hours, maybe."

He closed his eyes and sighed. All this time, he fought so hard to keep the virus, and it was his own actions that lead to him losing it. The disappointment read on the creased line between his brows, but he pushed it away to glance towards Rowan, locking onto the wound she cradled. He let his head fall again, groaning with regret before twisting around to stand.

"What are you doing?" Rowan asked after watching him limp towards her dresser, opening drawers and sorting through her clothes.

"We need to get you some help, I went deep... It won't stop bleeding on it's own," he replied, pulling out a pair of jeans and circling the bed to approach behind her. He helped her sit on the edge, getting down on his knees to guide her feet into the legs of the jeans.

"What about you?" she frowned at the dark, bruise-like coloring around his eyes and her blood all over his mouth. She reached out with her good arm, touching the discolored skin carefully.

He pulled himself away from her touch, wiping at the blood on the sleeve of his shirt, then looked up at her with a soft gaze. "I'll be fine. At least, for the next few hours, according to you." He stood, helping her to her feet. When she followed, her head swam and her vision went black. He held her up until the blood came back to her head, waiting anxiously until her unfocused sight came back. "You, on the other hand, need a hospital visit because of me."

"No." Rowan shook her head, blinking away the tunnel vision caused by her lightheadedness. "No hospital. They'll know exactly who you are. And besides, we'll never get out of here without the men outside seeing."

Lyall objected, "I can take care of them."

"They'll know you're in the city. They'll have men all over looking for you."

"So I'll kill every one of them while I still can." There was an angry note there, bitter with the impending outcome of the antiviral now in his system.

"No. I know where to go." She used Lyall's arm as a brace, leaning over to grab her phone from the bedside table. "First though, we have to go down and wake Cameron."

"Damn. How long was I out?" Cameron blinked away his sleep after she gently stirred him, gathering from the darkness around them that night had creeped up during his snooze.

Rowan offered a guess. "About an hour."

He rubbed his eyes, and once he did so, he settled to look at her, immediately frowning. "What's wrong?" He always knew. He always saw right through her.

It was a blessing and a curse.

She looked down, nervous and ashamed. What would he think of her if she told him how easily she let Lyall back in, after she confided in him only a few hours before about how much it had hurt when he left? On top of that, how would he react to the fact that the boy who had already hurt her once by leaving, had also just almost killed her?

She gnawed at her lip, scared to say it, but knowing she had to. Time was not on her side, the wet, bloody cloth around her arm a reminder. Swallowing her nerves, Rowan sat up a little to show more of the limb she was hiding.

"Don't panic, but... I need your help, Cam."

His eyes widened, sitting up to take her arm into his hands. He swore repeatedly under his breath, going to unwrap the fabric on her arm, but then deciding against it when he saw the amount of blood. "Shit. Rowan, *shit*. What happened? We have to get you to a hospital."

She moved to grab his arm, ready to protest, but Cameron stood too quickly for her to catch him, and once on his feet, he caught gaze with the cause of her injury. Lyall had his back leaned against the entryway to the living room, and when Cameron stopped in his tracks at the sight of him, the blue-eyed monster tilted his head.

"You," Cameron said, a bitter note on his tongue.

He was looking at exactly what happened, seeing the blood on

Lyall's face and connecting the dots. Thanks to her, Cameron knew exactly who Lyall was upon first sight, and his opinion was already colored red, no need for the extra blood.

"Me," Lyall replied, a simple confirmation. He didn't say it in pride or cockiness or even sarcasm, though. Lyall knew what he had done, and he actually sounded ashamed.

Cameron gave one short nod, looking back at Rowan briefly before striding out of the room. Confused and unsure where he disappeared to, she used the coffee table to pick herself up, intending to follow. He wasn't gone for long, though. He reentered the room only seconds later, his security guard issued pistol in hand. Before she could react, the hammer was pulled back, the barrel pressing Lyall's jaw.

"Pleasure to meet you." Lyall's sarcasm was thick.

"Cam, please. Is that necessary?"

Rowan tried to reason with him, but she could tell he wasn't even listening. Unfortunately, when it came to what Cameron thought was best, he didn't often listen to reason, pigheaded and ready to defend her even against a greatly unmatched opponent.

Lyall was also stubborn, but unlike Cameron, he was stubborn simply for the sake. He smirked, pushing his face even harder against the gun, staring Cameron in the eye the whole time.

"Shoot me, then. If you think you can."

She could tell it wasn't a real threat; it was one of Lyall's games. A dare, to play with Cameron and see how far he could push him. Cameron was not accustomed to being toyed with, though. He didn't take kindly to it.

He grabbed Lyall by the collar of his shirt and pushed him hard against the wall, repositioning the gun on his cheek. His hands trembled, and Lyall's eyes, even though they were tired and bloodshot and rimmed with purple, danced with laughter.

Rowan moved over to them as quickly as she could, putting

her hand on Cameron's arm. He was reluctant, but eventually gave in and looked at her.

"We'll need his help," she said, showing him her seriousness with a pointed, no words needed look, knowing he would understand because he always did.

He scowled, then turned back to Lyall, and shoved him hard against the wall one more time for good measure before removing his gun from the monster's face. Rowan offered an appreciative smile, turning back to sit down on the couch with Cameron following.

"You would have been doing him a favor shooting him anyway," she added sourly after a moment, glancing over her shoulder to confirm her suspicions. Lyall smirked as he rubbed at his cheek, caught red-handed in his little game.

"Why, got cancer or something, alien boy?" Cameron asked, even though he seemed uninterested in the answer.

Lyall's lip curled. "Worse. In a few hours, I'll be a completely healthy human being."

"The horror," Cameron said dull, and in response Rowan caught Lyall's grin grow a fraction wider. "Why do we need this freak again?"

"Because, if I can get a hold of the person I need to talk to, we're going to need someone to take care of our friends outside," she explained, pulling out her phone and searching through her contact list.

"Shouldn't we be getting you to a hospital? Who are you calling?"

She selected the number and held the phone up to her ear. "Phelps."

CHAPTER TWENTY-SIX

LYALL TOOK care of the men outside, knocking them both out before either realized what happened, and Phelps had the three of them picked up in an unmarked car. The car took them to his large, country style home on the other side of town; it was a long, quiet drive.

Rowan remembered him telling her once that he liked living this far out, because it was less likely you would be bothered. He always seemed to try so hard to distance himself from his work, and it was a trait she once frowned upon, seeing it as the reason why Phelps was not as successful as other doctors his age. Now though, she envied his ability to step away from the research, for his own good. If she had just taken his advice to leave when he had, perhaps everything would be different.

One thing was certain, she at least wouldn't be coming to him with her best friend and the monster who had just almost killed her, looking for medical help and refuge from the government men who would surely be looking for them in a short while.

The car drove around the backside of the house, where Phelps appeared from a cellar door, beckoning them in quickly. "In with you all, we don't want prying eyes."

The older man held the door open as Cameron helped Rowan out of the car and into the basement, Lyall on their flanks with his eyes on the ground. Rowan watched over her shoulder as Phelps eyed the boy he had only ever seen locked up and angry, a nervousness taking over his expression as Lyall passed, but he said nothing.

Once inside, Phelps sealed the doors and flicked on the lights, revealing a surprisingly roomy, personal laboratory. Rowan chuckled as she looked around the room, then said to him, "I thought you never took work home with you."

Phelp laughed also, moving forward to place a hand on her shoulder. "Sometimes we simply can't help ourselves. It's a good thing too, since it looks like this place will come in handy at the moment." He gestured to her arm, then walked passed her to gather a medical kit from a shelf in the corner of the room. "Come, sit, and we'll fix that up."

She crossed the room and took a seat in a chair Phelps collected. He picked out the last few things and placed them on the table next to her, then moved a rolling stool over to sit next to her with his supplies.

"I can't express how much this means to me, sir. Everything has been so messed up, and I didn't know who to turn to anymore." She offered her thanks as she watched Phelps put a pair of gloves on to prepare for stitching up her wound.

"Don't let it worry you. I know I made it seem like I wanted to keep out of this, and I did, but when I left that day, leaving you alone there with Margot and the rest of her brainwashed group of doctors, I knew I made a terrible mistake. I saw what was coming, and I didn't properly warn you, and that was selfish of me. This situation you're in is as much my fault as anyone's."

She stared for a moment, shocked briefly by his admission. "So you know what's happening? With the virus, and Miller?"

He frowned. "I have a hunch, and with my years knowing Miller, my hunches about her tend to be right. That's besides the point right now, though. We can talk about all that later, after we fix you up."

Rowan nodded, agreeing that she could use a moment to calm down and sort out her thoughts also, before they got into any talk about Miller. She held out her wrapped up, bloodied arm, and Phelps went to work, delicately peeling the matted fabric away.

When the wound was revealed, it was more grisly than she remembered it being. Cameron, who had been watching from a few steps away, sucked in a breath and came over to her side. Even though her skin was stained with red, it at least looked like the wound stopped bleeding for the most part.

"Your doing, I presume?" Phelps didn't look at Lyall, but his words were pointed in his direction.

Rowan looked up, spotting Lyall observing from back near the door, as if he felt it was inappropriate for him to be any closer. He responded to Phelps question by lowering his eyes back to the floor.

"It was an accident," she said, feeling like she needed to defend Lyall if he wasn't going to defend himself.

She knew he hadn't meant to hurt her. He had been hungry, overwhelmed, and her blood smelled of something he'd never smelled before. Besides, he suffered enough with the antiviral swirling in his veins.

Phelps raised an eyebrow at her quickness to defend, but held back whatever comment crossed his mind. Instead, he said, "Well, it's an accident that's going to leave a mark, but besides a scar, we should be able to stitch this up and it will heal just fine."

Cameron observed as Phelps sewed her wound together,

commenting about how gross it was and asking multiple times if she felt the needle. His personality distracted her, which Rowan appreciated since her thoughts were bleeding into concerns.

She didn't know what would happen to the project, if Miller intended to research the virus further and do human testing, or if it would be scrapped now that Lyall escaped. Or what would happen to Lyall now, since the government men and Miller were sure to catch wind soon that he was still in the city, losing his superhuman qualities quickly. She didn't even know what was going to happen to her.

It was a while later, when she was stitched up and attached to a saline drip to help her hydration, that she finally tried speaking more to Phelps about what was going on. "You knew Miller was going to use the virus? You knew she never intended to simply cure it?"

He sighed, taking his place on the stool again after putting away all his supplies. "It's not really Miller's speciality to cure things. That was more my deal. She was interested in virus biology and mutation. She liked to see what she could make viruses do by changing them. Her research was integral to our eventual development of the influenza virus cure, sure, but her motivation was never that focused on the actual antiviral. I didn't feel like it was unfair to assume she'd hold the same curiosities in this situation and would take advantage of it to try and come across something... 'Groundbreaking'."

Rowan scoffed. "If by 'groundbreaking' you mean potentially catastrophic..."

Phelps chuckled, though it was colored with a certain irony. "Miller has never been one to consider the consequences of her research. She's far more caught up on the actual discovery and what it will do for her than what the discovery might mean overall. On the bright side, this means as far as you and your escapee are concerned, she's probably not looking to have either of you back in her business."

She had already come to the conclusion that she was a minor problem on Miller's radar, and the men watching outside her house were to keep her and Cameron out of the woman's hair more than anything else.

"The downside?"

Phelps made a face. "If you want to do something about it, which I get the feeling that you probably do because you're as stubborn as Miller is, it means she's not going to let you interfere without a fight."

Rowan gnawed at her lip, considering her options briefly, but then shook her head to rid them from her mind. "No. I don't want to interfere with her research. I want nothing to do with it anymore, to be honest. There's really only one thing I want, one thing you might be able to help me with."

Phelps tilted his head, intrigued, and Rowan reconsidered her words carefully before finally deciding on them. "When Lyall bit me, he got a dose of Miller's antiviral, and he's losing the virus as we speak. It's not fair. Everything he's done has been simply defending himself, he doesn't deserve to have this part of him taken away, especially like this. I don't want to be the reason he had a part of his identity stolen from him. So, I want to get the virus sample back from the labs, then we can give it to Lyall."

Her proposition took everyone by surprise. The room was silent for a long moment as the three men stared at her.

Cameron spoke first. "He's finally going to be fixed, and you're going to break him again?"

Rowan glared. "He was never broken."

"God. You know what I mean, Row."

"I don't think I do, please elabor—"

"No." Lyall's objection was quiet, but firm, breaking through their bickering and silencing the room.

Rowan's reaction tumbled around in her mouth for a while before she got it out properly. "What do you mean, no?"

She didn't understand. It was everything he wanted, everything he had been fighting for all this time, and now that she wanted to give it back, he didn't want it? How could he say no, when he looked like he was dying?

He leaned back against the wall and moved his eyes away from her, giving no explanation. The silence left in the room was thick and heavy.

Phelps tried his best to be subtle as he broke it with a question. "You said he has an antiviral in his system, so Miller developed one?"

She tried not to let her frustration out on her tone, but it was hard to stifle it. "Yes. She gave me the injection in case Lyall..." She couldn't bring herself to finish that thought.

Phelps made a little sound to himself, understanding, then got up and rummaged around his supplies, coming back with a lancet and a blood slide. He walked past Rowan and moved over to Lyall. "You wouldn't mind me taking a small blood sample, just to take a look and see how Miller's treatment is working, would you?"

Lyall blinked, as if he was surprised anyone other than Rowan was talking to him. He glanced at Rowan before answering, as if questioning her about Phelps' intention, but she shrugged in reply, knowing as little as him.

"Okay," Lyall agreed, holding out his finger for Phelps to use the lancet on.

When he had Lyall's blood sample, he moved to Rowan. "How about you also? You said he got the antiviral from drinking your blood? I'd like to see if there is any left in there and what it's doing."

She eyed him, confused. "I really don't know what you're getting at with this." She voiced her concern with a skeptical gaze.

Phelps smiled. "I have another hunch, but I've always hated jumping to conclusions before having evidence. Would you?" He held out his hand, waiting for Rowan's agreement.

Curious as always, she gave him her finger.

PHELPS WORKED IMMEDIATELY, analyzing both their blood samples under a high-tech microscope at the other end of the room. Without the science talk, the silence thickened and weighed them down again. Rowan was glaring at Lyall, and Lyall was glaring back, and soon enough, Cameron dismissed himself to escape the stifling discomfort between them.

With the wall next to Rowan now vacant, Lyall gave a reluctant sigh, moving from the entrance to take the spot by her.

Neither of them were willing to start the argument, but Lyall offered words after the tension became painful. "I don't want the virus back. I told you I didn't want to go on just killing people anymore, and we proved tonight that I'm never going to be completely able to control it. It will eventually take over me. I can't have the virus and not kill." He leaned his head back against the wall and sighed again, closing his eyes. After a second without a response from her, he added bitterly, "Besides. This is how you wanted me from the start, right?"

Rowan practically growled. "This isn't about what I want."

"Maybe," he agreed, but shook his head after. "But maybe I'm tired of making decisions based solely on what I want. I'm tired of being... So out of control."

He was tired, that much was obvious. It wasn't just the purple around his eyes, but simply the look in them itself, like in the containment room when he accepted that he would die in there. He appeared defeated, broken. Lost.

Rowan shut her eyes briefly to gather her thoughts, taking in a calming breath. "This isn't about being selfish. I want to help you get it back because I don't think it's fair to take it away from you. It's part of who you are. And I also definitely don't want you to be without it simply because you think it's what I'd prefer. You can't put that kind of responsibility on me."

Lyall laughed a little. "But if I say it's for you, then I can blame you later when I'm bitter about it." He grinned mischievously when she scowled at him.

"Exactly." She wasn't able to hold her negativity for long, smirking back at him.

They quieted again, letting the heavy thoughts sit between them, untouched since neither of them had a good solution.

Lyall spoke again, offering another consideration. "I guess I just feel like it's time for me to learn who I am, without the hunger. After everything, maybe I owe that to not just myself, but you too."

She scoffed under her breath, but a smile played at her lips. "The way you're talking, it's almost like you're planning to stick around." She said it like it was absurd, but then she glanced up to see if he thought the same.

He caught her gaze, then looked away, a timidness coming over him, like he was afraid to admit it. "Maybe I was thinking about it. I haven't been human for a long time, so I'd need someone to help me get back into the swing of things."

Rowan couldn't help her lips, twitching up as she lowered her gaze to hide her softened expression.

From across the room, Phelps interrupted by clearing his throat, then sighing. "It's as I thought," he said, stepping away from the microscope and removing the gloves from his hands.

Rowan frowned. "What is?"

"The substance Miller put into your blood, that Lyall has in his system, is not an antiviral. Miller and her doctors would never be able to come up with a cure so quickly without me."

As his words settled in, Rowan found herself perking up a little. "But that means that Lyall still has the virus, right?" Her brief excitement faded with Phelps expression.

"He still has the virus, but it's not the same as it use to be, and it won't matter for long, anyway." Phelps paused, twistings his hands together uncomfortably. He was obviously reluctant to continue, but did so despite himself. "Whatever Miller created, it's reacting with the subject's virus to attack the other cells of his body. Miller likely intended to dispose of the subject with this substance."

The room was silent for a painful moment. Lyall spoke first. "Dispose of me?"

"You're not becoming human. You're dying. The substance you took from Rowan's blood is killing you. Rather quickly, actually."

Rowan shook her head, laughing in disbelief. "No. Absolutely not. Miller told me it was an antivirus. They were working on it for weeks."

"They were probably working on other things, developing this substance on the side to deal with the problem at hand. Miller would have considered having the subject around as a liability, and not worth trying to actually cure him. Miller... She's a manipulative woman, Rowan. She always has been. It's part of why she's where she is today.

"She's also not stupid. She saw your dedication as something valuable, even more so now that it opposed her. She probably considered you important to have around, therefore tried to offer you what you wanted as a means of restoring peace between you and keeping you around in case she needed you."

Phelps explanation was believable, reasonable even, but Rowan didn't want to accept it.

Frustration swelled up in her chest painfully, and she shut her eyes to fight the tears that threatened to erupt, exhaling smoothly to try and calm herself. She was able to get her next words out without her voice shaking. "What do we do then? Is there something you can do?"

Phelps inhaled deep and paced a few steps to the side, a thought festering in his head. "I'm not sure... But my best guess would be, if we had some of the original virus, we might be able to infuse it back into his system, and the new virus could overpower the damaging substance and fix the old cells. He'd, hopefully, be just like before. Unfortunately, you'd need probably an equal dose of the virus."

"For example, a test tube of infected blood?" Rowan offered, knowing immediately what Phelps suggested.

He nodded reluctantly. "It would be the only way, yes."

She stood, removing the IV from her arm with determination. "Then it's settled. We'll go to the labs, get the virus sample, and bring it back here so we can save Lyall."

"Rowan, please." Lyall objected with a strained voice, reaching out for her arm to try and get her to sit down again, but she avoided his grip.

"What? Doing this is the only way to save you. You're going to die otherwise."

He sighed, putting his head in his hands. "I almost killed you today. All because of this virus. And you want to get it back for me? I'm the issue in this situation, maybe it's about time I just disappear. Like I said I would. Maybe it's just easier that way."

"Oh, please." It was Cameron that spoke this time, a scoff from off to the side.

Lyall lifted his head, sending a sharp gaze in Cameron's direction. "Excuse me?"

Rolling his eyes, he elaborated. "You escaped from the ECBS earlier today to keep that virus intact. Rowan put everything on the line to *help,* for fuck sakes. And an hour of thinking you'd lost it has turned you soft? I didn't realize being human or finding out you're dying would turn you into such a coward. Or were you just always one?" Cameron laid on the attitude thick, purposely looking for a reaction from Lyall.

Rowan reacted first instead, snorting when she couldn't stifle her laugh any longer. Lyall's shocked expression was simply too rich.

Hearing her, Lyall moved his completely bewildered expression from Cameron to her, glaring at the fact she enjoyed his verbal bashing. Finally, he scoffed, leaning back and shaking his head.

"Fine. But no promises I won't kill you both once I get it back from how irritating you're being."

Cameron smirked. "I'll have to remember to insult you more. It gets results."

Rowan interrupted the bickering by clapping her hands together. "So *now* it's settled. To the labs to steal the virus back?"

Cameron nodded once curtly. "Definitely. And hey, while we're there, maybe we can mess up Miller's research for her army of superhumans she's planning too." He raised his hand to Rowan for a high five.

She smacked his palm with her good hand, grinning. "Viva la revolution!"

Phelps smiled also, but nervous tainted it, and as Lyall and Cameron got ready to go, he pulled Rowan to the side for a brief moment. "There was something else I needed to tell you. Something about your blood sample."

Her curiosity piqued, she stepped closer to him.

He paused for a long moment, then patted her shoulder and shook his head. "You know what, I'm going to take a second look. I'll tell you about it when you three get back from the labs."

She nodded, smiling, and turned back to the boys, not seeing when Phelps' expression fell.

CHAPTER TWENTY-SEVEN

THE ECBS WAS dark and quiet as they pulled up to the empty parking lot in the car Phelps loaned them. In fact, there was something unsettling about the stillness of it all; even when Rowan would visit Cameron in the middle of the night, the building never looked so abandoned.

"Something's wrong here," she said, mostly to herself, but Cameron chimed in with an agreeing sound.

"There's not even a guard tonight. Do you hear anyone, alien boy?"

They silenced for a moment to let Lyall listen, and he shook his head after. "I can't be sure, though. I think my hearing is going. Everything feels off, to be honest."

"Probably because you're poisoned and slowly dying," Cameron pointed out.

"Helpful. Thanks, Cam." Rowan scolded him on Lyall's behalf.

"Are you sure you're ok, Rowan? I feel the need to remind you again that I almost killed you about an hour ago. Aren't you tired?" Lyall's concern was obvious as they all stepped out of the car together. He came over to take her wrist and inspected the stitching, but she pulled her limb away from him.

"I'm fine. I feel good, actually. Maybe it's just the adrenaline, but what we're planning feels right. Miller shouldn't get away with this."

"She looks better than you do, Casper. That bite even seems like it's already healing."

Cameron's observation was innocent enough, but it made Rowan take a second glance at the wound on her forearm. It did appear to be healing, which was strange, but the thought left her mind as quickly as it entered, following Cameron as he approached the ECBS.

"You don't think it's some kind of trap?" He offered, although he seemed unfazed by the chance of it being so. As he unlocked the entry doors, he added with a cheeky grin, "A little action would be fun."

"Trigger happy, sarcastic, and a thrill junkie. And I thought I wasn't going to like you," Lyall said, following behind Rowan as they walked passed, into the ECBS.

"I'm going to take that as a compliment." Cameron shot back.

Rowan couldn't help her smile growing, the two boys' playful bickering bringing her a moment of joy. It wasn't often Cameron approved of people, and she got the feeling that the sentiment went the same for Lyall. It was an interesting experience bearing witness to their banter.

The fun was cut short as they approached the elevators, and she raised a finger to her mouth to quiet them. As she listened, her expression became confused. "The elevators are running."

"Do you think someone's downstairs?" Cameron asked.

She shook her head. "I don't know. Possibly..."

"So we should be careful, then," Lyall said, stepping towards the elevator and calling it with the button.

Cameron glanced at Rowan again as they listened. "It's coming up from downstairs."

"Someone's here." She nodded, catching his conclusion as the two of them followed Lyall into the empty elevator.

Rowan pulled out Phelps' key card again, along with a set of codes to reset the security system that Phelps had given her before they'd left, since he suspected she would have trouble getting back into the labs with the card's previous access if Miller wanted to keep her out for any reason. His suspicions had been spot on, the elevator requiring his reset codes before it would let Rowan go anywhere.

With the restrictions reset, she selected the underground floor, and the door closed on them, the elevator descending. Preparing for whoever was in the labs, Cameron held his gun up and aimed it for the elevator door. His paranoia rubbed off on Lyall as well; when the elevator chimed for its destination, he grabbed Rowan's arm, taking a step in front of her in a protective gesture.

She peered around him, out the elevator doors and down the stark, empty hallway. No one was there. Or at least, no one they could see.

Then she heard something. Beyond the sound of Cameron and Lyall's breathing, passed her own heart racing in her chest, there was something else. Tapping, like someone drumming their nails on a table as they sat and waited. It sounded like it was far away, but also like someone had taken the sound and thrown it at her. As she heard it, her mind focused in, and the noise became louder and louder until it felt like it was right there in the elevator with them.

Cameron stepped to move out into the hall, but Rowan stopped him. "Do you hear that?"

Both boys turned to her. Lyall was surprised, and with his surprise came Rowan's confusion.

"You don't hear that?" she asked, and Lyall became more bewildered, shaking his head. Had he lost so much of his abilities now, that he couldn't even hear what her human ears were hearing? He did look just about dead, after all.

She huffed and stepped forward to take Cameron's gun from his hands and lead the movement. She walked as lightly and carefully as she could, and the boys followed her example, making it easier for her to hear the tapping she led them towards.

Finally, she reached the door to the research labs, knowing that the sound was coming from inside. She used the keypad, and just like the elevator, it accepted her input without a key card. The door opened, and she entered cautiously, the two boys flanking her sides.

The room was dark at first, but her eyes adjusted quickly, perhaps more quickly than usual. It was like someone had bumped up the contrast, the darks were darker, but the lights were more defined. She still couldn't see well, but in the blackness of the room, she could make out the shape of a person: a tall, lean frame, and the gleam of rimless lenses.

"Dr. Miller."

"Good evening, Miss Platts. You're out late."

Lyall had never been one for conversation. In a characteristic reaction, he disappeared from Rowan's side, intent on eliminating the threat before the threat got an upper hand.

"Stop," Rowan said just as Lyall reached the woman, predicting exactly what he would do. He pulled back and looked at her, his hands on either side of Miller's head, ready to snap her neck.

"I don't need your permission," he growled after a moment, turning back to the woman between his palms. Miller stared with terror, but otherwise did not move in Lyall's grip, perhaps suspecting that attempting an escape would end worse for her.

"You said you didn't want to kill anymore." Rowan reminded

him, and watched as Lyall struggled for a moment before admitting defeat, moving his hands instead to Miller's collar and dragging her over.

"What are you doing here, doctor?" Rowan kept the gun up in front of her, but lowered it just a little to speak over the barrel.

Lyall shoved Miller towards her, and when the woman found her balance again on her heels, she cleared her voice, smoothed her messed hair. "I could ask you the same question. The others were afraid to continue the research, at least for now. I decided to stay." She glared momentarily, but when she glanced at Lyall, the sour expression stretched to a smirk. "From the looks of it, you got the dose of my *antivirus* after all."

"If you want to give your explanation, here's your chance. Why did you lie to me? If you planned on killing Lyall all along, why bother stringing me into it, making me think I was helping him." Rowan spat venom, feeling powerful with a gun in her hands and two males there to back her up. It didn't hurt that one of those males was also somewhat superhuman.

Miller sighed heavily, rubbing her temple under her glasses. "The subject was a liability, and you knew that. Even if we did cure him, he wasn't going to let us treat him as a human, either, and then he would have died anyway. It's easier and sounds nicer on the reports when someone infected dies, rather than when someone who was cured dies."

She seemed like she realized it sounded bad, but also didn't care much about it. When she continued, she forced herself to take on a more sympathetic tone. "And the reason I lied to you, was because I wanted you on my side. I admired your determination, I still do, although I wish it was focused on the same goals. I see so much of myself in you, Rowan. You could go so far, we could... together."

Rowan narrowed her eyes, anger boiling in her chest. "I

admired you as well, doctor. I did everything I could to please you. I risked my life for this project. But when I asked you to help me do something I felt was right, was just, you didn't trust my judgement. Even though it was my judgement that forged this project to begin with."

Miller blinked, discomfort filtering into her gaze as she forced a smile. "Perhaps you're right. Imagine if we could go back and change our decisions."

"Yes. Imagine." A suspicion twisted in her gut, but Rowan ignored it, lowering her gun a little more. Miller's words had a point. If she had the foresight to know what would happen by making the decision to join this project, would she have reconsidered? She'd already asked herself that so many times, coming up with a fairly easy answer. Now though, she couldn't imagine not having met Lyall, so much so that she was going to extreme lengths to save him. Would she give that up for the chance to avoid this altogether?

"Is there something I can do, to make this all up to you?" Miller asked after the silence dwelled for a moment too long.

Rowan raised the gun again, her suspicion making her feel unsettled again, but paused to consider her offer. "We're here for the virus. Phelps said it might be the best chance we have at saving Lyall from whatever you gave him."

Miller offered another stiff look, the expression in her eyes changing briefly. "You went to Phelps?"

"He helped me with my wound and was the one who told us about your antivirus not really being an antivirus." Rowan grinned a little as she considered an additional comment. "He said you've never been very good with cures."

Miller's fake smile soured a little, her eyes burning in annoyance. "He's also always been more compassionate. So much so it's been a detriment to himself." The jab was unnecessary, but it seemed to smooth Miller's upset, allowing her to continue. "You said you needed the virus? Phelps was correct, giving the subject a new dose of the original virus cells should counteract the effect of my substance. It might take a little while, but within a few days, the cell damage should be regenerated."

Rowan nodded. "If you let us have the virus, we'll leave, and you'll never see any of us again. I don't care what you do with the project after this. I won't interfere any longer. We'll be even."

Miller smiled briefly. "Very well, but it's hard to consider this a proper terms of agreement when you have a gun aimed at me."

Considering her point, Rowan glanced at Lyall and Cameron. Neither of them gave her anything to work on, so she looked back to Miller. What harm was there, just putting the gun down? Besides, if she tried anything, Lyall could always intervene.

Rowan lowered the weapon, putting the safety back on and handing it to Cameron, who returned it to the back of his jeans.

Satisfied, Miller's smile grew. "Let me put the sample in a syringe for you." She walked away to the other side of the room to retrieve it from the refrigerated storage.

Rowan had a moment of relief, glad that the whole thing was going so smoothly and that Miller seemed to have a phantom of a conscious erupting. She grinned when she caught Lyall's gaze.

"It feels like I'm long overdue to meet death, and I'm cheating it again," Lyall explained, forcing a sly look that was less than genuine.

Cameron was there immediately to offer his particular brand of reassurance. "Oh, get over yourself. No one wants to die. Everyone would do whatever it takes to stay alive another day, even turn themselves back into a monster."

Rowan backed up his statement. "It doesn't have to be permanent. With Phelps' help, we can find a real cure this time, if that's what you still want. It's just for now."

Lyall's gaze softened a little, considering her words, then nodding. "But just for now."

Caught up in the brief moment of positivity, the bright, cold blue of his eyes kept Rowan's gaze preoccupied for longer than she had meant to be, and her distraction was broken by Cameron pulling his gun out again.

It was too late, though. Even with Lyall reacting immediately, pinning Miller to a wall, the deed had already been done. An empty syringe hit the floor and Miller's arm bled where she had inserted it, laughing as Lyall choked her.

"Shut up! I'll crush your skull with my bare hands." Lyall's threats did nothing, and the reason for Miller's sudden confidence showed itself before Lyall was able to follow through.

Miller grabbed Lyall around the wrist and twisted, forcing Lyall to the ground to keep his arm from breaking. He yelled in pain, then groaned as she kicked him further to the floor.

"I see now why you wanted to keep this virus all to yourself." Miller paused to spread her fingers of the arm she injected the virus into, the veins in her wrist going dark as the new blood spread. "Why would anyone want to share *this*?"

Cameron fired his gun at Miller, pulling the trigger until it clicked empty, but Miller was already as fast as Lyall, faster maybe, and dodging bullets was child's play. Cameron's assault garnered nothing more than a laugh from her as she approached from the other side of the room.

"You know, I really wanted to use the virus to benefit people when I found out what it could do, but now that I have it, I'm wondering myself why I should let others in on the fun. No one is really worth this power, anyway. If everyone has it, then it's not very special anymore, is it?"

Rowan stood and stared, defenseless and very human compared to the approaching creature. Cameron tried to step in front of her, but he was shoved aside, hitting the other wall hard. Rowan cried out his name, turning to see if he was okay, but Miller grabbed her by the throat, forcing their gaze to meet.

"I really wanted to share this moment with you. We could have done so much together." Over the doctor's shoulder, Rowan saw Lyall trying to pick himself up off the floor. Giving a cruel grin in response to her concerned gaze, Miller added, "It was the virus you should have been infatuated with, not the host."

Rowan barely saw Lyall attack from behind, a fire extinguisher in his hands, hitting Miller across the back with it. Miller stumbled, tossing Rowan to the ground and twisting quick on Lyall to retaliate.

Even though Lyall was slower, he dodged Miller's attacks smoothly, until he was backed against a wall again. Nowhere to dodge anymore, she loomed over him and smiled, priming herself for an attack at his throat.

"Cameron, no!" Rowan yelled, because she knew he couldn't do anything, but it was too late. It happened too fast for her to stop it. He was already there, swinging his hand down to hit Miller with the butt of his pistol to help Lyall.

Miller swung around when Rowan shouted, snatching Cameron by his throat and throwing him against the ground. She heard him yell; then the yell stopped short, and her heart follow suit. In the moment between beats, she knew what happened, but refused to believe it. She inhaled, sharp and fast, and her heart pounded again, something waking up inside her. Something hungry.

It was like the monster that she had peacefully put to bed rose raging, filling her veins with an uncontrollable wildness that possessed her. Tears flooded her eyes, and the pounding of her heart was loud and deafening in her ears, but she didn't need to see or hear. The monster acted for her, and the monster saw only red.

She lunged across the room, tackling Miller's back and forcing her away from Cameron. Miller stumbled and flailed around, trying to get her off, but Rowan dug her nails into the other woman and held on tight, tearing at the skin of her eyes and face.

The doctor fell back, slamming Rowan between herself and a wall, then turned to deal with her. Rowan lunged again, barely winded from the hit. Miller stumbled on her heels, falling back onto a table, and Rowan straddled her torso, grabbed her by the hair, and began slamming her head against the table.

She didn't know how she was doing it, but she had overpowered the newly made monster, forcing her head against the tabletop over and over and over until...

"Rowan, stop!" Lyall's voice broke through the red somehow, and she paused. He was a blur past the tears, but she could tell by the way he stood there frozen, he was scared of something.

In the second she stopped, Miller threw her off, and Rowan hit the wall hard. Before she could even get her wind back, Miller disappeared.

Lyall ran over to help her up, but she threw her arms at him, her head still filled with rage. "I had her! Lyall, I had her, and you stopped me! Why?"

He broke through Rowan's anger by grabbing her face and forcing her to look him in the eye despite her struggle to push him away. "You don't want to be a killer," he said when she finally gave him her gaze, wiping at the fat, frustrated tears falling down her cheeks.

As quickly as the anger passed, the pain fell into place, and she remembered why her heart ached. "Cameron."

She pushed away from Lyall and searched for him in a panic, finding where he laid and scrambling on her hands and knees over to the body. She held back a scream as her palms came into contact with the blood on the floor.

"No." She shook her head and collapsed onto him, listening for a heartbeat. All she could hear was her own, pounding harder and harder in her skull. She wouldn't believe it. She couldn't. It wasn't true.

The sobs wracked her body as she gazed up and saw the wound on his neck, a wide, bloody hole tore through his skin and muscle. Her hands trembled as she reached out to touch his face, as if it might help, but all it did was leave bloody fingerprints on his cheeks and lips and eyelids. Her mouth trembled and she leaned down to kiss his chest, trying to will life into his body again.

It felt like her chest was ripping apart, like her throat was tearing open, like she would cry until her lungs stopped working. Everything hurt. She buried her face into his chest and breathed deep his smell one more time, hoping for some sort of comfort in the action, but with the inhale came the sharp, metallic scent of the blood that covered the both of them.

Still, something about the deep breath calmed her. The sobs slowed, her shaking settled, the pain in her chest numbed. She took another long inhale of his scent, and the smell of blood filled her nose again, sweeter this time. Rowan closed her eyes against the tears, sighing. One more inhale, one more, and she could leave and be ok, she told herself.

She breathed in, and her head felt more clear. When she opened her eyes the room was less dark. Her hands, gripped around Cameron's shirt, had stopped trembling. Was this what shock was like? Whatever it was, Rowan was thankful for it, because the pain disappeared and she could only smell him, the fresh cedar and peppermint of his aftershave with the hot, sharp smell of his blood.

Rowan looked back at the wound on his neck, and this time, she wasn't able to pull away. Locked onto the sight of the flesh and blood, it felt like her vision vibrated, like the shutter of a broken camera, trembling in and out, burning contrast. She exhaled a shallow breath.

Lyall's hand covered her eyes, and he pulled her face into his chest, picking her up in his arms and taking her away from the body. She wanted to object, she reached a hand out, but words failed her. Instead, she buried her face into Lyall's collar and let the hurt fill her again until it felt like her body would cave in on itself.

He brought her out to the car, put her in the passenger seat, then got into the driver's side. She didn't think about asking whether or not he could drive. She didn't think about anything. Just Cameron's mangled body, and the blood, all the blood. It was still on her hands, she could smell it as she wiped her eyes. It made her mouth water.

When Lyall got on the road, he leaned over and opened her window. The cool night air hit her hard in the face and chilled her lungs when she breathed. She realized then that she was sweating, and the air broke the heat like an ice bath broke a fever.

After a while, Rowan tried for words. "Lyall," she called for him, and saw from her peripherals as he turned towards her. She blinked, sighing, then looked out the window and said, "I'm hungry."

Again, the silence lingered for too long.

"I know," Lyall said finally, hiding something grave on his tone.

CHAPTER TWENTY-EIGHT

THEY WENT BACK TO PHELPS, hoping he could help them even though they were returning empty handed. But when they arrived, something was not right.

Papers littered the street and yard, rolling in the wind and fleeing from the car wheels as they drove up. Rowan got out of the car before it even stopped, spotting the cellar doors left wide open. The little bit of calm she obtained in the car faded into a deep dread. Someone had gotten here first, and she could only assume who.

They entered Phelps' cellar, his miniature laboratory completely trashed. Papers and files were thrown everywhere, equipment knocked over on tables and laid broken. A liquid leaked out onto the floor, and a gas spout burned.

Rowan hurried over quickly to extinguish the flame and turn the gas off. She swore under her breath all the while, a panic setting in again. This was her fault. She had been the one to mention Phelps. If she hadn't said anything, if she hadn't come here in the first place, maybe he would've been safe. This was the reason he left the project to begin with. To stay out of it. To stay safe.

She heard her name, called on a breath from the corner of the room. Rowan finally caught sight of him, sitting on the floor, almost under his desk, a shelf and filing cabinet knocked over and blocking his shape.

She hurried over, shoving the broken furniture aside to sit next to him. He breathed heavily, wincing with every inhale, sweat beaded on his forehead. He was as pale as a ghost, and Rowan's fingers shook as she checked his pulse and looked him over. He bled from his nose and mouth, signs of an internal injury.

"Miller," Phelps managed to strain out. She already connected the dots, nodding as he confirmed. If Miller attacked him in any way like how she had attacked them, it only made sense that the old man had broken. "She came... For my research."

Rowan had been trying to help Phelps sit up a little more, but stopped at his words. "Research, what research?"

"The cure. I was working on an antivirus. It was almost complete when I offered it to her, but she turned me down. She said it was a waste of resources. It was when I left." Phelps coughed as he finished, blood coming up into his hand. Rowan could hear his heart from where she sat, weak and strained, like the breaths of a dying bird. The smell of his blood was everywhere.

"She took the virus. When we were there, she injected it into herself. Why does she want your cure research?"

Rowan was confused. At the laboratories, it seemed Miller wasn't interested in the research anymore, overtaken by the intoxication of the virus' power. Why would she want anything to do with an antivirus now?

Phelps shook his head. "She didn't want to use it. She wanted to destroy it. So she destroyed everything and left me to die."

"You're not going to die, we're going to take you to the hospital." She beckoned for Lyall to come help her, but as they tried to pick Phelps up, he fell into another coughing fit and collapse to the floor again. More blood on his hands and lips, and Rowan tremble harder.

"It's too late," he said, his head falling back against the wall. "There's no time."

Rowan objected, tears filling her eyes. "Not you, too. Please. We need you."

She couldn't let Miller take someone else from her. No, she refused. She tried again to pick him up. He wasn't so heavy, but his limbs were awkward, and she could tell that moving him was causing him far more pain than he could handle. She cried out, letting him settle again on the floor, taking his hand in hers instead.

"I'm sorry. I'm so sorry."

He forced a smile, despite the fact that it caused him to cough again. After catching a breath, he wheezed out a few more words. "Miller is trying to erase the project's existence. She'll go after the others next. They were all staying... At the old Victorian Inn... Near the waterfront."

"Rowan, the cops are coming. If we're going to do something about Miller we need to go, now." Lyall said, at the door acting as lookout. When Rowan stretched her hearing, she caught the approaching sirens also.

She cursed, squeezing Phelps' hand, and prayed briefly that they would be able to help him. Maybe he had a chance, maybe it wasn't too late.

"My pocket, Rowan." Phelps' voice rasped and dry. He tried to take his free hand and get into his pant pocket, but Rowan did it for him, pulling out the object he was reaching for. A vial, with a clear liquid in it, sealed off tight.

"The antivirus. I made it while you were gone. One dose."

She gaped at him for a moment, bewildered. "I thought you said the research wasn't done."

Phelps spoke slow, barely whispers that Rowan had to lean close to him to hear. "My recipe was complete, I just never had what I needed to make it. I needed a sample of the original virus, and Miller never allowed it."

She shook her head, still not understanding. "Where did you get the sample of the virus? Lyall's blood was contaminated when you took it." Something turned in Rowan's gut, a part of her already knowing what he was going to say, but didn't want to believe it.

It was impossible.

Phelps grimaced, like he didn't want to tell her. It was not the time for secrets, though.

Not anymore.

"I used your blood, Rowan. It's what I was going to tell you before you left. You contracted the virus somehow. It's taking over your bloodstream as we speak."

Rowan sat motionless, too shocked, her mind running circles to deny it. "I didn't though. It's impossible, there's no way—" There was a way though. In her thoughtlessness, wrapped up in an inevitable moment with Lyall, she hadn't been thinking about protecting herself from a virus. She had completely forgotten all together that it was even a possibility. Even now, with her logic confirming it, it seemed unfeasible.

Then she remembered, though, all the little details that had been going overlooked, ignored, pushed aside. Her healing wound, her suddenly excellent hearing, her changing vision. She had taken Miller down because she was growing stronger, and over Cameron's bloody body, she experienced her first passing with the hunger that consumed Lyall while he was infected.

She stared at the wall, the shock dissipating into nervous panic. She shut her eyes tight to fight off the anxiety. Phelps squeezed her hand, getting her attention again. "It will be okay, Rowan. It'll all be ok. Take the antivirus. Once you stop Miller, you can take the antivirus and be human again. I made it for you."

Rowan nodded, her lips shaking as she leaned down to kiss his hand. He smiled, trying to repress another coughing fit as it overcame him.

"Cops. Rowan." Lyall reminded, more urgency in his voice this time.

She held back a sob, refusing herself tears as she whispered an apology and a thank you to Phelps. She then stood, hurrying over to the cabinet and grabbing a packaged syringe before following Lyall back to the car. He pulled out fast and started down the road. A group of cop cars passed them moments later, sirens wailing. The sound was assaulting to Rowan, hyper aware now of why it was now so intrusive.

She glanced down at her arm where the stitched up wound was. It no longer looked like it happened just a few hours before, but rather a few days. She swallowed down her discomfort, the vial twisting in her fingers.

"What's that?" Lyall asked, filling the quiet between them.

Rowan looked up at him, breaking away from her thoughts, then back at the tube she played with. "An antivirus. A real one this time."

"What else did he say to you?" It was an innocent enough question, but Rowan felt unsure if she wanted to tell him.

What if Phelps had been wrong? Her symptoms perhaps only a coincidence. After all, she had Miller's injection in her blood at the time... Maybe that protected her. Maybe, she just didn't want to accept it yet. Or couldn't.

Instead of answering his question, Rowan shook her head,

dismissing it as nothing, sliding the antivirus and the syringe into her jeans pocket. Lucky for her, he didn't press the matter, instead giving her a few extra minutes to gather her thoughts. She wasn't sure if his silence was a gift or a curse, since she didn't want to answer his question, but she also didn't want to be in her head. It was full of death and blood and darkness.

After a lengthy silence, minutes of just driving down empty roads through the darkness of the night, Lyall spoke again. "What should we do about Miller?"

She let the question sit for too long. When she did reply, her words weren't helpful. "I have no idea."

"We need to figure something out. I don't really have time," he said cautiously, like trying to get her to realize something while still being a delicate as possible.

Despite his attempts, his implication stung, and Rowan swallowed down a sob. "Can we maybe not talk about the fact that by morning you might be dead, too?"

She could save him, right now if she wanted, but it would mean accepting it, and she couldn't. Not yet. She just needed a little more time. Time that none of them had, unfortunately.

Lyall did as he was told, not saying a word, leaving Rowan to her destructive thoughts.

She'd kill Miller. It was decided. That woman had taken everything from her. She was the reason Lyall was dying, the reason Rowan's career was ruined, her life stolen from her. Miller murdered her best friend, her mentor, was killing Lyall, and now Rowan might also be...

If she had to bury her loved ones, then she would bury Miller also.

"Will the antivirus work on her?" Lyall asked, pulling Rowan away from the darkness in her head again.

She stared, then nodded. "It should."

"Then we'll do that. We'll use the antivirus on Miller. No one else has to die."

Rowan didn't reply, gnawing at her lip. He didn't know that the antivirus was made for her. Of course he assumed it was their answer for Miller. Of course his new, self-controlled attitude was searching for the most non-violent way, trying to prevent any more bloodshed. Rowan would have felt that way also, if she didn't have a monster growling in her chest for red. She didn't care if there was more carnage, as long as she was the one making it.

"Yeah. We'll use the antivirus on Miller." She agreed, nodding before opening the window and letting the air hit her face again. The numbness she felt over everything that had happened made it easy to lie to him while looking him right in the eye.

CHAPTER TWENTY-NINE

THEY FOLLOWED PHELPS' last tip and headed for downtown as fast as the old sedan would allow, still not completely sure of their final destination. There were a number of old Victorian-style buildings in the area, popular with the upper class, and the "waterfront" stretched almost two miles, meaning numerous, possible locations.

Lyall swerved through the city streets with ease though, following Rowan's directions as she multitasked between guiding him and searching up on her phone for any reports of disturbances in the city that might give them a better lead.

"I had no idea you could drive," she commented, only slightly sarcastic as she reached out to hold onto the dashboard as he turned and twisted the vehicle around sharp corners.

Lyall managed a chuckle. "There's a lot you don't know about me," he said, then his expression fell into the ghost of something bitter. "Wish we had some more time to share."

The dark circles around his eyes were going gray like his skin, like he was already dead and was drying up now instead. The vibrant blue had desaturated since the last time she noticed, making him ghostly. A sadness took over the space between them, and she nodded.

"Me too."

Maybe they could have more time. The possibility was right there, inside her veins, according to Phelps. If she had the virus, all she had to do was give it to Lyall, and he wouldn't have to die.

So why was she so scared? Why was she denying what she knew had awakened inside of her? Why was she selfishly hoarding the one thing they knew would right some of the damage Miller left in her wake? Why was she so reluctant to save Lyall now, when it had been her main goal for so long?

She knew the answer, but she was as reluctant to admit it as she was to accept the truth about herself. Phelps' survival was unlikely, and when he died he left behind only one dose of antiviral in his wake, meaning if she shared the virus with Lyall, one of them would have to keep it.

After the night they'd had, would he even want it? He'd been reluctant to go get the virus back in the first place, even after knowing it was the only way to save him. He only agreed under the pretenses they work together to cure him properly. He wanted to be human. He wanted to change, so who was she to give him the virus back, give him the suffering back, just to keep him alive? Was she so selfish?

She played with the vial in her palm, considering. She could always let him have the antiviral, and live with the virus herself. That would be the most selfless thing to do. But could she live with that? Rowan spent weeks watching, learning what it was like to be this kind of monster. The kind that attacked their lovers in blood-lust, that got hungry over the dead body of a friend. At least Lyall had spent his whole life with the virus. Rowan, she was only just becoming acquainted, and if Lyall was human, who would be left to stop her from making decisions she knew she didn't want to make? He'd already saved her so much regret that night, and she'd barely had the virus in her blood for a few hours. What would happen, when the same starvation that made him snap and almost drain her, seeped into her gut? Would she even be herself anymore? Would she ever be?

There wasn't time for her to figure out her feelings. As they neared the waterfront, smoke billowed in the sky from a burning building.

"Oh, no. Do you think we're too late?" she asked as Lyall stepped on the gas.

He hummed, unsure. "She'll be hungry by now. If we're lucky, she stuck around for a meal."

Rowan tried to swallow, but her throat went dry. Would she be able to keep her head, if there was blood around? Lyall would need her help to stop Miller, so she couldn't allow herself to become distracted. Even just the thought of all the blood made her mouth water, though.

They approached the burning building, onlookers keeping their distance, staying off the road for the approaching fire trucks, although Rowan could hear that they were still a few minutes away. She had no idea how she'd placed the noise, passed all the chatter, the roaring flames, and the old fire alarm in the building wailing over everything.

As they got out of the car and joined the crowd, Rowan overheard a woman, who looked like she could have been the owner of the inn, rambling in a crying panic to another. "The third floor is completely blocked off. They are all still up there."

Immediately Lyall had taken Rowan's wrist to drag her with him, round the building to the back, finding the fire escape.

What they were doing was against every one of Rowan's last instincts, but she allowed him to boost her up to the ladder, pulling him up after. As they continued up, the assault smell of ashe and heat left Rowan's lungs searing and her eyes watering, her head feeling like it was splitting with the noises around her. Under it all though, she could place another scent, which brought both a twisting dread to her gut and a hungry growl to the monster lurking under her skin.

They entered through the fire escape window, the smells and noises further amplified, the smoke and soot in the air forcing Rowan to pull the collar of her t-shirt up over her mouth. She regretted the decision immediately, when the scent of Cameron's dried blood filled her nose instead. Lyall took her elbow to lead her along with him, the touch grounding her back to reality a little and allowing her to keep her head for a moment longer.

The doors to the rooms were ajar, and there were fires started throughout the floor, but the largest one began at the stairwell, spreading across the walls at the corner of the building. Lyall moved them away from the flames, around a turn, to a safer part of the floor.

With the fire to their backs, Rowan could really smell the blood. She tried not to inhale, but couldn't help herself, needing a breath of fresher air after all the smoke. She had to blink away a wave of dizziness afterwards, the metallic sweetness momentarily leaving her intoxicated.

Lyall must have been able to smell it too, but he offered a morbid joke as he continued forward. "Follow the trail of blood…"

Every room they passed gave Rowan another waft of the scent, only each one was a little different, teasing Rowan's senses further. This was a mistake. She couldn't do this. She was going to lose it in here. Lyall at least had to know before she completely broke.

"Lyall I—"

He was already pulling her towards him, releasing her eyes from being locked onto a shadow of a body sprawled out on the bed in one of the rooms they passed. "Keep your eyes down, don't look," he whispered, leading her as he started walking again.

He must have thought she had trouble seeing all the bodies of her colleagues. She tried to take his advice regardless, but even with her eyes casted down, she salivated with every heavy breath she took.

They continued down the hallway, until the last few rooms approached, and a new scent entered the mix of fragrances in the air. It was much more pungent. Fresh and warm, making Rowan's stomach ache in desire. She was the one leading him now, as she pulled towards the smell, coming from the last room at the end of the hall.

They entered cautiously, concerned of being ambushed, but Miller wasn't hiding anywhere. In the middle of the well-furnished suite, Miller kneeled at the edge of a bed, sheets that had once been starkly white now pooled with wet, thick redness. Across the bed, bleeding from a reopened wound on his neck, was another familiar face that Rowan hadn't expected to see dead: William.

He had to have been the last of the doctors left, all eye witnesses of the events now destroyed, except for the three left alive in the room.

A sickly smile swept Miller's face as they approached, reminding Rowan too much of when Lyall had attacked William the first time. Miller was more blood than cotton in her lab coat now, soaked in a cocktail of different blood, her face and teeth stained with carnage. All at once, Rowan found herself rooted to the floor, terrified just like the first day she'd walked into that containment room, seeing a new monster all over again.

Then, the smile shifted a little on Miller's face, a ghost of something else crossing her expression. Something like, fear?

"What's happening to me? I can't stop..." Her mouth dripped

unswallowed blood when she spoke.

"I'm not surprised. Someone as self-serving and greedy as you with the virus. You've never had to deny yourself anything, have you, *doctor*? Well, don't worry. It's over now," Lyall said, taking a step forward, unafraid of the beast in front of him even though Rowan had the feeling that Miller could snap him in half like a twig.

Probably thinking the same thing, Miller laughed, viscous liquid dripping from her spread lips. "Are you going to stop me?" she asked, cackling again when Lyall's eyes became hard and determined.

It happened almost too quickly. Lyall attacked, and in a repeat of their last encounter, Miller caught him. This time, she slammed the dying boy down onto the floor with her, hard, and Rowan heard bones snapping. Lyall's pained expression confirmed it had been his body breaking. In less than a moment, the boy who Rowan thought would forever be unstoppable, was stopped.

Miller didn't milk her advantage, unwinding to her feet and looking over Lyall instead of inflicting more damage. "You forgot. I've fed now. I'm even stronger than earlier. And you're weaker. There's not even really a point in killing you now, is there? You must be on your last hour."

Lyall tried to catch his breath, winded and most likely fighting a few broken ribs. He tried to roll over, slowly and painfully. Miller helped, using her foot to kick him onto his side, making the boy on the floor scream in agony. She chuckled, finding pleasure in the torture, barely taking notice to Rowan.

"I would kill you, but it would be interesting to see you just waste away from my *antivirus*. I can't say I'm not curious to how exactly it will happen. I imagine dying on a cellular level will get painful." Miller pushed her foot into his side again, getting another scream. "You're not healing anymore, I see."

Rowan didn't know what to do. She was frozen with terror. She knew she had to do something, she knew that she had a better chance at taking Miller than Lyall ever did, but when she was terrified it was hard to feel like she had the ability to do anything. He was overpowered physically, and Rowan found herself overpowered mentally.

Miller shoved him again, and Rowan turned away to avoid seeing the pain on his face. Tears filled her eyes, of sadness and hopelessness and frustration. She tried to remember why they were there, tried to remember that angry growl of the animal inside her when she thought about tearing Miller apart. She tried to remember Cameron, his neck ripped open and mangled, and Phelps, coughing up blood as he died. She needed to do something, if not to save herself and Lyall and everyone else unfortunate enough to be in the area, but for the people Miller had already stolen from her.

She opened her eyes to blink away the wetness, and her gaze found the pool of blood on the bed around William's body, and this time she couldn't help but stare. Again, her vision shook, and the longer she stared, the more violent the tremor became. Rowan felt like her skin burned from the inside, her heart pounding, banging, urging her forward. The beast unwound and emerged from the deep, dark part of her abdomen, and it was like it was trying to force its way out through her chest and her throat.

Beside her, Miller was busy torturing Lyall, entertained like a child with a new toy, but the sound of her laugh and his yells of pain became distorted and murky to Rowan, like hearing a noise above the surface while underwater. All there was for her in that moment was the metallic smell around her, and the blood, drip, drip, dripping onto the floor from the drenched bed sheets. Her shaking vision stopped abruptly, and the monster shoved her forward.

Before she even realized what she was doing, her hand was in the pool of red, shiny and smooth and so tempting, and she licked it off her fingers. It tasted like everything she imagined and more. Her mouth watered, and her stomach twisting like she had been starving and had no idea until this very moment. It wasn't enough though, her thirst was unsatisfied.

Rowan grabbed William by the back of his head, then buried her face into the wound at his neck, a wound Lyall had made, Miller had reopened, and she was now feasting from, swallowing down the thick elixir as it leaked into her mouth. With every swallow, the monster inside her showed more of its skin, taking over her thoughts with insatiable growls.

"What on earth is going on here?" Miller said, the words barely registering past Rowan's untamed starvation. When the other woman laughed, she stopped, the monster hissing something dark as her eyes finally left her red feast to focused on something else.

Miller raised an eyebrow when Rowan finally raised her gaze. She hadn't noticed before, but her gray eyes had lightened with the new addition to her blood, becoming an almost ghostly silver. It made the woman look even more unnatural, even more terrifying, just like Lyall's ice blue gaze had made him. Human Rowan would have been scared stiff, but monster Rowan was in control now.

"I knew something was strange about how you almost killed me back at the laboratory. Seems like we have another little blood sucker after all." Miller was having a grand time messing with the two of them. Everytime she laughed, Rowan felt her pupils shudder and refocus, the animal taking a new target.

"Here, wait, let me guess. Our lovebirds had a romantic night, that ended in someone accidently making a meal of the other. You must have forgotten how the virus worked, didn't you? I don't blame you, most people have trouble worrying about *protection* when the moment strikes them."

A toothy grin spread wide across her face and Miller finally took a step away from Lyall and moved towards Rowan. She leaned over the bed and grabbed her under the chin, holding her face up to look her in the eye. Rowan watched the woman's pupils, wide and black like when Lyall was possessed with the hunger. Was she also so terrifying?

Miller rubbed her thumb across Rowan's cheek, like the way a parent wipes a smudge off a child's face. Her hand came back red. "Look at us. Still following down the same path, more alike than ever, I'd dare say. Imagine what we could do now. Together, Rowan. We could be unstoppable."

She felt the monster rear inside her, thrashing against the walls that contained it. She felt like if she let it, it would explode from her flesh, and she'd no longer even be human anymore. Just the dark, shadowy *thing* inside of her. The idea felt wonderful. She wanted to let it tear her apart. She wanted to let it tear the world apart.

She looked at Miller, most likely a mirror image of herself just as the woman had suggested; blood on their faces and hunger in their eyes, fire dancing in the deep darkness of the woman's pupils, because she thought that she had everything in her control, including Rowan.

But the human inside her remembered.

Rowan remembered red, but the red of Cameron's blood, spilt all over the floor, flooding around him. She remembered Phelps, coughing, his heart barely fluttering as he spoke to her. She remembered the rooms of bodies they had to pass just to get here, face to face with the woman who'd stolen everything away with her greed.

She remembered that Miller had to die for this to end, and she had to be the one to do it.

They didn't want any more bodies, but to make sure there wasn't, she had to make one more with her own hands, and she didn't mind the idea at all. Lyall told her that she didn't want to be a killer, but the monster disagreed. Her eyes went down to Miller's throat, and it purred at the idea of tearing it opened. More blood. She wanted more blood. She was ready for it. Her first kill.

Miller didn't expect Rowan to do anything, because she raised an eyebrow when she reached out for her neck. Rowan clawed at the skin, but Miller only laughed, prying her fingers away dragging her to her feet by her hair. She had no chance of winning a power struggle against the other woman. She was already far stronger than her, even with the hunger fueling Rowan's rage. She caught Miller by surprise last time in the labs, and it seems like the doctor was not going to allowed that opportunity again.

Lyall, on the other hand, had been completely forgotten by both of them. So when Rowan saw his shape slide carefully to his feet behind Miller, she reacted, twisting and struggling to distract the woman that held her.

Miller growled, tossing her to the ground forcefully. The humor was gone from her face. Now she was just annoyed.

"I've offered you so much, and this is really how you repay me? I should have known any assistant of Phelps' would be an ungrateful little brat. I thought you would be smarter than this, Rowan. You *are* smarter than this. This boy has already given you all he has to offer; immortality and a good fucking. It's time to grow up now. Come with me instead, and we could have everything." She leaned down again, placing her hand on Rowan's head, and sweeping back a strand of matted blonde hair. Miller offered one last, tender smile, and added a stolen line, "You look so much more appropriate in red, anyway."

Rowan gazed up at the woman, letting her face soften to see

the darkness in Miller's eyes shift to satisfaction, and then down to angry disappointment again when Rowan shook her head. "I'm sorry, doctor. Even with the same virus, I could never be the same kind of monster as you."

Miller had just enough time to snarl and tighten her grip in Rowan's hair before her expression shifted to surprise and her fingers slacked. Behind her, Lyall pushed the plunger down on the syringe that he'd stuck deep into Miller's neck, adding to Rowan's words, "Besides, red is a terrible color on you."

Miller yelled, swinging around wildly in reaction to the unforeseen assault. Lyall retreated immediately, but his injuries made him slow, and Miller connected a limb, knocking the dying boy to the floor again. Miller dove for him, murder in her eyes, obviously intending to finish the boy off, but Rowan lunged forward also, grabbing her around the neck and wrestling her back.

Miller growled loudly again, turning her sights back to Rowan, twisting and bending to try and get her off. Just like at the labs though, she held on tight and dug her nails into the woman's skin, letting herself be crushed against the floor but never letting go. If she just waited long enough for the antivirus to set in, she would win. She just needed to *hold on.*

It happened faster than she expected. Miller's struggles became more wild and desperate, but her strength diminished rapidly. Becoming confused herself, she yelled as she wrestled, "What have you done to me?"

"Just a little antivirus, courtesy of Robert Phelps. You should be happy. Unlike yours, this one won't kill you," Rowan strained out an answer, twisting her body to lock her arm around the woman's neck tight.

She tightened her hold around Miller's throat, cutting off her air. The woman continued to struggle hard, but she simply did not have the strength anymore to fight now that Rowan was the only one with the virus. After a long moment of gasping and choking, Miller fell limp, and Rowan released her grip and shoved her body away.

There was no time to catch her breath. The fire had spread during their confrontation and she could hear the beams giving under the heat, the building ready to collapse at any moment. She dragged Miller out of the room, down the flaming hall and out to the fire escape, then returned for Lyall. She managed to get them both down to ground level before a flash fire blew out one of the windows from the floor they had been on. Rowan could hear the firemen coming, so she left Miller, disappearing into the alleys behind the hotel with Lyall's nearly unconscious body.

Once she was far enough away from the scene, the smoke and blood and loud sirens less assaulting to her senses, she stopped to recuperate. Laying Lyall down, she sat on her knees and let her head fall back, taking in a deep inhale. The smell of blood saturated the air, but she closed her eyes and focused on her heart, beating loud and steady, and it calmed her, pulling her away from the bloodlust lingering within her. She wouldn't let it take her again. Once was enough.

Her head finally a little clearer, she remembered, the pieces of everything that happened falling into place and a dreadful realization taking over. She moved quickly again, panicking, patting her fingers over the pockets of her bloody jeans, the antivirus and syringe gone.

"Why? Why did you do that?" Rowan turned to Lyall, who clutched at his ribs while propped up against a back alley wall. There was fire in her eyes, but her anger dissipated the moment she saw him. She heard his pulse immediately, the beat so slow and weak. While her heart punched against her ribs, his barely pattered.

She touched him suddenly, petting over his hair and face, panic in her chest and her lungs, like knives through her ribs, making every breath hurt. "No, no, no," she muttered in denial, calling for him to not give up on her. She tried to help him sit up further, but he winced against his broken bones. She hadn't known he'd been injured so badly.

His eyes lacked color and life when he lifted them. When he inhaled, his throat sounded arid as a desert. "You lied to me," he said, barely a whisper, trying to sound playful but failing horribly.

Rowan bowed her head, putting her cheek to his chest to hear that tiny flutter of a heart beat. She willed it not to stop. "I didn't know what to say. I didn't know if you'd want it back. I—"

"I knew you had it. With Cameron. Your eyes..." His words were short, strained, painful.

Tears drowned her vision. "If you knew, why didn't you ask for it?"

She felt stupid, selfish. She should have just given it to him. He wouldn't be here, dying painfully if she had just given it to him. He would have been able to fight Miller if she had just given the virus back.

But she held it, selfishly, and now she worried it was too late.

"I didn't want it... Not like that. I didn't want... To be alone with it again." He barely got the words out, shutting his eyes and taking a deep breath after them. His heart skipped.

Rowan panicked, grabbing at him, not hearing the little flit of the muscle in his chest. Not yet. No. It couldn't be too late. She bit violently at the palm of her hand, until it hurt, until she couldn't take it, and then, until the skin tore open, and the wound poured blood. With shaking fingers, she opened his mouth and put her palm to his lips. The blood dripped to his tongue, out the corner of his mouth. She flexed her fingers to get more flow, but the wound was already healing.

"Don't do this, Lyall," she whispered, desperately begging, putting her head to his chest to search for that tiny little noise again.

When she didn't hear it everything crashed down on her, and the sobs swelled up in her chest. She lost everyone to this, even the one person that she had the opportunity to save, and now she was where Lyall started: a monster, all alone.

"You can't leave me like this. I need you. I don't want to be alone either..."

His heart had stopped fluttering though, and for a second the dark alley was too silent. Even the monster in her stopped its growling to weep instead.

Then, he inhaled.

Sharp and strong and so loud to her sensitive ears, his heart beating again wildly, like he'd woken up from a bad nightmare. Rowan sat up, shocked, and stared as he panted. She watched with wide eyes and shallow lungs as he came back to life, still not sure if what she was seeing was really happening.

She counted the times his chest rose and fell, then when she confirmed he had caught enough air, she stole his mouth, kissing him with wet, bloody, sobbing kisses until he had to reach up and grab her face to stop her smothering. His forehead to hers, she gave a small, breathless, thankful laugh to his lips, and she felt his curl against hers. She smiled, kissing him again, only to get a whisper muttered against her lips.

"Whoever you've been eating tastes familiar."

With the grim joke Rowan growled and shoved at him, but Lyall caught her around the back of her neck to keep her close, and she waited as he opened his eyes. They focused on her, and she was trapped by icy blue once again. Her wolf was back, and the monster in her bones purred.

Danielle Koste is born and raised Canadian, but currently lives with her significant other in the equally snowy and cold Stockholm, Sweden. While working a day job and learning the language of the locals, she spent her free time honing the craft she always had a passion for. Movies, music, and video games are among her favorite time-wasters.

PULSE is Danielle Koste's first published book. You can experience more of her work online at one of the following locations.

www.daniellekoste.com
www.facebook.com/DanielleKoste
www.patreon.com/DanielleKoste
or @DanielleKoste on twitter